Re

"Mink's brisk com
ture is what street in is an about . . .
of women orbiting the hip-hop world . . . Luscious is both a
villain and a heroine whom readers will embrace. Order in
anticipation of high demand."

—Library Journal

"A gritty new urban series with a down and dirty intensity
that's heartbreaking."

—Publishers Weekly

"Unexpected storylines . . . very realistic . . . a quick read
with an engaging main character."

—Huffington Post

Praise for
Real Wifeys: On the Grind

"Marking her solo debut with this new series launch,
Mink . . . gives Kaeyla a snappy and profane voi~~~
sarcasm. She's a charismatic v
tough. Female readers will lov
check their own woman's purse
shelves with multiple copies."

—Library Journal

"Move over Wisteria Lane. Drama and scandal have permanently moved to Bentley Manor. . . . A wonderfully written novel that is sassy, smart, and unadulterated!"
—Danielle Santiago, *Essence* bestselling author

"A sexy tale that will keep you gasping as you turn the pages."
—Miasha, *Essence* bestselling author

Praise for
Shameless Hoodwives

"Diamond and Mink deliver a compelling hood tale that is a true page-turner."
—RAWSISTAZ

"This is the ghetto Wisteria Lane, called Bentley Manor, and anything can and will happen here."
—Coast 2 Coast Readers

"Invigorating plots magnify the intensity of each scene that creates a breathless anticipation as you delve further and further into the sordid lives of the people that occupy this notorious neighborhood."
—Urban Reviews

Praise for
The Hood Life

"A great page-turner! It's easy to get lost in this novel. The story is so vivid . . . it will keep you on the edge of your seat the whole ride of this book about four men in their story of struggle in Urban America."

—Savvy Book Club

"A scandalous tale of four men who found themselves always at the wrong end of the track. They ultimately got what they deserved. This book was definitely a page-turner."

—Q.U.E.E.N.S. Book Club of Mississippi

REAL WIFEYS

Hustle Hard

AN URBAN TALE

MEESHA MINK

A Touchstone Book
Published by Simon & Schuster
New York   London   Toronto   Sydney   New Delhi

Touchstone
A Division of Simon & Schuster, Inc.
1230 Avenue of the Americas
New York, NY 10020

First Touchstone trade paperback edition January 2013

TOUCHSTONE and colophon are registered trademarks of Simon & Schuster, Inc.

For information about special discounts for bulk purchases, please contact Simon & Schuster Special Sales at 1-866-506-1949 or business@simonandschuster.com.

The Simon & Schuster Speakers Bureau can bring authors to your live event. For more information or to book an event contact the Simon & Schuster Speakers Bureau at 1-866-248-3049 or visit our website at www.simonspeakers.com.

Designed by Akasha Archer

Manufactured in the United States of America

10   9   8   7   6   5   4   3   2   1

ISBN 978-1-4516-8897-9
ISBN 978-1-4516-8898-6 (ebook)

*For those with big dreams
and the inner hustle to make them come true.*

Wifey: *(n.) a girlfriend, usually live-in, who does all the work of a wife without being legally married.*

"Hustle 'caine, hustle clothes, or hustle music/
But hustle hard in any hustle that you pick . . ."

Jay-Z, "No Hook"

Prologue

$\mathcal{I}$ am all about *my* business. Be it my career or my man, I go hard for mine. I put in work like I'm starving and I love him like a drug that has me fucked all the way up. I hustle with the same intensity of any hip-hop entertainer or dope boy.

I've busted my ass for the last six years climbing the corporate ladder. Good grades in high school. Better grades in college. Dean's List. Internships. Graduating magna cum laude with a job offer that I was too smart to even think about turning down. I was on track to become a chief financial officer at the same firm and then my income would damn near triple.

Yes, this little mixed African American and Puerto Rican girl from Newark, New Jersey, was one of those "success stories" that the press makes you think is so damn rare in this "inner" city, "ghetto," or "hood." Don't let the news fool you into thinking nothing good grows in Newark. That's bullshit. I know plenty of people who thrived: graduated college, worked hard every day, owned homes and paid rent with no problems, but those stories were outshined by the bad elements that every city has—even whitewashed middle America. I rep just as hard for my hometown as I rep for myself.

Growing up in this city, I am that mix of common sense, street smarts, and book smarts. *Humph.* Fuck with me. Don't get it twisted. When pushed, I am not a bitch you want to try lightly. I mean, I can't front like I'm the kind of chick to hide a razor blade under my tongue ready for a fight but I go hard for mine, "25/8," like Mary J. Blige: *"Every minute of every hour, Still it ain't enough time . . ."* I have the skills, brains, and the class to broker a seven-figure deal and the right hook to straight knock a bitch out if she make the mistake of *thinking* I'm too bougie to fight.

I float between two worlds and although I'm comfortable in both, I am ready for some changes. The man I love doesn't live within the law. Not slinging dope or gang banging or some shit like that; but nothing about his job is nine-to-five. Nothing about his hustle is safe or easy. See, living in fear of your man getting killed or arrested is torture.

When he is out in those streets, deep into the world that he keeps from me, I can't sleep or eat right. When he's not by me, where I can lay eyes on him and feel him, I live life on the edge of sanity. I have fear that the wrong move on his part will lead to the feds taking him from me or some nigga on the come-up taking his life. And then where will I be?

And on some real shit, the thought of losing him in any way scares me so much that I stay on the move. I stay busy. I'm a hamster on a fucking wheel. Going. Going. Going. Going. Going.

Trying like hell to keep my fear from making my sanity completely . . . gone.

Because I care about him. I love that motherfucker for real. I love to say it and think it and feel it. Emphasize it. Declare my shit.

But our worlds are different and there ain't shit about it that's easy.

All I need—all *we* need—is to make our shit legit. Professionally and personally.

I sit down in front of my dressing table and use my brush to work the tangles from my hair. I do my makeup. I almost get by without really looking into my own eyes. Almost.

The sadness I see in the chocolate depths has been there for such a long time.

I glance at the clock. It's just after midnight. Dane wasn't home and the house felt empty as hell.

My mind wasn't on dumb shit like another bitch or nothing like that. His tricking and treating whores isn't our issue at all. I just wanted him safe.

For a second I look at myself. I mean really sit back and take a hard-core look at me. But I don't see the pretty face people always tell me about. Or the hair a lot of women groan about me cutting. Or the curvy body my man loves. Or the smarts that were certified by Rutgers University.

No, I don't see any of that shit.

All I see is a woman afraid of being left alone by a game I don't even understand or have any part in.

Somehow, I gotta figure out how to convince my man to get out the game before the game get us completely fucked up, because losing him isn't a fucking option.

Part One

Same old shit, just a different day

Out here tryna get it, each and every way . . .

Times are getting hard, guess what I'm gonna do . . .

—Ace Hood, "Hustle Hard"

$\mathcal{J}$ was so fucking tired it didn't make any sense. Not even sitting in the club with the bass of the music beating against my body could keep the yawn from escaping through my gloss-covered lips. Sipping on a glass of Moscato wasn't helping a damn thing either. Really I wanted to carry my ass home to our comfy king-size bed in our beautifully renovated home in Weequahic in Newark, New Jersey, and not be sitting in the VIP of Club 973 in Newark. I put in nine hours of work today with another full day waiting for me at 9 a.m. sharp while a lot of these motherfuckers *just* woke up out of their bed a few hours ago.

Great club. Good drinks. Banging music. I just wasn't in the mood for this shit. Hell with it.

"You lookin' good as fuck, Suga," my fiancé, Daniel "Dane" Greenley, whispered into my ear, pressing his large and warm hand onto my bare thigh.

I instantly felt the heat of his touch and that crazy "can't keep my hands off of you" fire that burned steady between us. In the six years we been together, our sex was *loco,* our love was *atractivo,* and our friendship was mad *refresque.* Crazy, sexy, and cool. Cutting my eyes over to him, I slightly opened my thighs in the fuchsia sequined skirt I wore with a white silk tank.

I arched my eyebrow and smiled when he looked over at me like: "Word?"

I licked my lips and opened my legs wider even as I moved my bare shoulders to the sound of Ace Hood's "Hustle Hard"—a 2011 oldie but goodie and my inner theme song.

We were sitting in a dark corner of VIP behind a table covered with buckets upon buckets holding our bottle service. I didn't need my bachelor's degree in finance to know my man had already easily blown a couple of grand or better. That was nothing to Dane, not with Friday right around the corner. Thursdays was party night because on Fridays, Dane and his crew were all about collecting money he was owed.

Behind the table, he slid my black lace panties to the side and eased one thick finger against my pussy lips. I leaned over to lightly lick the side of his mouth as he pressed that finger inside my wetness. "*¿Quiere al me carajo?*" I asked in a whisper with a soft moan against his ear before sucking the lobe.

His body tensed as he leaned into me. Dane loved when I talked nasty to him in Spanish during sex. He couldn't speak a lick of it—hell, I wasn't that fluent—but he recognized whenever I asked him did he want to fuck me. I felt a shiver race across his body and I leaned back to look at his profile. My man was fine. Caramel-brown complexion. Jet-black hair cut into a low caesar. High cheekbones. Strong jaw. Slanted eyes surrounded by long ebony lashes. Lips built to kiss me—and only me—everywhere. Strong and muscled athletic body built to please me in every way.

Dane turned his head to eye me with a smile on his lips as he used his thumb to press against my juicy clit.

It was my turn to shiver. My mouth opened a bit as my eyes closed just a little.

This sexy motherfucker just did it for me. Not even the faded scar just above his right eye could fuck up the pretty picture. "Let's get out of here," I said, taking in the deep navy V-neck sweater he wore with a long diamond chain glittering around his neck and in full competition with the rest of his diamond jewelry.

I wasn't envious of his shine. Dane made sure I had plenty of my own. Four-carat diamond studs. Watch. Encrusted heart-shaped locket on a long platinum chain. Rings. Bracelets. And that's only what I wore at the moment. He loved to surprise and I loved to be surprised.

And let's not get it twisted. I did the same for him. My job provided me the funds to spoil him at times and also to pay my share of the bills—I wouldn't have it any other way.

Dane nodded and slipped out his finger to suck my sweet juices before he rose to his Gucci-covered feet and removed a wad of bills from the front pocket of his jeans to peel off enough hundred-dollar bills to cover his tab and the tip for the waitress already included on it.

Yes, let's be out!

He held out his hand for mine and I grabbed my crystal heart-shaped purse as I rose to my five-inch hot-pink satin heels. It felt like heaven to ease my hand into his. A perfect fit.

As we made our way downstairs and through the crowded club, I made sure to stay close to him and he made sure his grip on my hand was unbreakable. When we came to a sudden stop, I looked past his broad shoulder to see some bitch with more weave than clothes backing her ass up against him. I straight eyed her from the top of her Beyoncé blonde weave to her Trina outfit and Nicki Minaj ass.

Dane tried to sidestep her but I sidestepped him and stood there looking at her now grind her ass against my skirt. I lightly mushed that trick against the back of her head and she looked over her shoulder to see me posted up and looking really ready to slap the hell out of her.

The look of shock on her face was priceless.

I arched my brow and raised my hand to shoo the bitch away dismissively.

Even though Dane kept tugging on my hand, I stayed my ass locked in place as I eyed this chick hard. Females were always trying to push up on Dane. He looked good as hell and he made a lot of money. Bitches were forever trying to fill a spot that wasn't vacant. Thirsty tricks dying to be a side chick and then fight hard for their come-up.

And since I wasn't always at his side in the club or always with him when he was handling his business in the streets, some bitches really tried me like I was a joke or some weak spineless chick. And yes, I made it a point to school a bitch on how big a mistake it was.

Never underestimate me.

She slowly straightened up and turned to move away with a stank-ass walk.

"Come on, girl," Dane said jokingly, tugging my wrist one last time. "Like you can beat somebody."

I laughed and playfully pinched his arm. "I ain't no killa but don't try me," I said as I let him lead me out of the club and into the warm summer night.

"I'm glad we goin' home. I'm tired as fuck," Dane admitted as he reached up to stroke my hair from my face as we

strolled the short distance down the street to the gated
parking lot.

"You didn't get in until three this morning," I said, trying
hard as hell not to sound like his mother or prison guard or
some shit.

Dane looked over at me. "I thought you were sleeping
when I got in bed."

I shrugged it off. "I can't really fall too deep asleep until
you get into bed with me," I admitted.

He grabbed my waist and came to a stop as he pulled my
body against his. My heart pounded as he pressed his mouth
to mine. I moaned in the back of my throat as he traced my
bottom lip with the tip of his tongue. *Damn.*

Right there on the street as cars whizzed by and people
passed us on their way in or out of the club, Dane kissed
me like I was water for his thirst. One hand on my ass. The
other twisting my hair. His hot body. His hard dick.

Damn. It was always like that between us and the older
we got the better we got *together.*

My nipples and clit was just as hard as his dick. "I'ma
ride the fuck out of you tonight," I moaned into his mouth
before hotly licking at his lips.

Dane leaned back and looked down at me with a smile.
"Backward?" he asked, his voice deep and rough.

I nodded in earnest as I let my hand ease between us to
stroke the long and thick length of his dick in his denims.
"Shit, backward . . . sideways . . ."

Dane slapped my ass, making it jiggle like Jell-O.

"Damn, at least take that shit to one of y'all rides."

Dane gave my ass one last tap and my lips one last kiss
before he turned around. I leaned my head to the side to

look over his shoulder at his best friend, Keno, and his wifey, Hunga, standing behind us enjoying the show.

I forced a smile to my face. I really didn't give a fuck about either one of them.

Keno and Hunga were cliché as hell. The thug and his ride-or-die chick. Bonnie and Clyde. Just him and his bitch. They lived together. Did dirt together. Didn't give a fuck about much out of life but clothes, partying, and smoking weed . . . together. In hood heaven all that bullshit sounded real good . . . if I didn't know the real on their relationship. Both of them were fucking around on each other and those fools fought each other so hard that weapons were drawn.

So uhmmm . . . yeah. What the fuck ever.

Me and Dane's love wasn't shit like theirs but I wouldn't judge them if they didn't make it clear they side-eyed us.

"Hey, Suga," Hunga said, tossing her waist-length jet-black weave over her shoulder with her four-inch colorful fingernails, eyeing me up and down, from where she stood behind Keno's tall and thin frame in a body-hugging blue sequin jumpsuit and some "fuck me like a ten-dollar corner ho" heels.

Hunga had that smooth and dark "black don't crack" complexion with a curvy body and china-doll features.

I gave her another fake smile and a hand wave.

"Y'all out?" Keno asked, barely glancing in my direction before locking his coal-black eyes on Dane's face.

"Yeah," Dane said, releasing my hand to press his palm to the small of my back.

"A'ight then. Call me tomorrow. There's a problem with—"

Dane raised his hand and motioned it across his neck.

Keno instantly closed his mouth, his eyes darting over to me real quick before he nodded in understanding. Hunga sucked her teeth and let out air pressure.

Dane never talked business in front of me. Never. He felt like the less I knew the better it was for me if the shit hit the fan. He always promised that his business would never affect our home. We'd been together since before I graduated college—more than six years. So far, so good.

"Yo, ain't that Poppi?"

I felt Dane's body go stiff as he whipped his head to look where Keno pointed to one of those old-school, long-ass Cadillacs pulling into the parking lot at the other entrance. "Hell yeah. That's that motherfucka."

Just that quick the energy flipped.

Keno went striding across the parking lot at a run-walk that looked mad crazy. Soon the sound of raised and angry voices filled the air along with the *thump-thump* of the club's bass-heavy music.

"Oh fuck no," Hunga snapped before she took off toward the scene in her high heels.

She damn near fell as she turned the corner of the building.

"What the fuck is going on, Dane?" I asked, my nerves completely shot. This did not feel right.

"Stay here, Sophie," he said, surprising me by using my real name.

He always called me Suga. Ever since I told him that was the nickname my mother gave me when I was a baby, he hardly ever called me Sophie. It seemed silly and insignificant but I knew shit was about to get real. And that scared me.

"Dane," I called out, reaching out to grab his arm as he took off at a run.

He shook off my touch. "Just stay here," he stressed, his deep brown eyes hard and cold and serious. Too fucking serious.

With one last stare, Dane raced down the street and around the corner to the closest opening of the gate surrounding the parking lot.

I felt dumb as hell standing there not doing shit but literally kicking at the tiny rocks of concrete from cracks in the street. My heart was racing and pounding as I paced. As far as I knew, Poppi was a good friend of Dane and Keno's. He'd been to our house plenty of times just to chill with Dane and the rest of the squad. I frowned as I looked down the street. *What the fuck was this shit all about?*

"No, Dane, man! My bad man. Damn!" a male voice hollered before he cried out in a high-pitched tone like a bitch. A bitch in pain.

I felt my heart leap up into my throat as I turned and raced toward the parking lot. My pulse was pounding as hard as my stilettos to the pavement. I came to a stop at the entrance to the gate and my eyes got big as hell.

Dane was standing there as Keno beat the shit out of Poppi's short ass until his face was a bloodied mess. He was on the ground, his slight-built body curled into a ball. I wanted to turn away but I couldn't, even as I felt like I could throw the fuck up. Blow after blow of Keno's fists landed. And landed. And landed. Echoing against the night, it was like the sound of meat being pounded to tenderness.

"Motherfuckin' sneaky-ass thief!" Hunga spat, stepping

forward from her spot behind Keno to viciously kick Poppi's ribs.

I cried out as his ball became smaller. "Stop it!" I screamed from behind the hand I held to my mouth in shock.

They all turned and looked over at me.

Dane's face was tight with anger.

Keno's eyes were crazed.

Hunga's face was filled with annoyance.

Poppi's eyes were closed in what could only be relief as he enjoyed the end of the destruction of his face.

I trembled in my stilettos as I rushed over to them. Dane met me and stood in my path before I could get any closer. I cringed at the sight of blood on his knuckles and his shirt. "Dane," I said softly. That one soft mumble of my man's name was filled with surprise, question, confusion, and disgust.

It was obvious he got in a few swings too.

My eyes searched his but he didn't do shit but turn away from me. "Keno, let Hunga take Suga home for me?" Dane asked, even though that shit sounded more like a demand to me.

"No," I snapped, reaching out to grab his arm.

"I gotta handle this, Suga," Dane said, as he turned back to grip my face and press a kiss to the side of my mouth.

"What the hell is going on, Daniel?" I asked, switching to his given name to let him up on the fact that this shit was real as hell for me. To let him know that *I* was serious as hell.

He leaned back and looked down into my eyes. "Business is—"

"Business," I finished, shaking my head as my anger filled me in a snap. That's the bullshit line he fed me when he didn't want me mixed up in his hustle and everything that went along with it.

Hunga gave Poppi another mean kick and then spat down on him before she turned and strutted away like she was starring in a music video or some shit. "Let's ride, Suga," she called out before lighting a cigarette and climbing into the driver's seat of Keno's tricked-out silver Dodge Charger.

With one last look at Keno dragging Poppi's body into the back of Dane's all-black Benz R-Class, I walked away from Dane and climbed into the passenger seat of the Charger. I just wanted to get the fuck away from there—even if Hunga's crazy ass was my driver.

I was trembling a little as I raised my hand to stroke my thumb against my diamond locket. Inside was a picture of my mother holding me as a newborn. I unlocked it and leaned it closer to the window to use the streetlights to look down at the pretty dark-skinned woman with a curly 'fro that framed her face like a halo. That made sense because she was my angel now watching me from heaven, and moments that was crazy like this, I called on her.

"Damn, that ninja got me tracking blood in this motherfucker. Ugh!" Hunga snapped in exasperation as she pulled to a stop at a red light and reached up to turn on the light before she looked down at the mats.

I side-eyed this bitch like she was dumb as hell. "I'm sure Poppi's main motivation when he kept slamming his face into Keno's fists and rolled into your foot was to track blood all in this *motherfucker*," I said, finishing with emphasis meant to mock her silly ass.

Hunga glanced over at me as she took one long drag off her cigarette before she lowered the driver-side window and plucked the still lit cigarette out onto the street. "Poppi don't deserve pity," she began, reaching over to lower the satellite radio softly playing some Jeezy banger. "See, *you* may not give a fuck about some punk pussy bitch stealing five figures from your man but *I do* 'cause his money affect Keno's money and Keno's money affects me."

I turned my head to eye her as the streetlight turned green. A car laid on the horn behind us but Hunga didn't even flinch as she turned in the seat to settle her back against the closed driver's door to eye me right back. "See, my job ain't no nine-to-five working with dem slick-ass white-collar thugs like you. My job is to have the back of my street thug out their hustling to make sure we have a place to live, eat, sleep, fuck, smoke that good as Bob Marley and do whatever else *we* want in that motherfucker."

"Go park your shit if you talking!" the driver screamed through the open passenger window of his Explorer as he roared past them.

Hunga turned her head to the side just long enough to scream out the window. "Fuck youuuuuuu!"

I rolled my eyes. *Crazy bitch.* "So Poppi stole money?" I asked, fighting the urge to pull out my cell phone and call Dane. I couldn't lie that I was worried right along with being disgusted by the shit I saw go down. *What if Poppi got free and shot Dane and Keno for the beating he took? And just what was they going to do with him now?*

"You know, Suga, when a dude out there in dem streets making money he got a lot of shit on his mind and a lot of people on his back . . . he need to be able to come home and have his chick to talk to and get all of that bullshit off his chest." With the tips of her nails she raked the blunt bangs that blended with the tips of her long fake lashes.

I heard Hunga but I didn't say shit else to her as she turned in her seat and finally accelerated the Charger forward toward the Weequahic section, where Dane and I lived. Still, her words were on my mind as I looked out the tinted window at the streets of Newark, crowded with people either walking fast to get somewhere or standing in one spot either waiting for public transportation or just content to go nowhere. I focused on them as I fought like crazy to not give her words of advice any importance. To not let her judgment of me make me judge my damn self.

Thing was, how could I be all that she thought I should be for Dane when I wanted nothing more than for him to get out of the game? No, Dane didn't sell drugs, rob, or steal, but his gambling and loan-sharking business still left my man—my everything—open to getting locked up, robbed, or worse. Much worse. So how the hell was I supposed to support him in putting himself at risk? Just being with him and loving him in spite of it all was the limit of my riding or dying as his chick.

It was crazy being in a world where a wild chick like Hunga might be the better chick than me. Fuck my college education and my finance career making over fifty grand. Fuck my good credit and my good name. Fuck that I kept a clean house and a clean ass and a clean history on my pussy . . . . No, fuck all of *that*. My worth was all wrapped up in me chinning and grinning and holding him down while he did whatever, whenever, in those streets.

Hunga was a better chick than me because she was willing to break a rib with her foot while Keno whupped some man's ass, while I screamed out for Dane not to even swing?

For the millionth time I knew this world was not for me.

The Charger jerked to a stop and I opened my eyes to look out at Dane's and my house: a two-story with a fully furnished basement. The brick of the four-bedroom colonial home was refurbished and the black shutters were new. The sixty-year-old house had new life with all of the renovations we did inside and out just a few months ago. It was our home. I moved in a rush to open the passenger door and climbed out. "Thanks, Hunga," I said, closing the door.

"I can come in and wait with you if you want," she offered, reaching in her purse to pull out a blunt. "We can smoke this White Widow and chill 'til they get done handling Poppi's no-good ass."

Picture that shit. "Nah, I'm good. I have to get up early in the morning," I lied. "You get home safe."

Hunga lit the blunt. "Home? Shit. I'm headed back to the club to get my sip-and-dip on. See you when I see you."

With a quick toot of the horn and long stream of exhaled silver haze blown out the open window, she pulled off and eventually turned the corner.

I climbed the two levels of redbrick stairs and used my keys to enter the house. As soon as the door closed behind me, I released a breath in the darkness that was dimly lit by the lights on in the living room just off the foyer to the right. It felt damn good to be home and it would feel even better when Dane was here with me.

For me to hold him. For me to know he was safe. For him to answer my questions.

Kicking off my shoes, I climbed the stairs to one of four

bedrooms. In the darkness I tossed my bag on the bed and crossed the space to the adjoining bathroom. I flipped the switch to turn on the ceiling light and my reflection in the mirror above the sink made me jump back.

Blood was smeared across my cheek and the front of my shirt. Poppi's blood.

I flinched as the sight of his bloody face flashed before me like a vision. The man had just been to our house last week watching sports and eating the dinner I cooked for Dane and the rest of his crew. When they all finally brought their asses up from the basement—Dane's man cave—Poppi was the first one to tell me how much he enjoyed the smothered pork chops and mashed potatoes I cooked using one of the recipes in my mother's favorite cookbook.

And now his blood was on my face . . . put there by the blood on the hands of my man.

I grabbed the bottle of alcohol from underneath the sink and plenty of tissue to scrub the blood from my face. I scrubbed until my cheek felt raw. Almost as raw as I felt inside.

I dropped the tissues into the sink and grabbed the edges of the cool porcelain. My eyes fell on my engagement ring but the image blurred with my tears. Just last week, I reminded Dane of his promise to go completely legit before we even thought about setting a date and making plans for a wedding.

It was a promise he wasn't keeping.

"He so fucking hardheaded," I said aloud to myself, turning to press my ass to the sink as I rubbed my face with my hands.

When I met Dane we were both college students. The

draw of money from hustling pulled him from school and I stayed with him while I studied hard in school. I graduated college and got a job as a junior account executive at a large corporation. As I used my education and instincts to climb the ranks at the company, he was just as busy climbing the ranks until he was running the hustle and not just a runner in the hustle.

I loved him strong like God never created another man before or after him. That was cool because I knew without a damn doubt that he loved me just the same. Our love was real—the realest ever.

But I was tired of it all. The late nights. Constantly being on the go. The business calls on the cell all day and damn night. The sketchy-ass friends. The bitches throwing pussy at him. The even thirstier bitches wanting to claim my spot in all the nice cars and walk in my five-inch stilettos.

And the violence I saw tonight?

That was a side of Dane I never saw before and a side of Keno that just made total sense.

Releasing a breath heavy with my anxieties, I reached up to pull my thick curly hair into a loose topknot. Stripping naked, I turned on the shower and was happy as hell to step inside and let the heat and steam press against the curves of my body. Being half African American and half Puerto Rican gave me a double dose of ass and thighs.

The hairs on the back of my neck stood on end and I turned to look through the frosted glass at Dane stripping off his own clothes. I felt pure relief that he was home safe.

He opened the shower door and my eyes took him in. Broad shoulders. Tight stomach. Strong thighs. Long and thick dick.

Dane stepped inside the shower and reached for me. "Damn that water look good running down your body, baby," he said low in his throat as he brought both hands up to cup my small but plump breasts.

As good as he looked . . . and felt . . . I used one arm to move him from in front of me before coming around his body to step out of the shower dripping wet.

"Damn, Suga, what's up?" Dane asked, looking down meaningfully at his milk-chocolate dick, long and curving as it hung from his body with weight.

"Enough is enough, Dane," I said, my voice hard as hell, standing there naked and a little cold as I eyed him.

"Man, not now, Suga," he complained, his voice just as hard.

"Enough is enough," I said again. This was an old argument and he knew exactly what the fuck I meant.

Dane avoided my eyes as he slammed the glass door of the shower closed.

I stepped right up and opened that motherfucker right back, giving him a stare filled with more than enough attitude.

Dane was already lathering his body with soap as he glanced over his shoulder at my face. Once and then again. He made a face filled with aggravation as he threw his hands up and looked at me. "A'ight, Suga. Damn. I know. A'ight. I got it. I got you."

"Just remember that we're traveling steady on two different roads that's gonna take us in two different directions," I said, softening my tone and my stance. This was my man. This was the dude I love. This was the motherfucker I would die for.

He stopped soaping his dick to look over at me as water beat down on his belly. "Oh, so you gone leave me?" Dane asked.

His voice sounded like he was challenging me. Daring me. Not believing me. Knowing my ass wasn't going anywhere.

"No, maybe the bullshit gone take you from me," I told him in a soft voice filled with my fears.

Dane shook his head as he dropped the soap and stepped out the shower to pull me into his arms and up against his body.

I felt weak at the knees, but he was strong enough to hold me up as I gave in and wrapped my arms around his damn shoulders to hold that nigga tight as hell.

"Suga, I promise you I'm not going nowhere. There ain't no jail cell or coffin built for me. You heard me?" Dane whispered against my ear as he pressed kisses to my cheek.

I just wished I had as much faith in his words as he did.

2 ///

*T*he next morning I was up and out of our bed before my alarm clock had a chance to sound off. I snatched an outfit, shoes, and accessories from my new walk-in closet so fast that I had to hope the shit matched until I got into one of the guest bedrooms with its own adjoining bath.

I was more than cool with leaving Dane on his back, snoring with his mouth open and his dick sleeping just as hard as he was. Usually I'd wake him up with his dick in my mouth to suck him hard and fast until he got rock *hard* and came *fast*. A little something-something for him to think about for the rest of the day. I liked to leave my man with a nice BJ before his OJ. Usually his nut would send him right back to sleep until early afternoon when he finally rose to start his day.

And I just knew after he went to bed earlier that morning with a bad case of the dry dick that he was really banking on that head game. Tough shit. To me, that would be like cosigning what happened last night.

It was hard to think about riding or sucking dick when you were fighting not to throw up in disgust. That was a side of Dane I didn't like to see. I couldn't stand to see. And usually I didn't. He made sure of that. The violence and anger was nothing like the man he was with me.

I couldn't help but wonder which of his two sides was the realest of him.

When we met we both were freshmen at Rutgers University–New Brunswick. Before we finished our first year he was into the game with his uncle Stripes, who used to work as a runner for some Mafia crime boss back in the seventies. I didn't like it but I knew that from the jump. Over the next couple of years, Dane took over the business as his uncle's health began to fade and Stripes eventually succumbed to his diagnosis of stomach cancer. The money flowed into his pockets like crazy and he made sure to spend it on fly shit to put on my back, feet, and wrists.

Through loan-sharking and running a couple underground gambling houses where they played nothing but sky's the limit poker, Dane was getting money. *That* I knew about. He wasn't hustling dope but a lot of his major clients did. *That* I knew. He stayed strapped to make sure no one came gunning for him and got away with his money or his life. I knew *that* too.

And I knew when it came to his money, Dane didn't play. He was all about his business. I can understand taking a heavy risk with someone walking away with your cash, especially if it wasn't clear as fuck that the loan needed to be paid back. And Dane didn't deal in small numbers. He wasn't the type to be chasing Negroes down for two or three hundred dollars on Friday nights when they cashed their paychecks.

But beating some dude's ass until he was bloody and limp? What's next? Murder?

Was the man I loved willing to put a shot to the dome to someone who crossed him? Shit, had he already? Loving a man in the hustle was one thing. But riding for a murderer?

Don't get me wrong. I'm a chick who grew up in Newark, New Jersey. The Weequahic part of Newark wasn't as congested as other sections of the city and a *little* safer, but it still wasn't any kind of place to walk around with your head up your ass. No place really was. I've seen some shit. I've heard about plenty of shit. I've been through some shit. The streets could get wild as hell and some of the people smelled fear and jumped on it—sometimes it was even worse for a chick with a light complexion and curly hair that people *assumed* thought she was better than the next bitch. I never did think that but still I had to learn early how to stay sharp at the tongue, fierce in the eyes, and thorough with my fist-work—when pushed.

Satisfied with the designer linen V-neck dress I wore with a mix of wooden, turquoise, and coral beaded neck-laces, I left the guest room and made my way down the stairs with my cork high-heeled shoes in my hand. I pulled my jet-black hair up into a tight topknot and thanked God I could get through the workday with just a tube of lip gloss in my purse.

It didn't matter anyway. I just wanted to get the hell away from the house. My pussy was directly connected to my brain and my heart and like most of the men in the world, Dane couldn't comprehend that shit. When I was pissed or sad or just had something heavy on my mind, I didn't feel like fucking.

I paused on the steps leading from the second level of our home and looked over at one of the many leather-framed mirrors lining the wall in an organized pattern meant to draw the eye. My eyes were troubled. The what-ifs were a bitch and every day I lived in fear that the phone would ring.

What if Dane was killed?

What if Dane got locked up?

Either way . . . what if I had to learn to live without him?

Dane really was the only person in my life that was constant.

My eyes filled with sadness. My mother, Martha, passed away when I was real young but I remembered the smell of her favorite perfume, the feel of her kisses to my cheeks, the sound of her voice as she said my nightly prayers with me before bed, and the sight of the sadness in her eyes caused by my father. His drinking tantrums. His yelling at her . . . at me. I truly believed that she absolutely loved me and I was the goodness in her life. I was what mattered. I knew she was proud of me and guiding my steps from heaven.

I couldn't say the same for my father.

He didn't really know how to show me he loved me outside of making sure I had clothes on my back, food in my belly and that I carried my behind to school. He spent any time outside of his job as a school janitor loving the liquor he thought he was hiding from me in his coffee cup. I was happy as hell to graduate high school and leave for college. I was freed from his drinking and his distance.

No hugs. No kisses. No affection.

All the things my mama gave me without hesitation. All of the things I rediscovered when Dane came into my life. He was my man, my lover, my backbone, my friend, my defender, my supporter.

I didn't want to lose any of that.

The streets were tough enough for a man on the right side of the law. You could be minding your own, walking home with a can of tea and Skittles, and be side-eyed that you were up to no good. Dane was taking a helluva chance. As far as the feds and the locals were concerned he wasn't shit but a criminal and that made the target on his back even bigger.

We already owned our beautifully decorated home. Cars. Jewelry. Designer clothes. Money in the bank. Loot hidden around the house—and God knows where else. On top of all that I made damn good money and was on my own hustle to climb the corporate ladder to make more.

Why not go legit? We weren't millionaires but we were straight.

If only he wasn't so fucking hardheaded.

With a heavy sigh I grabbed my briefcase, purse, and keys from the top of the leather and studded foyer table under a large round mirror with an ostrich feather frame. I hated that I always peeped out the window before I left the house. Straight up, I didn't know what the fuck I was looking for but whatever might await me—be it the police or a stick-up kid, or worse—I wanted to know. Fuck it. I didn't like surprises. Never did.

Although Dane also updated our detached two-car garage in the backyard, I always parked on the street. I'd rather his Benz, convertible Jag, and motorcycles were off the street. Plus the houses on our street didn't have the largest lots, and without much yard and just one long driveway leading to the garage behind the house, it was much easier to pull my convertible Volvo on and off the street in front of the house.

As I walked to the driver's side door I looked up and down the tree-lined street. The four-block radius where

Dane and I lived in Weequahic was a middle-class community of hardworking career people. Hell, an officer for the Newark Police Department lived around the corner from us and we even socialized at his house for holiday cookouts. I could just imagine the look on our neighbors' faces if the police flooded the neighborhood to storm our house.

I shook my head and smoothed my hands over the steering wheel before I pulled away. It only took me a good ten or fifteen minutes to make it downtown to the fifteen-story building on Broad Street that housed the three floors of offices for the financial planning and investment firm where I worked.

After parking in the lot, I grabbed my extra tube of lip gloss to coat my lips real quick before sliding on my shades. With briefcase in hand and my Michael Kors straw clutch under my arm, I made my way out of the lot. I smiled in polite greeting at two women standing and talking at the rear of a Range Rover. The telecommunications firm where they worked was housed on a floor of offices in the building.

"Oh no, I always make sure to be on the Garden State Parkway before the clocks hit five after five," one of them said.

"I heard on the news on the way in to work that a nine-year-old kid got shot last night," the other said in a raspy-ass voice like she lived on cigarette ashes and shots of hard liquor. "Newark revitalization my ass."

Now see, I really wasn't paying these broads any real attention. In *my* mind, their conversation was interrupting my day because I really didn't want to hear nothing they had to say. But for me to check in and realize they was shitting on my city? And I was in a fucked-up mood *anyway*? Nada.

I turned on the heels of my Miu Miu pumps and politely strolled my ass back over to them. "Excuse me, ladies," I said, with a smile that didn't have a hint of happiness or pleasantry in it.

They both looked at me. All nice and shit. All unsuspecting and shit.

See, I'm not a black man. I have a light complexion slightly tanned by my African American mother. My Puerto Rican features inherited from my father were "J-Lo safe" to them. I was professionally and stylishly dressed. In their eyes I was safe. See, even a dark-skinned woman—whether African American or Latina—dressed in jeans and larger in size would've made them clutch their purse a bit tighter.

"I couldn't help but overhear your little convo," I said, removing my shades as I turned my head to lock my eyes on each of them. "If you're so afraid of this city then why come here to work and sap up the income to carry to another city or county or even state to spend? Because you're leeches on the city that's why."

Their mouths fell open and they looked offended. Fuck 'em. Maybe on another day—in another moment—I could have just ignored their ignorant fear. *Maybe.*

"See, qualified Newark residents have to compete with those of you from subpar suburbia scrounging for jobs like rats," I said, without raising my voice. "If you're gonna commute your asses into the city to make the money then at least have enough respect for the city not to sit up in it and act like your life is in danger at any given moment. It's simple-minded, prejudicial, and a bunch of bullshit."

"We never—"

I shook my head and held up my hand.

Many of the workers in the towering office buildings found in the area surrounding Newark Penn Station, Military Park, and Market Street, commuted to work from New York or the other surrounding cities. A lot—not all—but a lot had slick shit to say about the city. And yes, I calmly and coolly checked each and every one of their asses. I felt damn good that I was born and raised in Newark, made my money in the city, and paid taxes there as well.

I took a breath as they looked at me like I was one stroke from being *muy loco*. "What you need to never do is offend a Newark resident while standing in Newark and preparing to walk in an office building . . . *in Newark* to work and collect a paycheck that you made in . . . *Newark*. If nothing else, have some manners."

With one last disparaging glare, I slipped on my shades, turned on my heels, and walked away with an extra sashay of the hips, buttocks, and thighs that Dane was real appreciative of. Ow!

I frowned as I entered the building. I didn't want to think about Dane, especially when it was clear my big ass and thighs couldn't do shit to convince him to go motherfucking legit.

Long after I rode the elevator to the fourteenth floor and entered my small office that really wasn't shit but a glorified walk-in closet with a window overlooking Penn Station, I sat at my desk and tried hard to focus on starting my work day as a senior accounting specialist. Tried and failed like a mother.

Brrrnnnggg.

I shifted my eyes to the phone before reaching to pick up the handset. "Sophia Alvarez speaking."

"What's wrong with you?"

Dane.

I glanced at my two-tone Movado watch. Barely ten in the morning but he was up. "Hey. Can I call you back, I was just about to walk into a meeting," I lied, arching my eyebrow.

The line went quiet.

"I'm a grown-ass man, Suga," Dane said, his voice hard. "Stop fuckin' playing with me."

Dane and I always kept it real with each other. Always. "Do I think you love me? Yes. Do I think you're faithful? Yes. Do I think you would fight the world for me? Hell yes. Do I know I will love you for the rest of my life? Yes. But . . . do I think you will ever keep your word about changing your business? No. No, Dane. You're lying to me. And that shit hurts. That *shit* hurts like hell."

"I can't just fuckin' quit like it's Popeye's or some shit, Suga," he snapped.

I rolled my eyes and sat up straight in my chair. "I really gotta go, Dane. There's a room filled with people who recognize I'm *not* fucking stupid."

Click.

I dropped the phone back onto its cradle before reaching into my clutch for my cell phone. Dane hardly ever called my office line. I had ten missed calls from him and one from my dad. My ringer was on silent.

Knock-knock.

I looked up as I locked the screen of my phone. "Come in," I called out, setting it on the corner of my desk before opening up some profit-and-loss report a junior level clerk submitted for my approval. Whoopie-fucking doo. When I was done I had to submit it to my immediate supervisor for *their* approval.

My promotion meant a small-ass office, new title, and pay raise, but I was still a bottom feeder around this mother-fucker when it came to making major moves within the company. Still, at twenty-four I knew I was ahead of the game and on the right track.

The door opened and one of my coworkers, Leo Hunt, leaned in the doorway dressed in all gray. Like me, Leo was recently promoted and also under twenty-five. He was tall and cute with a smooth bald head and chocolate complex-ion. To make sure he kept white folks at ease, he always kept his face clean-shaven and wore a pair of cheap glasses from Walgreen's . . . that didn't have a bit of prescription in them.

"Whassup, Leo?" I asked, shaking my head as he pushed the frames up on the top of his bald head.

"I wanted to drop this off for you to look over," he said, stepping into the office to sit the glossy folder he held in front of me.

I cut my eyes over at him as he folded his tall frame into one of the leather club chairs in front of my desk. Anything more than that would keep the door from opening . . . seri-ously. It was some real bullshit but it gave a girl more privacy than the cubicle I came out of before my promotion.

"I know you said you were going to work some before you considered going back to school for your MBA but I thought I'd give you a little push," Leo said.

I nodded as I flipped through the info on New York Uni-versity's twenty-two-month MBA program. "I'll think about it *but,* I've been out of college for a few years and it feels real

Meesha Mink

good not to have a paper due or have to study all week for an exam."

Leo laughed.

"But I wish you the best going for yours and still working full-time," I told him, lifting off my ass a little bit to reach across the desk and playfully swat his knee.

Just that quick, his hand reached out to cover mine. I'm talking quick as hell. I eased my hand right back across my desk as I eyed him. "How's Nia?" I asked, reminding him of his girlfriend.

Leo smiled. "She's good," he said, leaning forward to pick up my framed photo of me and Dane living it up on a yacht he chartered during our vacay in the Bahamas last year. "How's Dane?"

"I'm straight as a motherfucker. Why?"

My eyes got big as hell as I shifted them to Dane standing in the doorway of my office. I could tell by the sound of his voice and the look on his face that his ass was on ten. That spelled—in my Bernie Mac from *The Players Club* voice—"trouble-trouble." I hopped to my feet and came around my desk, trying to play it cool and not show that I wasn't a hundred percent sure Dane wasn't about to knock Leo the fuck out. "Hey baby, this is Leo my coworker," I said as I pressed my hand to Dane's chest and a soothing kiss to the corner of his mouth.

"Nice to finally meet you," Leo said as he rose to his feet and extended his hand.

Dane made a face like "Negro please" before he slid his arm around my waist and hugged me closer to his side. "I'm sure there's some work you have to do around here some-where," he said.

Okay . . . my bottom lip literally dropped low enough to hit the floor.

Leo made a confused face before he just shook his head. "Yo, Sophie. Talk to you later," he said, before leaving the office.

"Much later," Dane emphasized.

I let out a breath before pulling Dane farther into the office so that I could reach behind him and push the door shut. "Don't come to my job tryna mob out on my coworkers. Really, Dane, really?" I said, looking up at him like he was straight crazy.

He sat down on the edge of my desk, looking good in a basic white V-neck tee that fit his frame without clinging and denims with some Prada sneakers I bought him a few weeks ago. "One . . . don't give me a reason to come to your job. Two . . . when I do come, baby, I definitely don't want to run up on some lame-duck-ass nigga making a slick-ass move on you."

I tilted my head to the side as I crossed my arms over my chest. "One . . . I didn't give you a reason to come. Two . . . he didn't step out of line but if he did I know how to check a man. I don't lend money, clothes, or pussy."

Dane reached out to grab my thigh. "And that's my pussy, ain't it?" he asked, his voice too deep and too sexy.

My pussy was a no-good traitor because his touch, his voice, and that look in his eyes made it come to life. This is why I snuck out the house like I ran his pockets. The pressure he put on me to fuck always won out over my anger or disappointment. Always.

Dane's hand came up to grip my ass and he jerked me forward until I stood between his legs. I kept my arms crossed over my chest and face in a definite "No haps" expression . . . but my heart was already beating fast and hard in my chest. My pussy? She been gone off to a world where nothing but sliding on Dane's dick mattered.

Dick addiction was real as hell. Don't sleep.

His hands eased under my dress and gripped my buttocks before he massaged them as he leaned forward to lightly bite and then kiss the slight dimple in my cheek.

I shivered.

He chuckled.

"No, Dane. I'm good," I said, bringing my hands up to his broad shoulders and fighting like hell to step back.

He held me tighter and buried his face against my neck as he pulled my panties to the side.

"I skipped a big meeting to come and get this good pussy," Dane whispered against my pulse.

I gasped even as I shook my head and pressed my hands against them shoulders, all weak as hell. "Dane—"

He stood up to kiss me and shut me up all at once. And it was so good. All soft and moist at first before he traced my lips with his tongue.

My hands slid right up his shoulders to surround his neck as his hands slid my panties to the side to play in my pussy.

My clit was throbbing.

My nipples got hard.

I was hot. Ready. Gone. So gone.

Damn.

I tried to break his hold on me. He held me tighter. "I need to lock the door," I said, turning with his arms still around me. I leaned forward and turned the latch as he pressed a hand to my back and ground his hard dick against my ass. Felt like a damn anaconda or some shit.

I turned and stood back up to press my hands to my man's fine face as he jerked my dress up around my waist. "I can't believe you came down here for some ass," I whispered against his mouth in between our heated kisses.

"I can't believe you left the house without giving me some," Dane told me, about to suck my bottom lip.

I leaned back from him. "Six months. Six more months for you to go legit or I'm out," I told him, making sure my voice and my eyes were hard. "I love you but I will leave your ass, because if you can't leave it for me then you love it more than me. And I'm not coming second to nothing or nobody in your life."

Dane lifted me up onto the desk and stepped back with a cocky-ass expression to unzip his denims and release that beautiful beast. It was thick and long and hard with the veins pulsing all along the dark chocolate. "Baby, you want this dick or you wanna talk?" he asked, wrapping his strong caramel fingers around it to shake at me.

Oh really? Really?

I reached to undo my side zip and then eased my dress up over my head until I sat before him in nothing but a sheer ivory bra and matching bikinis. *Thank God for locked doors*, I thought, and I lay back on the desk, ignoring the stapler pressing into my side like a motherfucker, as I arched my back and then spread my legs wide in front of him. His head dropped to take it all in. Trust me, the sheerness of the lingerie wasn't hiding shit from his eyes.

"You want to have all this or all of *that*?" I asked with emphasis.

We both knew damn well what *that* was.

Dane's eyes were serious as hell as he licked his lips and stepped forward to rip my panties with one strong tug before that sexy motherfucker stroked the length of his dick across my moist and swollen clit.

I hissed in pleasure but closed my legs, gently catching his eleven inches between my thighs until nothing but the thick tip poked between the firm flesh. I rocked my legs back and forth, jacking his dick with my thighs. "Six months?" I asked again.

Dane was looking down at his dick between my thighs as he pressed his strong hips forward. He cut his eyes up to look at my face. "Six months," he agreed.

I moved my legs until my knees were on either side of my shoulders, causing my ass to lift up off the desk. Oh, I was flexible as hell . . . and he loved it. *"Ido y lo consigue, el bebé,"* I whispered to him, my eyes half-closed as I looked up at him. I knew he understood me. After the first time I spoke the words to him, he asked me what they meant.

"I'ma get this pussy good too," Dane warned and promised all at once.

I knew this Negro was gone try and make a point.

He used the slight drizzle of his juice from the tip to rub against my core before he worked that dick inside me with tiny back-and-forth thrusts of his hips. I worked my walls to help guide that strong long motherfucker inside me. Inch by inch. *Whoo!*

Dane grunted and he thrust the last thick inch of the base inside me as he bent over to shift my bra down and circle one hard brown nipple with his tongue. And just like that I forgot about every-damn-thing. The six-month compromise. The fact only a locked door separated our fuck session from the receptionist. Any memories of him whipping someone's ass. The bloody smear he left on my cheek. The slight smell of weed in his mouth. Even the knowledge that he was so intent on getting this pussy because we both knew he wouldn't get home until a few hours before dawn. Just. Like. That.

Dane looked down at me all fierce and shit as he raised my ass higher in the air and pumped his dick inside me like it would save his life. Fuck CPR. This dude—my dude—was delivering GDR—good dick resuscitation.

I loved it. It was . . . hot. It was . . . hard. It was . . . good. It was . . . fiery. It was . . . on. It was motherfucking on. Ooh. And my face shown it all to him because his face showed me that my reaction to him was turning him the fuck on even more.

"Good, ain't it?" I asked hotly, pulling him down by his neck to lick his chin . . . his cheeks . . . his mouth.

I felt his dick get harder inside me and against me and . . .

"I'm cumming," I whispered against his mouth as these familiar—but still good as hell—tiny explosions went off in my pussy and everything else about me that made me a woman. My clit. My breasts. My nipples. My core. My instincts. Every-damn-thing.

Shit. I just closed my eyes and gave in. Enjoyed it. Savored that shit for every bit of good it was. And this the shit . . . this wasn't even us on a level ten.

Dane leaned up and I knew by the look on his face and the way he bit his bottom lip that he was about to nut it up. He grunted loud as shit as he flung his head back with all the veins in his neck straining and shit. My mouth fell open and I undid one of my legs and kicked off a shoe to stick my toes in his mouth.

Knock-knock.

My heart damn near stopped. "Ssssh," I whispered up to Dane as he sucked my toes and fucked me hard as he came in me.

Knock-knock.

The doorknob rattled.

Knock-knock.

Dane gave me three or four final thrusts and sucks before his body went slack and he lowered his upper body onto mine. "They persistent like a motherfucker," he whispered in my ear before his ass had the nerve to laugh. "Sure it's not your boy?"

I worked my pussy walls and shot his now limp—but still thick—dick out of me. "Fuck him and fuck you because now I have to go all day without panties," I whispered back, playfully swatting the back of his head.

He nuzzled his face against my neck. "I love you," he whispered against the sweat dripping there.

"Love you too," I answered, and I did.

We were young now and even younger when we first met. Everybody with a tongue and not enough sense to mind their business told us we would never make it. Said we were too different. Too young. Too much left in the world to still see . . . and do . . . and feel.

But fuck them. Fuck 'em all.

There was only one thing that could fuck us up. Just one damn thing.

We got up and Dane took off his shirt to give me the

beater he wore to clean up as best I could until I could get my nasty ass to the bathroom. He even balled it up and rammed it in his pocket to get the hell out of the office. With one last kiss, I unlocked the door and peeped out.

"Call me later," Dane said.

I grabbed his arm.

He turned back.

"Six months, Dane," I said, knowing I was nagging him and not really giving a fuck. I wished his mother hadn't died from cancer a few years back, because she was my ride or die on Dane going legit.

"Six months," he promised with another kiss to my dome before he turned and walked to the elevator with all the swagger he had even back when we were college kids.

The receptionist walked back to her desk and spotted me. "Oh, you're back," she said. "Mr. Wilkin wants to see you."

I nodded even though I barely heard her as I watched Dane until the elevator started to close. He winked at me and smiled.

I made sure to smile back even though those crazy-ass "what-ifs" came floating back to me. Just like every other day, I could only pray that nothing happened to take him from me for good.

3 //

$\mathcal{I}$ woke up to the warm feeling of Dane's arm around me and I smiled as I snuggled my body back against the heat of his body. I lived for weekend mornings. I didn't have to get up early and Dane didn't usually bother to get out the bed before one or two in the afternoon. Hell with it. We slept in.

I checked the bedside clock as my stomach grumbled. It was a little after ten. I decided to treat us both to some breakfast in bed. I would feed him food, then feed him this good pussy, and send his ass right back to sleep.

I made a move to get up and his arm tightened around my waist. I smiled. "I'm going to cook," I told him.

That arm lifted right on up and then so did I. I slapped his bare ass before crossing the hardwood floors and stepping into the bathroom for a quick shower before I pulled on his thick, heavy black robe. When I stepped back into the bedroom, I was surprised the bed was empty. Frowning, I made my way downstairs and then followed the noises coming from our kitchen.

The sight of Dane butt naked, smoking a blunt and flipping pancakes on the griddle, was a hot fucking mess. I leaned against the door frame and watched him. Dirty dick and all. And the dick was dirty. He'd made sure of that when he finally got home around three. He woke me up with his head buried between my thighs just as he started to eat my pussy. Two nuts later he flipped me onto my stomach, slid the dick in deep, and fucked me real good to a third. So my juices was *all* over that dick.

"You want bacon, baby?" he asked, taking a deep toke on his blunt.

I lifted my eyes from the hardness of his ass to find him looking at me. "I said I would cook," I reminded.

He shrugged them square shoulders. "When you was in the shower, I decided to jack your surprise and make breakfast for you."

Pushing off the doorframe, I strolled over to him and kissed his shoulder as I slapped his ass. HARD.

WHAP.

"I owed you that from this morning," I reminded him, lifting my face up to him.

Dane pinched the blunt lightly as he inhaled the kush. His eyes squinted as he pursed them suckable lips to blow a stream of the thick smoke into my nostrils.

I leaned back but his hand came up to lightly grip the back of my neck and hold my head steady as the stream filled my nose. I inhaled it as I locked my eyes with his. His free hand came down to open the robe and slide across my belly to my back.

"You think you slick," I told him, smoke escaping through my mouth as I spoke. "You know weed makes me not give a fuck."

Dane raised the blunt to take another deep inhale before he released another stream that I inhaled. "Exactly."

I didn't mess with weed that often. I never fucked with

it unless I was with Dane and it was the weekend. I can't lie that getting high made me hot as shit. "Last time I fucked with you with this shit I woke up with a sore asshole, mo'fucka."

Dane laughed and whistled as he shook his head. "You said you wanted to try it," he said as he turned to flip the pancakes. "Don't worry, I barely got the head in before you farted and that killed it for me."

Brrrnnnggg.

"Shit, I thought you was about to shit on my dick so I got the fuck out that hole," he teased.

"Shut up," I said, walking over to the cordless phone sitting on the counter.

"Nobody but your pops call the house phone," Dane called over to me.

Brrrnnnggg.

True. That shit made my hand ease back from the phone like it had just turned into a snake. I loved my daddy. For real. But he never called unless he needed me to do something, and his ass never thought about doing something until he was tipsy.

Since he retired last year from being a school custodian he really had all day to get fucked up off whatever cheap-ass brown liquor he loved.

Pulling the robe closed, I looked over my shoulder at Dane as he used the remote to turn on the small flat-screen on the counter beneath the cabinets. Soon the sounds of MTV2's "Sucker Free" filled the air. Dane loved for music to be playing in the house. It was like his Linus blanket or something.

Brrrnnnggg . . .

"*Maldito,*" I swore.

"I know that one," Dane said around a mouthful of pancakes.

Ignoring him, I answered the call. *"Hola, Papi."*

"Hi, stranger," he said in English, his Spanish accent present. Although my father was full-blood Puerto Rican, he was born and raised in Newark and barely spoke in Spanish. It was by choice because, unlike me, he was fluent in it.

I remembered when I was little, he would mumble in Spanish when he was drunk and feeling spiteful because he knew my mother hated that shit since she couldn't understand him. To get back at him, my moms would talk shit to him in pig Latin. "Uckfay ouyay!" was her favorite. Pushing aside that memory with a shake of my head, I reached up to twist my hair into a topknot. "You needed something?" I asked, wishing I didn't feel so much dread because any time me and my father spent more than ten minutes together it was always awkward as hell.

"I needed a ride from the hospital—"

"Hospital?" I said. "What's wrong?"

"I was cleaning fish and cut myself by mistake. Just a few stitches."

"You okay?" I asked as I let my body lean against the wall. I was a lightweight and that little bit of weed smoke just hit me.

"Yup. I'm at Beth Israel."

"I'm on the way," I said.

"I know," he said, before the line went dead.

My mouth fell open. My father was a trip. He *stayed* on one. *And how the hell could he cut himself?*

The sounds of Method Man and Mary J. Blige on "You're All I Need" suddenly filled the air. Dane had turned it up as

soon as I got off the phone. This was his all-time favorite rap
and R & B collabo. Fuck the rest.

Kanye West and Jaime Foxx's "Gold Digger."

Biggie and Faith Evans's "One More Chance" remix.

Not even Jay-Z and Mary's "Can't Knock the Hustle."

I am always the Mary to his Meth.

Butt naked, without a care in the world, he jumped to
his feet using the syrup bottle as mic and came over to me
straight doing Method Man's part. "For real girl, it's me and
your world believe me—"

I lowered my chin to my chest and did the Mary dance with
one arm in the air. I loved when we remembered we were still
young as hell and could have fun. We both were hustlers with
our nose to the grind, but moments like these made our life
cool as hell together. "Like sweet morning dew . . ."

It didn't even matter that I was off-key as hell as I took
over Mary's chorus. I wanted him to know I was there for
him any time he needed me.

Living in Newark was such a wild card. Depending on the
ward or the street or even the particular home on a block,
you could be living the life of suburbia or struggling like a
bitch among brick urban landscapes, working forty hours
a week or hustling like if you ever stopped your life would
stop. You could look out your window and see a beautiful
park or a business or high-rise building or passing train or
baseball stadium or abandoned homes or bodegas or graffiti or corners littered with young men thinking they could
only find themselves and their future through colors or affil-
iations or their homeboys. Or those young men hiding the

fact they cling to those things outside homes filled with drug use, yelling, hitting, and hunger.

This city was huge—the largest in New Jersey—and the stories being lived and told within the limits were so varied. The people calling it home were so different in skin color and ethnicity and careers but still the same because of a love for the city. A desire to see the city continue to do better even when the news reports the moments that should be looked upon with shame and regret . . . like any other city. But still the love and the hope remained.

I repped hard for my city.

As I drove the few blocks to my father's house, I looked out at the neighborhood where I grew up. Certain houses brought back certain memories. Certain friends. Playing hopscotch and doing dances in the street between parked cars. Sleepovers. First day of school. My first house party. Walking up one of the many uphill streets—or downhill depending on your direction—in my first pair of heels.

When I parked in front of my father's house, the memory—as always, was the day my mother died, but I pushed the pain of that thought away, as always. Even though I was so young at the time, I could remember everything about that day so clear, but I still couldn't remember the name of my eighth grade teacher for shit.

I had just turned the corner onto my father's street when I spotted a woman in a pink maxi dress jogging up the stairs of my father's next-door neighbors, the Jordans. My eyes got a little big to see one of my ex–childhood friends, Harriet Jordan. Now she goes by Luscious.

For as long as I could remember, our parents lived next door to each other and we had been best friends until we both got onto that campus in New Brunswick and Harriet lost her damn mind. The sudden freedom was too much.

That bitch started acting real ratchet, skipping classes, partying, smoking weed, and God knows what else. Her rep on campus was fucked—especially when her and her white roommate started stripping at some club back in Newark. That silly chick wouldn't go home unless the campus shut down but rode the hour-and-a-half drive to Newark to shake it fast for dollars.

Her dumb ass had a way better home life than I did so I didn't even cram to understand her purpose. I had my eyes on the goal of graduating—and enjoying Dane—so I cut her loose. After a while we barely spoke when we saw each other in the dorm or on campus. I wasn't shocked when she finally dropped/flunked/whatever out of school. I had already dropped her out of my life.

The chick she became was nothing—NOTHING—like the girl I grew up with or the young woman I first walked onto the Rutgers campus with. This bitch became reckless and I had no time for her ass. In this case foresight was 20/20 like a motherfucker. Straight reckless.

The last time I saw her I was dropping something off to my father's house after work. As I was leaving his house, he made me walk over to where he was already outside standing with Harriet and her mother, Naomi. I *hated* that shit and kept it moving to my Volvo like I didn't see or hear him. I didn't spare breath to speak to her in all these years and now he was forcing the issue.

"Suga," he had called out to me by my nickname.

Still faking it I put on a fake-ass smile and waved without even looking their way.

He called my name again and I remember thinking those swigs of E&J brandy he had was kicking in. And that ticked me off even more. I hated dealing with him when he was drunk or drinking.

Yeah, I threw a little shade that day. It was clear to a blind and mute monkey I didn't want to walk over and I damn sure didn't want to speak . . .

I closed the car door and walked over to them. "Sí, Papi?"I said.

"It's Harriet, your childhood friend," he said.

I looked at Harriet with this blank-ass expression like I never met her. Like we never were as close as sisters. "That was a long time ago," I said, shady as hell.

Harriet and her mom looked offended.

"Maybe not long enough," Harriet said . . .

I was glad to get the hell out of their company that day. Truth was, Harriet hurt my feelings tossing me aside because I was focused on school and she was focused on fun. A piece of me felt real good looking down my nose at her. Childish? Yup. Real? Real as hell.

That is a fly-ass Jag, though, I thought as I passed her whip parked on the street. I heard she was living with that rapper Make$—before his one-hit-wonderboy ass got arrested for helping two dudes from his crew try to get away with raping one of his dancers on tour. Then the rumors were hot that she started fucking Tek-9—one of Make$'s rapper friends—before he was locked up for selling drugs.

I didn't know what she was doing to make ends meet these days but they had to be meeting like a motherfucker.

The only open parking spot was in front of my father's house so I went to the end of the street to turn around.

"So she's out of jail. *Joder perra*," my father said as he reached in the backseat for his cane.

My mouth fell open. I didn't know what had me fucked up more, the gossip on Harriet getting locked up or my father looking so angry as he called her a "fucking bitch." I whipped my head to the right so hard to look at him that my topknot fell over like a limp dick. The hell?

"The police arrested her on her parent's porch last night," he said.

"For what?" I asked.

"I don't know and I caught a cab to the hospital not long after they took her," her father said, sounding tired . . . and probably wanting a drink.

I could see Harriet was on the porch with her parents as I did a little U-turn to come back down the street on the other side. I know they had to be ashamed to have their daughter hauled off to jail in front of their house. In all the years of us living next door to each other the Jordans never had police to their house. *And* they was bougie as hell . . .

Oooh. They were arguing . . . and their voices were carrying. I lowered the window. Fuck it.

"Calm down, Harriet," her father, Kendrick, said.

"Calm down. Calm down. You two have no clue what I been through and I really don't think you care."

"Anything that you have been through that is too much for you to bear was at your own doing," her father said.

I looked over and almost laughed to see my father had lowered his window too. We were ear hustling like a motherfucker and driving slow like we were gonna shoot up the damn block!

"I got arrested because that detective was a dirty cop

blackmailing me into having sex with him and I put a stop to it. The charges were dropped this morning. See, you didn't do a damn thing to protect me last night. I told you I was afraid that he was going to hurt me and not even take me to jail. I begged you . . . I BEGGED YOU to be there for me. And you let me down."

Damn. I frowned. This some cinematic type shit. Dirty cop? Blackmailed for sex? I wasn't even about her life. Fuck no.

I parallel-parked in the spot just as Harriet turned and walked down the steps to her Jag. She eyed us as my father used his cane to get out the car.

"Hi, Sophie," she said with a wave that was as fake as the smile I gave her in return as I climbed out my whip.

"Are you okay, Mr. Alvarez?" Harriet called out to him.

I came around the car to help him. He stopped in his tracks and turned to look over his shoulder at her. "Just an accident while I was cleaning some fish last night," he said.

I frowned because his body felt tight as hell. Tense.

I looked up at him. He was tall and thin with shiny silver hair looking like the poor man's Ricky Ricardo. Everything I am is the feminine—and softer—version of this man. My wide ebony eyes and long lashes. High cheekbones and long nose. Slightly downturned mouth and full lips. Even my dimpled chin. I was Victor Alvarez in a long-ass black wig. Our only difference was the thicker texture to my hair and the brown tint to my complexion. Those things were all from my mama.

"You all right?" I asked him as a car drove by blasting Wale.

He was still staring at Harriet as she climbed into her car and pulled off.

"Damn, what she do to piss you off?" I asked as he finally limped his way toward the porch.

Victor looked down at me as we moved up the first step. "Just all that ruckus she caused last night," he said.

The smell of liquor was already on his breath but it was light. Real light. Usually the smell of alcohol would be strong enough for me to get tipsy off the fumes. He was nowhere near finished for the day.

I cooked my father a big pot of my mama's chicken and sausage stew with a pot of seasoned rice. He always said he loved her cooking and that was his favorite dish. I made sure he ate a big plate of it and packed the rest in small plastic containers for him to warm up easily. After setting him up in his favorite recliner with his cane and the remote nearby— and ignoring the bottle of E&J brandy he thought he was hiding on the other side of his chair—I gave him a pat on the back and hauled ass. My daughter duties were done and most of my afternoon shot to hell.

As soon as I stepped outside I slid my shades on and took a deep breath of the summer air as I made my way to my car and slid beneath the wheel. I had just started the engine when my cell phone rang. I dug it out of my purse and used my nude-painted thumbnail to unlock the touch screen.

I never saved info to contacts so it took me a second to recognize the cell phone number of Johnica Brantley. I hadn't heard from my little mentee in a minute.

Last year my job had started a mentoring program for "at-risk" inner-city youth. Of course Leo, myself, and the few other chocolate drops scattered about the company had stepped right up to participate. I'll be damned if I have to listen to these white folks bragging about what all they do for the poor "at-risk" Newark youths. Hell to the no. *No bueno.*

The mentoring program ran during the school year but I told Johnica to feel free to call me during the summer if she needed to talk. Still I hesitated like a motherfucker to answer her call. She could be a handful. From the moment I met Johnica—her father's name was Johnny of course—in the conference room of our offices, the teenager had been bold and brash and upfront. She walked up to me and introduced herself. She was fifteen with a face like a twelve-year-old and the body of a grown-ass woman—a thick and curvy grown-ass woman. Sometimes I thought she would tell me or just ask me shit to see how big she could make my eyes from shock.

Really I wasn't in the mood for whatever drama she might be serving up. I dropped the phone and decided to let it go to voice mail. *I'll call her Monday.*

I turned the corner onto our street. A cherry red car suddenly switched lanes and rolled to a stop about ten feet ahead of me. I squinted my eyes as I slowed down waiting for it to switch back to its lane.

It didn't.

"Man, shit. What the fuck?" I swore, turning the wheel and accelerating to move the car forward and into the opposite lane to pass.

The red car came over to block me in that lane as well.

I slammed on my brakes and looked up at my rearview mirror as my heart started to beat like crazy. The sight of a blacked-out dark car sitting at the end of the block made the hairs on my neck stand on end. "Oh shit," I whispered.

Something was up. I was blocked. I can't front. This shit

right here had me scared. I didn't want to be a fucking statistic. Another woman shot dead in the streets of Newark. I put my hand on the driver's-side door, thinking I should risk it and jump the hell out of the car. I kept shifting my eyes from the red car in front of me and then the black car in the rearview mirror behind me. I let the door handle go. *But what if they shoot at me while I'm running?*

Closing my hand into a fist, I reached for my cell phone with my other hand. It rang as soon as I picked it up. "Hello."

"Suga, stop by the store and get some cards—"

"Two cars got me blocked in the street down from the house," I said in a rush, feeling stupid for whispering as I waited for one or all of these motherfuckers in the cars to make a move.

Suddenly I heard Dane running through the house. His feet pounded the stairs just as hard as my heart beat in my chest. I fought the urge to mash the pedal and race forward to move that red motherfucker out my way. But then what?

"Don't hang up, Suga," Dane said in the phone.

My stomach lurched at the sound of him loading a clip into the gun. *Shit.*

I hated sitting here like a duck.

"I see you," Dane said.

I looked past the car and saw Dane running down the middle of the street at full speed in his bare feet and shirtless.

Suddenly the red car straightened up and zoomed forward in the opposite lane. It screeched to halt right beside me.

Don't shoot me.

I ducked down, covering my head with my hands as I squeezed my eyes shut, swearing I was about to be shot. I screamed the top of my lungs so hard a sharp pain hit the back of my throat.

I heard the car door open and in that moment a bitch was wishing for a gun.

Don't shoot me.

I felt hands on my body and I sat up swinging, landing two quick blows to something. *Bap-dhap.* I turned in my seat to start kicking like my daddy was Jackie Chan and not Victor Alvarez.

Please let me live.

"Suga . . . Suga . . . it's a'ight, baby. I got you."

Dane.

"Dane," I said in a whisper while my heart pounded like thunder as my body went slack with relief.

He pulled me out the car and up against his body. "I got you," he promised again as his hands stroked my back and my hair.

What the fuck was that shit about?

I felt his heart pounding against my chest and I buried my face into his neck, trembling my ass off. There was so much shit I wanted to say. To bitch about. To even blame him about. But I couldn't form words. I couldn't say shit. It was all about what I was feeling in that moment: Dane's arms and my fear.

4 //

$\mathcal{I}$t took Dane a week to convince me nobody was gunning for him or me and another whole week for me to stop looking for a red car—or any other strange car—sitting outside my door or following me when I left the house. I can't lie. That shit had me shook. How couldn't it? Every damn day I live my life afraid to lose Dane. Every day. But I never really thought about my own life. My own safety. Being collateral fucking damage.

I didn't know if all that craziness that day was about Dane's shit or just some randoms out and about looking to have some dumb fun on a chick. I didn't know. We didn't know. But I wasn't stuck on stupid. And Dane didn't come running his ass down the street like Will Smith in *Bad Boys* because he took it lightly either.

"Sophie, what you think about this?"

I shook my head to clear it and licked my lips as I looked over at Johnica standing in the doorway of one of the dressing rooms of the On Your Back boutique. She was in a satiny strapless mint-green bodysuit and flashy gold heels. Every piece of shine in that material highlighted her titties and ass. She started booty popping and snapping her fingers.

"This is me, right, Sophie?" Johnica asked, grinding her hips to the floor and bringing it back up.

"Miss Sophie," I reminded her just as I spotted the security guard standing in his post by the front door looking across the downtown Newark boutique eyeing the teen's show. I strolled over to him in my five-inch heels and the fool still didn't take his eyes off Johnica to look down at me standing in front of his horny ass. I had to fight the urge to grab his nuts in my fist. "She's fourteen," I snapped on him.

He frowned, cleared his throat and turned away, pushing his hands into the pockets of his dark blue uniform pants.

Rolling my eyes I came across the polished hardwood floors to gently nudge her back inside the dressing room. "When did you even take those in there, little girl?" I asked.

Johnica laughed. "It was worth a try," she said.

I smiled as I pulled the curtain closed. I turned and strolled around the boutique, smoothing my hands on the hips of my dark jeggings. I hadn't planned on spending my day off with my mentee but when she asked me to please free her from the two-bedroom apartment she shared with her mother, little sister, aunt, five younger cousins, and a pit-bull named Goon, I said hell with it and scooped her up. I didn't know shit else to do with a teenager that didn't involve me breaking a sweat but shopping, mani-pedis, catching a movie, and grabbing something to eat.

Thankfully, On Your Back recently started carrying the younger and edgier urban fashion they did when they first opened back in the 1990s. In time they had transitioned to the more upscale designer pieces they were now known for. I climbed the stairs to the newly renovated loft where they moved all the good shit.

I was breezing through a rack of linen dresses when I looked down and spotted a blacked-out Tahoe parking outside the boutique on the corner. I paused because I could have sworn I seen the same Tahoe when we left the nail salon. I hated the way my stomach got tight as hell and my heart pounded when I remembered that day the cars blocked me in the street.

"I haven't seen you here in a while."

I turned to find Armina Gunns, the store manager, standing beside me in this bad-ass gray linen ruffle dress that I instantly wanted. The length was just long enough for me to wear it to work. "I want that in a size ten," I told her as we did the double air kiss to the cheeks.

Armina nodded. "In gray or fuchsia?"

I didn't get a chance to say shit.

CRASH!

"I'm sick of your shit, DA-MI-EN!!!"

I looked down over the railing to see an older woman following close behind a dude in his forties or fifties who was every bit of six feet nine inches. She swore as she hit him with her fists hard as hell before she raised both her hands to push into his back. He stumbled forward into one of the clothes racks, knocking that bitch over as he struggled not to fall.

The hell? This shit was crazy . . . especially since they were so up in age and acting up in public like they were in their twenties. This was some World Star Hip Hop shit.

Side note: *That's one bad built bitch. Looking like Spongebob about the shoulders and waist without a bit of ass.* "What young bitch you fucking now, DA-MI-EN?" the woman screeched, her face twisted as she swung on him and stumbled forward herself. "Say something. Say something, Dyme. That's what this one call you too, right? Just like the last ho I had to check because of your nosy dick. *Dyme.*"

What was crazy to me is how the security guard and the store's staff were not getting involved. They really were letting these old folks wild out in their store? Definitely wasn't the luxury experience they advertised about.

"No harm, Armina, I mean, I'm enjoying the show. But . . . really?" I asked, knowing I sounded like the bullshit was beneath me. Fuck it, it was. I really didn't need to know the couple was arguing about him getting caught cheating . . . and obviously it wasn't the first time.

Armina pinched the bridge of her nose. "It's hard to stop them when they own the store . . . and they're my parents," she said, looking ashamed. "Excuse me."

"Oh," I said, as she turned and made her way down the stairs quick as hell on her heels.

I looked back down over the railing as Armina stepped in between her parents just in time to catch the slap her mother was about to lay on her father.

WHAP!

"Oh shit," I whispered with a cringe.

How about her mother still mushed Armina out the way and headed out the door behind her husband that was quick-stepping it to the front door. "Damn, that's fucked up," I muttered, watching Armina hold her face and dash for the boutique's restroom as her father climbed in a silver Jaguar and pulled off with a hard squeal of his tires as his wife went running behind him still cussing and fussing.

I heard giggles and looked down to see Johnica poking her head through the curtains of her dressing room. I gave her a serious face and motioned for her to meet me at the register. I paused just long enough to grab the dress I saw Armina wearing and a few other cute pieces. Since Armina was busy probably putting ice on her face and no one had bothered to send an employee upstairs to replace her, I carried my items downstairs to the register.

Armina came out the restroom with her hand still covering the side of her face. She said nothing. Nada. Not one word. She just left the boutique and climbed behind the wheel of a black Benz. She took off just as hard as her father. Drama.

"Will this be all for you, Ms. Alvarez?" one of the sales clerks asked, taking everything from my arms to quickly scan and remove the security tags.

"No . . . not quite," I said, looking over my shoulder just as Johnica walked up to me carrying the clothes she wanted.

"Your subtotal is nine hundred and twenty," the clerk offered.

I nodded and quickly went through Johnica's stack, selecting two outfits that were age appropriate. I knew I was overstepping my mentor role with the mini shopping spree, but dropping a couple hundred on some clothes for her wasn't gonna hurt me at all. Plus, I could tell from her faded shirt that was a size too small and jeans that *used* to be a dark rinse that she could use them. "My job as your mentor is to help keep you off the pole," I told her, handing her back the shiny jumpsuit, gold heels, and a few skirts short enough to give her a cold directly in her ass.

"Your total is one thousand fifty-nine and eighty-six cents."

"Neeci don't care," Johnica said, swiping her reddish brown bangs back from her face before she patted her jet-black ponytail.

"Neeci?" I asked as I reached in my wallet for my bank debit card.

"My mama," she said, staring at the clerk place her new clothes in the shopping bags.

I didn't bother to ask why she called her mother by her first name. I didn't agree with it. To me that was the first step to a child feeling like they were an adult's equal. Plus it wasn't my world to run my way. If her mama Neeci didn't give a fuck, why should I?

"I want to do whatever you do when I grow up," Johnica said as we left the boutique.

I eyed her. I didn't dare tell her that my loansharking man made our shopping spree possible. I made good money, but if I had to pay all my bills—and hella school loans—alone, there was no way I could drop a grand or better on any damn thing. I bitched to Dane about being in the game even as I benefited from him doing it.

Would he take me more seriously if I turned down the money he gave me? Hell, did I want him to do that? It was hard not to visualize the word *hypocrite* across my forehead.

Johnica was standing by the passenger door waiting for me to say something. So I gave her the "college is your savior" speech.

"Keep your mind and your hot spots off boys and graduate college and you can be whatever you want," I said, sliding on my shades as we climbed inside my Volvo.

I was tired as hell by the time I headed my Volvo toward King Court to take Johnica home. Martin Luther King Court Housing Projects was a collection of brick low-rise apartment buildings lined up on the corner of the block like pieces on a chessboard or dominoes . . . ready to fall back and take out the one directly behind it.

It was July in the city and the brick buildings held cold in the winter and heat in the summer. Those box fans in lots of the windows couldn't be doing much of anything to beat the heat. The lucky ones had AC units, and they were few and far between.

I felt for them. It was hot as fuck outside and the temps had to be at least ten degrees higher or more inside. Fuck that. It seemed like most of the people living there were outside fanning themselves with something, sweat dripping off their bodies and darkening their clothes with sweat on their necks, chest, between their titties and the cracks of their asses.

I couldn't even fathom them dudes shirtless as they balled on the playground. Or the ladies with a child pressed between their legs as they braided hair. Or the kids ripping and running like they didn't feel the sun and the heat.

I just wanted to drop Johnica off and head my ass back to my house and its central air that was set on a cool sixty degrees. I was part Puerto Rican but neither side of me was feeling the heat.

Johnica lowered the passenger window as we turned the corner. I spotted four teenage boys in beaters and shorts posted up against the fence surrounding the entire complex. "Hey, Mook," she said sweetly with a wave of her fingers, smiling and flirting like she saw Mindless Behavior or something.

I politely used my controls to raise the window.

She whirled around in her seat. "Sophie!" she whined.

"Girl, you letting out all this good air," I told her, as I

turned the car through the leaning gates to the parking lot.

"It *is* hot," she agreed. "But I wanted him to see me in your car so they wouldn't get it when you come upstairs."

I didn't know which bomb she dropped had me more shook—having to put a safety alert on my ride or her thinking I was going up to their apartment. "I can't come up today. I have to get home," I told her, as my eyes shot up to the rearview mirror to see if they were eyeing my ride.

"Don't worry, you're good. I am too good to Mook for him to rob somebody I'm cool—"

I pulled the car into a parking spot, careful not to run over a dog walking slow enough to be on his final walk to doggie heaven. "Good to him how?" I asked.

"We just cool. That's all," she said, climbing from the car.

I didn't believe that, but I wasn't sure if discussing sex was a part of my mentor duties. That was some shit her mama needed to handle because if Johnica got pregnant, Neeci would be the one rocking the baby. Not me.

I opened the trunk for her to get her bags.

"Thanks again, Sophie," Johnica called to me before she walked to her building.

She stood at the door for a few moments before it opened and she disappeared through it.

I looked over my shoulder as I slowly reversed out the parking spot. Just as I looked forward, I spotted a black Tahoe drive by on the street running alongside the complex. I paused before I eased out the parking lot and turned onto the street. *What the fuck?*

Was I fucking paranoid?

I eased out the parking lot and looked down the long and narrow street to my left. I turned right, eventually passing the same boys leaning against the fence before I made the right onto Martin Luther King Boulevard. The wide four-lane street was just as crowded with people.

A lot of people. A lot of eyewitnesses.

I pulled into a parking spot behind a rusted Ford Escort. My heart pounded as I grabbed my cell phone and shut the car off before I climbed out, locked it, and walked up onto the sidewalk to a Chinese restaurant. It was hot as hell in there and smelled like old frying grease. A girl was sitting at one of the few tables next to a stroller with a blank face like she didn't hear the baby sitting in it crying.

I turned and looked out the window as I chewed the last of my lip gloss off.

Sure enough it didn't take long before the Tahoe turned the corner. I turned my back to the smudged glass window just before the SUV passed by the restaurant. I felt like I was in some kind of dumb-ass B-list movie. Some kind of whack-ass ghetto espionage shit.

I turned back around just in time to see the Tahoe parked up the street on the corner with ten cars between us. *Slick motherfuckers.*

BAM-BAM-BAM!

I whirled back around and a little Chinese man was pounding his fist on the bulletproof glass separating him from his customers.

"You buy something or get out! No trouble. No trouble!" he said through the holes drilled into the glass.

I frowned at him. My days of eating food that had to be passed to me through a bulletproof glass were a wrap. Hell, if they don't trust me, why the hell should I trust them? "That right there is not called for," I told him as I pulled the heavy glass door open. "Plus I don't eat General Tso Cat or Kung Pow Puppy."

"Fuck you!" he yelled.

BAM-BAM-BAM!

I left the restaurant and pretended to browse at the different street vendors until I got closer to the Tahoe. Fuck it. The passenger window was lowered and a stream of smoke drifted out. A hand came out the window to flick the ashes from the cigarette.

My mouth fell open at the sight of a name tattooed on the back of the caramel hand of a man.

"No the fuck he didn't." I stalked the short distance to the Tahoe.

The brake lights suddenly flashed and I knew I was spotted. They was about to haul ass. I rushed to step down off the sidewalk and in front of the Tahoe. Through the windshield I eyed AaRon and Lil Wil—two of Dane's runners.

I arched my brow and pointed my finger at both of them before I headed up the street to my own car. I was behind the wheel and speeding up the street before either one of them mofos could call my name.

Dane ran two gambling houses: one in a backroom of a small run-down club on Springfield Avenue that went damn near 24/7—just like the bar—and then the pretty brick house on Eighteenth Avenue for the high-stakes poker games. Less hours of operation and less players but more money.

I pulled up in front of the house—one of only two still left on the entire block, and a huge lot separated the two homes, where five houses once sat. Across the street was a huge apartment building that was abandoned. There wasn't much stop-and-go traffic on the street because there were only stop signs and no traffic lights. To the unsuspecting eye, it was just another little house in Newark that most people drove by and paid no attention.

I already knew whichever cars Dane and Keno were driving that day were in the garage. They always parked in the back and entered the house through the rear because Dane didn't want a lot of younger dudes in flashy cars drawing too much attention.

My cell phone rang as soon I parked in front of the house. I knew it was Dane. I ignored it as I hopped out to hit the sidewalk and jog up the steps. I could almost giggle at the flowery welcome mat and lace curtains . . . *if* I wasn't so pissed. And I was hot.

I made a fist and knocked on the door. It opened before I could go for a second round. Stepping inside, I looked over my shoulder to eye Keno's tall and thin figure closing the door behind me. There wasn't shit in the house but poker tables and folded chairs with cases of liquor lined up on the wall. I remembered when I offered to decorate the house and they laughed at me like I was Kevin Hart.

"Whaddup, Suga," he said, before turning to head back to a table with three electronic money counters on it.

The stacks of money on the table didn't faze me. I've seen plenty more. It was the two chicks sitting in the corner in skintight jeans passing a blunt that made me pause. Both of them looked like they lived off semen.

"Who are you two?" I asked.

One looked nervous and the other boldly turned to eye Keno like she expected him to check me. So I eyed Keno too but he didn't do shit but shrug and go back to loading money into the counter.

"Exactly," I snapped. That Negro did not want me to miss and tell Hunga shit. "Bye-bye."

They rose to their feet slow as hell. I could tell the one with the short haircut was fucking Keno or wanted to. I couldn't call it on the other one. Either way . . .

"But we don't have a way home," one of them said.

I opened the front door and waved them out. "Call a cab," I suggested.

"But we don't have cab money."

"Next time trick smarter," I told them as they crossed the threshold onto the porch.

WHAM.

They had to feel the breeze of the slammed door against them.

Overlooking Keno, I made my way across the empty house to the stairs. Before I could press a Giuseppe footprint to a step, Dane came jogging down the stairs with two empty duffel bags. I pointed my finger at him.

"I did it for your own good, Suga," he said before I could open my mouth, as he tossed the bags to Keno. "Just like me telling you not to come here is for your own good."

"First off, having some of your damn goons following me to the point that I am scared was a huge fucking fail, Dane," I told him as he lightly grasped my elbow and led me up the stairs. "Especially since you argued me down that I had nothing to worry about. So why the security if you're not worried?"

Dane opened one of four doors and we walked into a room with nothing but a desk, chair, and a flat-screen TV on the wall. There was White Castle takeout on the desk.

I knew it was Dane's because he loved that shit. "I'm sorry AaRon and Lil Wil fucked up and let you see them looking out for you. I just wanted to make sure that nothing happens to you when I'm not with you, Suga," Dane said, reaching for the hands I had tucked under my arms.

I let him have my hands but I held on to my anger like a motherfucker. "No, you don't want me to be able to see that somebody—maybe even Poppi—is out for payback and that makes me even more right that your ass needs to quit."

Dane dropped my hands to throw his own up in the air. "Don't start this shit with me, Suga!" he shouted.

I leaned back—way back—on that. "Something's going on and you're not telling me everything, which is equal to lying as far as I'm concerned."

Dane rubbed his eyes with his hands and flexed his shoulders as he rolled his head.

He was mad. But so was I.

"And before you ask, Keno trying to fuck one of them bitches and called her over here," Dane said. "I told him to get rid of them but if he don't give a fuck about them that's their problem. Me? I don't want you here. It's not safe."

I shook my head as I made my way to the door. "You admit it's not safe but you expect me to walk away and leave you here. The same way you want to protect me, I want to protect you," I told him, my voice soft, before I opened the door and left.

When I came down the stairs, AaRon and Lil Wil were there. I gave them a hard stare and they both held up their hands like it was out of their control. By the time I walked down the stairs and climbed into my car, I saw them coming out the house. I didn't bother to argue or lose them.

If Dane ordered them to watch out for me then that's what they were going to do.

I spotted the two girls walking and I shook my damn head. I honestly thought Keno would go behind me and give his birds a ride or at least cab fare. Five-inch heels was hectic enough. Five-inch cheap heels? Crucial.

Slowing down, I lowered the passenger window. They both looked nervous as shit at me. "Where do y'all live?" I asked, feeling sorry for them.

We were probably all in our early twenties but I felt older than them. More mature. More together.

"Ivy Hill," the quiet one said.

I looked at them like they were crazy. Ivy Hill was a section of Newark on the other side of South Orange and every bit of twenty minutes or better . . . by car. "Get in," I told them, unlocking the doors. They would've broke heels and split the seam of them shoes before they even made it ten blocks.

Keno's recruit looked hesitant but the quiet one pulled her inside. "Next time don't ever go anywhere without money—*especially* not anything concerning a fucking dude you don't really know. If you trying to be out there at least be smart about it," I told them before I pulled off with the Tahoe on my tail.

5 //

Knock-knock.

I looked up from the reports I was reading. "Come in," I called out, working my pen between my index and middle finger.

The door opened and Leo poked his head inside with a big grin. "Are you busy?" he asked.

I leaned back in my chair. I really wasn't in the mood for chitchat but in the corporate world a sistah needed allies and Leo was a damn good one. Still, I had a lot of shit on my mind with worrying about just what Dane was keeping from me.

"Come in," I finally said, actually smiling at the odd look on his face from my pause.

Leo folded his tall frame into one of the chairs. "I came to share my good news," he said, smiling and showing every tooth in his head.

"I can use some good news . . . even if it's somebody's else's."

"I proposed to my girl this weekend," Leo said.

"Oh shit," I said, eyeing him in surprise. "Congratulations."

He nodded. "Thank you. Thank you."

"So when's the wedding?" I asked, crossing my legs in

the navy pinstriped pencil skirt I wore with sky-high red heels.

Leo's eyes dipped down to take in the move.

I arched my eyebrow. "Really, Leo?" I asked.

His eyes shot up to my face and he smiled big as hell before he shook his head.

"Didn't you just say you got engaged?' I asked him with a smile.

"I'm engaged. Not dead," he said.

I grabbed the edge of the desk and rolled my chair—and legs—under it. "An-y-way, congratulations, Leo," I told him truthfully, plus I was ready to keep it moving. I had work to do. "Be sure to send my invitation."

Leo licked his bottom lip as he eyed my three-carat solitaire ring. "Your fiancé's still threatening people?"

"Your point?" I asked him, as I leaned forward to sit my chin in my hand as I pressed my elbow on the desk.

Leo held up his hands. "I mean you really think old boy is faithful?" he asked.

My eyes got big as I eyed him. Leo and I were cool. When it came to work we kept it all the way one hundred with each other and made sure we had each other's back. The line laid flat in the middle of my work business and my personal business. He was about to cross that mother-fucker.

"I really think it's none of your business," I snapped.

"I'm just saying, that was really crazy of him to act up in your workplace that way," he said adamantly, as he smoothed his hand over tie. "You're lucky it was me and not somebody else."

"I'm pretty sure somebody else wouldn't have been playing tag with my hand and got caught," I reminded his ass gently.

Leo had never really come at me strong but the hint of flirtation was always there.

He smiled a little and then shook his head before he got up to his feet. "God forbid he caught me standing beside you if touching you hand was that serious," Leo said. "If you're okay with being with someone so . . . different, then I'm out of it."

And that was best because if he kept on I was going to use that motherfucking tie to choke his ass.

"Don't sound like a hater, Leo. You're smarter than that. Right?" I asked, leaning back in my chair as I tapped my fingernails against my desk.

Leo leaned against my door as he eyed me. "And so are you."

I jumped to my feet. "Leo, are we really having this conversation at work? Like, really, Leo?"

"I just never thought I would see you with some dude wearing all his assets around his neck, stunting in a fly-ass whip ridin' 'round and gettin' it."

I actually chuckled at his play on 2 Chainz's song "Spend It" because what he thought sounded like he was mocking Dane sounded more like pure jealousy to me. "I'll tell you what, Leo. Let's hit rewind on this conversation," I said, very easily, very calmly, as I came around my desk.

"Okay, I was just trying to help," he said.

"Yes, but what are you trying to help yourself to, Leo?" I asked, leaning against the door as I crossed my ankles and looked up at him.

Leo eased his hands inside the pockets of his pants. "I'll

admit when I first met you I liked you . . . but now I see I'm not your type."

I just shrugged. There wasn't shit to say because he was right.

Bzzzzzzzzzzzz.

I turned my head to eye my vibrating cell phone. "Excuse me. I gotta take this call," I told him. "Let's pretend this convo never went down. Seriously."

With a smile, I pushed him through the door even as he chuckled before I closed it and turned to scoop up my cell phone.

It was Johnica. I was not in the mood for her. For real. Plus it was close to the end of the workday, so I let the call go to voice mail and started getting my shit together. Before I could gather my files into my briefcase my cell phone vibrated again. I checked it. Johnica again. It was unusual for her to call back to back. I answered. "Hello."

"Sophie. I mean Miss Sophie. This Johnica. Could you come and get me?"

The fuck, I look like a damn taxi? "Not today. I got some things to do," I told her, pushing the layers of my loosely curled hair behind my ear as I left my office.

"Sophie, will you come and get me? *Please.*"

I stepped into the elevator. "Are you crying?" I asked, leaning back against the wall.

"Please, Sophie."

"Where are you?"

Her next words made me weak. *Oh Lord, Johnica.* I closed my eyes and lightly tapped the back of my head against the wall. When I opened them, several of my coworkers, including my immediate supervisor, were giving me all kinds of odd looks. "I'm on my way," I said into the phone, turning my back on them with a smile.

"Please don't hang up," she asked, her voice sounding small. And afraid. And alone.

"I won't," I promised her, my heart already racing.

As I shuffled off the elevator with the rest of the corporate rat race, I had to admit I was happy as hell that Dane had a security team on me.

I pulled up in front of the row of burnt and abandoned buildings, looking around at the empty dirt lots that once held homes and now were scattered with broken glass, abandoned cars blackened from being burnt by owners looking to file insurance claims or thieves hoping to hide evidence of their crime, and bags of trash bitten through and scattered by dogs and cats. Nothing about the entire street said that life existed or was even respected.

With the phone still pressed to my face, I climbed out of my car, hating that the rain from the night before made everything even more depressing and wilted. "Johnica, I'm here," I said into the phone before ending the call. "Suga."

I turned just as AaRon climbed from the passenger seat of the Tahoe to lumber over to me. *That's one big-ass dude.* He was tall and solid with a baby face that made you foolishly trust him . . . until he got his big beefy hands around your neck and straight handled bones like paper.

"I don't trust this," AaRon said, looking around. "With the robbery and all the threats, somebody might be setting you up. They got plenty of places to hide and shoot."

Robberies? Threats? What the fuck? But I pushed that info aside for now as I shifted my eyes from his and up to the many fucking empty windows. But this was Johnica . . .

"Just get back in your car and I'll go in," AaRon said, turning to walk back to the Tahoe.

I eyed him as he went to the rear of it. I knew he was getting a gun.

The sound of movement caused us both to whirl our head just as Johnica stepped into the doorway of the middle building. I gasped deeply at the sight of her eyes puffy and swollen as she emerged from what resembled a vertical war zone. I raced to her in my heels and I didn't stop even as AaRon called my name. "What happened to you?"

Johnica dropped her head on my shoulder and cried so hard that her shoulders shook. "I was at the corner store by my house and this cute dude in a Benz asked me to go for a ride in his car," she began, sounding so much like the child she was rushing not to be.

I bit my lip to keep from getting in her ass.

"He took me in that building and asked me to go down on him—"

I dropped my head.

"And when I got done he left me in there and ran out the building laughing," she said, her voice trembling.

I looked over at her as we walked up to my car and big fat teardrops fell from her eyes. My heart ached for her but this little girl needed a reality check. A hard one. "Get in the car," I told her.

AaRon turned and walked back to the Tahoe. I spotted the handle of the gun poking through his oversized white T-shirt.

Giving myself a moment to shake off the fuckery, I climbed in my car and pulled off. "You know what, Johnica, I'ma talk to you like I ain't never talk to your ass before," I began as I sped up. "One, getting in a car with a dude you don't know was dumb as fuck, but going in an abandoned building with this clown was crazy. He coulda killed you and left your ass in that building to rot and nobody woulda knew."

Johnica's bottom lip trembled.

"You really around here sucking dick like it's lollipops for dudes you *don't* know?" I snapped.

"It's not sex," she said with a shrug, her tears drying up. "I done it before."

My eyes got big. "One of the first things a bitch got to lose in this world is her reputation. Once you're considered a ho . . . you a ho and you gone get treated like a ho. You get old . . . you an old ho. You stop hoing . . . you used to be a ho. That shit follows you 'cause dudes talk."

"I'm not a ho!" Johnica snapped.

"No, you just a young chick who got left in an abandoned building with the taste of some dude's dirty dick and nut still in your mouth," I told her.

She had the nerve to smack her lips like she was checking the taste of him.

"Look, I'm just trying to come at you and let you know this is your life. And sex ain't to be traded for attention, money, a ride, a meal, a favor. Nothing," I told her as I pulled to a red light with the Tahoe right behind. "This a fucked-up world sometimes but how you chose to live it makes it better or worse. Please believe me that people only gonna treat you as good as you treat yourself. So no more random-ass blow jobs. Hand jobs. Fucking. Hopping in the whip with dudes you don't know. None of that."

"But—"

"But nothing. Is your life worth something?" I asked her softly.

"Yes," she answered with a hint of attitude that I knew was fired up by her shame.

"Then act like it."

Johnica didn't say anything else as I took her home. I could only hope my words stuck in her head. I doubted it but what the fuck was I supposed to do?

I reached over and turned on the radio. Jay-Z's classic "Hard Knock Life" filled the car. Johnica started moving her head to the bass-filled beat. I wondered if it was too late for her to reclaim being a teenager who liked listening to music and just *flirting* with boys.

I drove inside King Court and pulled into one of the parking spots. Nothing looked different from the last time I was there. It was like life around this motherfucker was on pause. I shut the car off and climbed out.

"You coming in?" Johnica shrieked, rushing around the car to stand in front of me.

"Yes," I stressed. "I need to talk to your mother."

"You a snitch, Sophie?" she asked, her round face filled with disbelief.

"Uhm, your mother ain't the police—"

She crossed her arms over her ample chest. "Yeah, but if I wanted my mama to know I woulda called her . . . and not you."

"Excuse me," I said, walking past her to climb the few steps of the building.

I stopped at the STAY OUT spray-painted on the outer door. I can't front and say I didn't want to turn my ass around and follow the directions. I looked over my shoulder and sure enough the Tahoe was parked across from the building.

I tried to pull the door handle but the door was locked.

A slit in the door opened and a pair of glossy eyes filled it. "What you want?" a deep male voice asked.

I cocked my brow. "To get in," I said in a tone like "what the fuck you think I want?"

"You don't live in this building," the voice said. "Get the fuck outta here."

The eyes were replaced with the barrel of a gun.

I can't lie. I stepped back and almost fell the fuck down the concrete stoop. *The hell?*

"She's with me," Johnica said, brushing past me to stand on the top of the step.

"She straight?" the voice asked.

"Yeah."

The gun disappeared and the little door on the slit closed.

What in the holy fuckery was this *shit?*

My heart was pounding like a motherfucker as the heavy metal sound of the door being unlocked echoed before Johnica pulled the door. I was hesitant as hell to go in that bitch. Would I be able to get the fuck out or was there a code word or some shit?

The smell of weed was thick as we stepped into the dark hall. Nothing but the shadows of whoever was in that motherfucker could be seen. The sound of somebody slobbering on something—dick or tongue—came from the darkest corner. I kept my head straight ahead and followed Johnica's thick figure as she jogged up the stairs.

I didn't feel any better until we left the stairwell and came through the metal door to the second-floor apartments. Suddenly there was light streaming in from the windows at either end of the halls. My eyes had to get adjusted. I reached out for her wrist. "Johnica," I snapped.

She looked at me. "Huh?"

"Uhmmm . . . you wanna school me on what just happened downstairs?" I asked.

Johnica shrugged. "Just business as usual," she said. "They just tripped a little bit 'cause they don't know you."

Mind-fuck.

For real.

These people were really living with a building locked down by some dope boys? And Johnica was so blasé about the shit. Like it was nothing that a gun was just pointed at me. I was learning a lot about my mentee. Two things she seemed to be used to: dicks and guns.

How could her mother or any other parent be okay with that?

I followed her to one of the doors in the middle of the hallway. She pulled out her key and unlocked it. Before she opened it she gave me one last big-eyed look that reminded me of those anime cartoons. "Please, Sophie," she mouthed.

I just notched my chin higher.

Johnica shook her head before she walked in the apartment. As soon as I stepped in the doorway I felt heat hit every part of my body. *Hell can't fuck with this shit,* I thought, already feeling sweat pop up on my body as Johnica closed the door behind me.

Must be six pairs of eyes of children of various ages fell on me and I didn't have but a second to blink hard before a huge rottweiler came running down the hall full speed at me.

"Aaaaaaaaaaaaaaaggggggggggggggg," I screamed at the top of my lungs until my tonsils hurt.

"Stop, Gucci!" Johnica said.

Gucci tried to but he ended up sliding down the rest of the hall. I had to jump back to keep him from knocking me over like a bowling pin. He slid past me and into the wall. BAM!

Johnica grabbed his collar and I pressed my back against the wall as the dog stood up on his hind legs and barked in my face. Spit spray. Shitty breath. Ringing balls. *Fuck this dog.*

"Put him in the room, Johni . . . since she scared."

"A'ight, Neeci," Johnica said.

Neeci. Johnica's mother. I looked as a tall heavy woman with a gut that hung low over her pussy strolled in the hall in a short tank dress that emphasized that gut and her nipples that hung toward the floor. She had on a ton of gold makeup and her curly 'fro looked like she blasted it with dynamite and sent the blonde ends to the sky. A hot fucking mess . . . and a face filled with attitude.

Do I know this bitch? Shit, do she know me?

As Johnica struggled like a motherfucker to drag the barking dog back into one the bedrooms, I tried to give her mother a friendly smile. I could tell the woman had already sized me up and decided she had no use for me. "I'm Sophie Alvarez—"

"I know who you is," she said, waving her hand dismissively before she plodded over to drop down onto this futon that was *already* struggling and bent her leg to press her foot against the edge, exposing that her inner thighs were dark as hell from friction. "Turn that fucking channel. I ain't watching no fucking cartoons."

I used my hand to wipe the sweat that drizzled down my neck and between my breasts. The fans in the windows were a waste of time and energy. The entire apartment felt sticky and smelled like a mix of old grease and even older piss. A baby of about two with a diaper that was swollen and about to pop waddled over to me with the remnants of something sticky on his hands.

All I could think about was if I picked him up, that Pamper would burst on me.

I took a step forward and sidestepped him all at once. I had to unstick my foot from the floor. "I wanted to talk to you about Johnica—"

Neeci cut her eyes up to me as she lit a blunt. "What the fuck you got to tell me about *my* child that came out of *my* pussy?"

I hated that my eyes darted down to what was at the end of them dark inner thighs. I forced them back up as I fought the urge to twist my face. Now this the shit. You have to know when to hold them and when to fold them.

This big swollen Kim Coles reject–looking bitch wasn't bright or just didn't give a fuck about nothing including her child. She was okay with living in a building that was blockaded by dope boys. She was okay with piling a million and one motherfuckers in a small-ass apartment. She was sitting in a living room with no circulation giving a bunch of kids a purple haze contact.

I had to give myself a three-count pause when she flicked her blunt ashes just as one of the babies crawled under her leg and that shit landed in her hair. She drew another toke off the blunt and then purposefully picked up the remote and turned the TV up loud.

This chick right here was certifiably crazy.

I'm out.

I turned and Johnica was standing behind me leaning against the wall while she played with her fingers. "Call me," I whispered to her, squeezing her hand before I opened the door and left that madness behind.

"Don't bring that bitch back to my house!" Johnica's mother yelled at her as soon as I closed the door. "I got to hear you talk about her all the time. You think I want to look in her face too?"

Johnica mumbled something.

"You think that bitch Michelle Barack or something?"

Johnica mumbled something else.

"SHUDDAFUKUP!"

I shook my head as I finally walked away from the door. I know Johnica corrected her mother. How the hell can you not know the president and his wife's last name? Michelle Barack?

I walked down the hall and into the stairwell.

BOOM!

That made me pause.

BOOM!

I stood on the top step and looked down the stairs. I was clutching my keys so hard they pressed into my flesh. I didn't know what the fuck to do. Was the police raiding the building? Were these fools about to be robbed?

BOOM!

The sound of something metal giving way echoed and suddenly the hall flooded with light. I blinked as my eyes adjusted. My hand clutched the railing and my heart was beating fast as I paused on the steps like a rat caught on a glue trap. *This can't be life.*

Suddenly Lil Wil came up the stairs. "You good?" he asked.

I nodded as I followed him down the stairs. Now that daylight ran all though the stairwell, I was surprised that the halls were clear of graffiti and trash. *Does the maintenance man have to get permission to come do his job, though?*

I paused on the steps again as soon as I spotted AaRon standing by the door that was now lying flat to the floor. The stairwell was empty and there was a crowd of onlookers standing outside the building. It was obvious the door came down and everybody behinds its false security had scattered like roaches from funky boric acid.

"Dane said go in and get you," AaRon offered.

He led us out the building and I could see him looking at all the faces in the crowd that was gathering outside the building. They didn't leave my side until I unlocked my car and was behind the wheel. I reversed out of the parking spot and they walked behind the car until I turned onto the street. By the time I reached the traffic light at the corner, the Tahoe was behind me.

Sometimes I still had to think of how crazy it was that I rode around the city with security detail like I was Beyoncé. That shit was almost laughable. But then I remembered the little tidbit of info AaRon dropped on me and I sobered right the fuck up.

"With the robbery and all the threats somebody might be setting you up. They got plenty of places to hide and shoot."

Robberies. Threats. Shooting. How the hell is an accountant in the middle of this mafioso-type shit?

I drove through the streets of Newark and was happy to see our home. I parked in front of the house and was surprised to see Dane's motorcycle parked in the driveway next to the side door leading into our kitchen. My heart pounded at the thought of seeing him, like we were still in the first year of our relationship.

I walked in the house and finally kicked off my heels before I made my way into the kitchen. I heard music thumping against the walls of the basement and the faint smell of weed reaching me. Shaking my head, I grabbed a bottle of water from the stainless steel fridge and walked over to the carved wooden door leading into the basement. I opened the door and started on my way down the stairs just as the music ended.

I paused. I don't know why I did, but I did.

"Oh, so it was *that* nigga," Dane said.

I could see the shadow of him pacing against the wall.

"So he 'round this motherfucker bragging on robbing the house?" Dane said, his voice tight with rage.

My mouth opened and I squinted my eyes as I kept right on ear hustling. Dane wasn't going to tell me shit.

"Keno, when y'all catch up to that grimy punk-ass motherfucker, you make sure that fuck-ass nigga know he don't walk away with fifty stacks of my money and live to spend it."

My grip on the railing tightened until my knuckles stretched across my skin.

"Find him," Dane ordered.

Seconds later his cell phone crashed against the leather-covered wall.

I backed up the stairs but before I could turn and walk through the door, Dane appeared at the foot of the stairs dressed in all white. He was as surprised to see me as I was to be caught eavesdropping.

Dane opened his mouth to say something and then shook his head before he jogged up the stairs, squeezed past me, and then rushed out the house. Not too long after that I heard his motorcycle as he took off down the street full speed.

6 ///

I can't remember shit around my house being so tense. Ever.

Dane barely spoke when he was home and he spent so much time down in the basement smoking and listening to music filled with enough bass to rattle the walls that I was expecting his ass to come up one night looking like one of the Marleys. I wasn't talking too much either. All I could think about was his threat to have someone killed. I can't lie. I was afraid as hell that the order was done.

I didn't want to know Dane was really capable of that. I didn't want to know. So I was burying my head in the sand and not even fucking with arguing or questioning him about it. We just started speaking earlier that day and I could only hope we both got our "act right" on.

"All done, Suga."

I focused on my hairstylist and makeup artist, June, stepping back from me as she checked out her handiwork. I checked my reflection, thinking I looked like an even more polished version of me. Arched brows. Metallic eye shadow that smoked out my eyes and made them even brighter.

Glossy lips. Bronzed complexion. She doobie-wrapped my hair and curled it before pulling it into an updo that highlighted my cheekbones and showed off the dangling black diamond earrings I wore.

June had been doing my hair since my high school days and now that I could afford it, she would come to my house to get me ready for events or just because I didn't feel like the hustle and bustle of the hair salon all the time. She charged well for her little ventures outside the salon but she was worth every penny.

"Thank ya, thank ya," I told her, rising from a padded leather high chair and still feeling like my ass cheeks was numb from sitting.

I grabbed my wallet and wrote her a check as she gathered her equipment. We were upstairs in the one of the empty bedrooms that I planned to turn into a home office one day—not that I was ever loving bringing work home but sometimes it happened. I handed her the check.

"Have fun tonight," June said as she headed for the door pulling the bright pink hard carry-on she used to hold her equipment.

"It's a work thing so I'll do my best," I told her as we went down the stairs.

The company I worked for was having its annual charity banquet and every employee was expected to attend. Dry dinner. Dry-ass music. Dryer speeches. Dry-ass time.

And Dane was going with me, even though it was Friday night and I know he'd rather be somewhere collecting or counting money. I recognized that he was putting me first and I appreciated it. Plus I needed him and we needed this. We would laugh and share long looks at some of my duck-ass supervisors and his presence would make sure Leo kept his distance. Win and motherfucking win.

As soon as I made sure June made it to her SUV and pulled off, I closed the door and headed through the kitchen and down the stairs to the basement. Like any other man, Dane had turned the entire basement into a man cave. Luckily he let me decorate it for him so it didn't look like a real cave. Leather-covered walls. Ebony hardwood floors. Faux mink area rugs. Suede sectional and ottomans. One-hundred-inch high-def projection screen. Surround sound. Fully stocked bar. Fridge. A half bathroom that was all black.

Dane was lounging on the sectional in a black beater and sweatpants cleaning one of his guns as he watched the news and smoked a cigar. He glanced over at me for a hot second before shifting his eyes back to the news and then shifting them right back to me. "Damn, baby, you look good," he said.

I smiled at this man I loved as I came over to plop down on the sectional next to him. His arm came around me and cupped my ass. It felt good to feel his touch again. "We gotta get dressed for that banquet in a little bit," I reminded him, waving my hand as he let out a thick stream of cigar smoke up into the air.

He grunted as he set the cigar in the ashtray atop the end table sitting next to the corner of the sectional. "We got a little time though," Dane said, shifting in the chair to pull open the edges of my robe.

I tilted my head to the side and eyed him as he playfully tweaked my brown nipples. "No time for that," I said, all easy and breezy.

"There's always time for pussy," he said, easing forward

to drag his tongue against that nipple before he sucked it into his mouth.

I hissed at the feel of it as I brought one hand around to cup the back of his head. I can't front and say I didn't want the dick. Dane's been so tense lately that we hadn't even done shit in the last week. His dick was already standing up tall in his sweats.

Even a fast and freaky fuck would beat a dry spell.

"You ready to knock the dust off this pussy, huh?" I asked.

He lifted his head and looked up at me as I reached down to pull his dick free until I had that hot and throbbing motherfucker in my hand. His hips arched up off the chair a little bit as I stroked him from the base to the smooth tip. Up and down. Slow and easy. A smooth twist and turn. Leaning down I circled the tip of his dick with my tongue before I sucked it into my mouth.

It felt smooth and warm against my tongue. I sucked him deeper between my lips.

Dane moaned. "Fuck," he gasped.

I felt his hand come up my back and as soon as I felt it near my neck I shook away his touch. *Humph. Don't touch the hair. Fuck that.*

He reached down and edged his sweatpants and boxers down around his knees. "Get *all* that dick."

And I did until I felt the curly dark hairs surrounding his dick tickle my lips and the tip tickle my throat. I lightly squeezed his nuts as I eased off it enough to work my head back and forth as I attacked the tip like I was milking that motherfucker. The sounds of my head game echoed and smacked in the air.

I was on it.

"Ahh, Suga," Dane moaned, letting his head fall back against the couch as he worked his hips.

I can't front. Sucking his dick had me just as hot as him, especially when I saw how much he loved it. My pussy was throbbing and I moved to get up on my knees with the robe hanging loosely around my body. His hand came up between my thighs to touch my clit and I spread my knees with a moan and a deeper suck of his dick.

He slipped one finger and then another inside me, twirling them around my slickly wet walls as his thumb worked smooth circles against my clit. I closed my eyes in pleasure as I worked my hips against his hand.

"Get on this dick," Dane said thickly. "I want to cum inside you."

With one last long moan of pleasure and flicker of my tongue against the tip, I released his dick with a smack as he eased his fingers from my body. Flinging back the edges of the robe, I straddled his hip and eased down on the dick as he pressed his moist fingers in my mouth. I looked him boldly in the eye as I sucked my own juices from them.

I slid down until his entire dick filled me. Spread me. Fuck me.

Dane's free hand gripped my ass as his eyes glazed over.

I smiled around his fingers and gripped the back of the couch on either side of his head as I started to work my wide hips back and forth to glide back and forth on every one of his thick inches.

"Pussy hot, baby," he moaned against my wrist.

I worked my walls as I rode him.

"You wanted this dick, didn't you?" he asked, looking up into my eyes.

I nodded as I fucked him a little harder.

Dane brought his hands around to massage and stroke my belly. "Let's make a baby, Suga," he said so low that I barely heard him.

I wished that I hadn't, because he knew our deal. No baby until he was legit.

Not wanting to fuck up the mood, I freed his fingers from my mouth and leaned forward and kissed him, enjoying the feel of his tongue in my mouth and his dick gliding against my walls.

Dane slapped my ass before he brought his hands up to hold both of my jiggling breasts. I leaned back to enjoy it. He knew the feel of his fingers on my nipples made me hotter. I let my head fall back with a moan.

His hands came up my back to pull me forward until his mouth covered one of my nipples. I lowered my head to press kisses and hot licks against his forehead as I kept riding the dick like I was the jockey on a racehorse. My heart pounded. A fine sheen of sweat coated our bodies. I felt almost out of my mind. Light-headed. A little dizzy.

And I didn't give a fuck.

My focus was on making us both cum like crazy.

I felt his dick get harder inside me while that familiar warm buzz started building inside the core of my pussy until I felt anxious and wanting . . . and waiting for the explosion.

And the excitement building in those hot moments just before we came together was *everything*. Fireworks on the Fourth of July. Ice cream on hot summer days. The warmth of a fireplace on a freezing winter night. Every holiday and birthday rolled into one. Skydiving. Free falling.

We both hollered out roughly as we clutched each other tight as hell and worked our bodies, struggling for control of them as we came together in one fiery explosion after another. We couldn't speak and could barely breathe.

I didn't know a damn thing else in the world that felt better.

"Whoo," I sighed when I finally came off my high and fell off the dick to lay on my side on the sofa.

I didn't give a damn that my lip gloss was smeared on both our lips and I was lying on my hair. I was too busy trying to breathe through my heart racing and pounding in my chest so hard like it wanted to be freed.

"I'm still ready to have kids, Suga."

My eyes opened. For a few moments I didn't say shit, but I knew he was waiting for just that. "Let's talk later. The sooner we get there, the sooner we can haul ass outta there," I said.

I didn't turn to look at him but I could swear I felt his body tense. I didn't feel like another argument. It would've been nice to enjoy a few more moments of being in a sex daze before we headed to the benefit. I rolled off the couch, ignoring the feel of our sticky juices between my thighs as I headed to the staircase.

I was just coming out of the bathroom after taking a quick bath when Dane walked into our bedroom. We didn't really say too much to each other as we moved about the room getting dressed. Even as I helped him put his diamond cuff links onto his monogrammed tuxedo shirt and he zipped me up in my black strapless dress, we said nothing.

The air was pregnant—no pun intended—with everything we *wanted* to say though.

Ding-dong.

"I'll get it," Dane said, pulling on his tuxedo jacket before he headed out the bedroom.

Standing in the mirror over the sink in the bathroom, I let myself have a moment to just relax and get myself together. I had lot of other shit on my mind besides Dane and work.

My father's leg wound became infected because his ass was too drunk most times to take care of it. Now I had to go over there every day and make sure he took his antibiotics and kept the bandages clean.

I hadn't heard from Johnica since I took her home that day. She hadn't called me and her cell phone was off. I hoped that with the new school year this week, she would sign up for the internship program again and I would see her. I wanted to go by her apartment and check on her, but after the way Dane got in my ass about going into a building *after* a gun was pointed at me . . . I wasn't even trying to fuck with that. Dane wasn't in the dope game but he knew plenty of dudes who were, and the building Johnica and her family lived in in King Court was infamous for having that bitch on lock by the dope boys for years. Of course, my ass didn't know shit about it.

I heard a female laughing downstairs and I frowned as I stopped touching up my makeup. Nobody but Hunga laughed like that. Loud and abrasive and over-the-top. The shit sounded so damn phony, like she was just trying to draw attention or make people think she was in the middle of a convo that was so fucking fabulous or something.

Needless to say, I coulda gone without seeing her ass for the night . . . and that went double for her man. If Hunga was here, then Keno's ass was too.

I stalled like a motherfucker hoping Dane would send them on their way before I came down. No such luck. Twenty minutes ticked by and I was sitting on the edge of the bed trying not to pull out my own fucking teeth every time Hunga's laughter floated up the damn stairs. I didn't have any choice but to float my ass down the stairs and bust the shit up.

Grabbing my black sequined purse and a feathery wrap that was about as daring and fly as I would get for a work function, I left the bedroom. I held the railing as I came down the stairs but I damn near stumbled down the last few steps I spotted Hunga straddling—and grinding against—Keno's lap . . . on my custom suede and leather chaise lounge. I didn't even really like people in my living room. I damn sure didn't want their ass dry-humping in it. The fuck?

I made noises coming down the stairs and these fools didn't even stop.

Dane came walking out the kitchen carrying a bottle of Heineken. He paused at the sight of me. "You ready?" he asked.

I nodded my head toward the living room. "Yes . . . for Hunga and Keno to stop dry humpin' on our sofa."

Dane took a few steps forward and looked in the living room. "Oh man, come on *man*. Y'all carry that shit the fuck home," he said as he walked into the room.

The tone of Dane's voice made me smile.

By the time I made it into the living room, Hunga and

her multicolored catsuit—that only emphasized the hugeness of her hips, thighs, and ass—was sitting on the sofa next to Keno.

"Suga . . . you look . . . nice," Hunga said, her hazel contact-covered eyes looking me up and down as she fingered her new blonde blunt bob with elaborately decorated 3-D nails.

I eyed the bright hair and eyes and even brighter Rainbow Brite outfit that was colorful down to her yellow patent leather peep-toe heels and neon-colored toes. Thankfully summer would be a rap in a few weeks and the coolness of fall would bring out more clothes for this heifer to put on. "Hunga, you're looking . . . the same," I said. *Like a fucking bag of Skittles exploded on her ass.*

But it was so Hunga. Loud. Obnoxious. Needing to be seen.

She laughed as she reached in the deep vee of her catsuit and pulled out a prerolled blunt. "We was just telling Dane we got tickets for all of us to see the Kevin Hart comedy show coming up. Front row."

Dane nodded. "That little nigga is funny as shit. Good looking out," he said.

Another night out with Keno and Hunga—the fake-ass Beyoncé and Jay-Z of the hood. "I can use a good laugh," I lied, forcing my face to be nice.

"We all can," Keno said.

Dane and he shared a look that I didn't miss.

Hunga reached in her bright turquoise bag and pulled out a lighter. I didn't give a fuck if she sucked that blunt until it was as wet as her coochie in them synthetic-ass pants but light it? *Bitch, you stupid . . .*

"Hunga, y'all have to smoke that outside. We can't go to a banquet smelling like weed," I told her.

She rolled her eyes. "Oh, so nobody at your job smoke? Fuck outta here," she said, flicking her motherfucking Bic.

I eyed Dane. Dane eyed Keno. Keno patted Hunga's thigh. "Let's be out. I gotta quick stop to make," he said, rising to his feet.

And then Hunga eyed me. There was a hierarchy in this little clique and she just got a reminder that Suga trumped Hunga every motherfucking time. "Y'all have a good night," I said, already walking to the door to ease it open.

Dane and Keno talked low together while Hunga took her time climbing to her feet and sashaying over to the door. As soon as she stepped onto the porch she sucked her blunt like a dick and then lit it. "How is the air up there on your high horse, Suga?" she asked, as she tapped the ashes from her blunt onto my porch.

I took a deep inhale and then shrugged as I eyed her. "It's straight," I told her.

"Careful. That fall is a bitch," she told me before she turned and made her way down the stairs.

I eyed her, and her words—even though I didn't think there was shit true about them—still made my heart double-pump.

With the speeches and lackluster music, the banquet was just as dry as it was last year and the year before that, but I had to admit that The Newark Club was beautifully decorated, with its recessed ceilings and elaborate flower and glass vase centerpieces. Plus my promotion meant a slightly better table on the edge of the room in front of the wide windows with the city's lit skyline as my backdrop. Well, *our* backdrop, since the table seated eight.

I was just glad they didn't pull that "group all the black employees together" stunt like my first year. I thought they were going to serve our table fried chicken, watermelon, and Kool-Aid cocktails that year. Thank God somebody bought their ass a clue and several seats.

Dane reached under the table to squeeze my thigh. I looked at him. "You okay?" I asked, my voice amused as hell because I knew he'd rather have his asshole licked by a pit bull then be at the banquet.

He raised his brows and shrugged. "I'm good," he assured me, adjusting his seat on the padded chair. "You think there's enough cops and politicians here?"

I was hoping he wouldn't notice that. The mayor, several councilmen, and a few high-ranking police officers were in attendance. "The company donated a lot of money to the city and the Police Athletic League."

Dane just grunted and shifted his eyes about the room.

I was still watching his profile when he sat up a little straighter. His body tensed and his eyes opened just a smidge wider. Turning my head I followed his line of vision to a balding heavy-set black dude that I didn't recognize. Turning back to Dane, I saw that his gaze had shifted away but his body was still tight.

I leaned in close to him. "How much does he owe you?" I asked softly near his ear.

Dane's grip on my thigh tightened. "Fifteen," he admitted.

My eyes went back to the man. Dane only dealt in the

thousands and that meant the man—whoever he was—owed him fifteen stacks.

Police. Politicians. And now clients?

"Time to go," I said, pushing back in my chair.

The servers were just beginning to bring the desserts but it wasn't even that motherfucking serious to stay around for. All I could think about was the night Dane and Keno handled Poppi outside the club. I didn't need anything even remotely similar to that shit going down at one of my work functions . . . and in front of the cops.

"Good, we can hit IHOP or something 'cause I'm hungry as fuck," Dane said, rising to his Gucci-covered feet and buttoning his tuxedo jacket. "I'll go and get the car from the garage."

"You're heading home?"

I looked over to find six sets of eyes on me. The questioner was Bob Kingsley and I could barely see his eyes through the layer of glass in his bifocals.

"Family emergency," I lied, my mind already focused on ordering a stack of pancakes for my damn self. "Get home safe, everyone. Good night."

I headed across the dimly lit room making my rounds and speaking to those I wanted to be sure saw that I made my appearance. I was socializing with the CEO of the company and his wife when I spotted Leo heading across the room toward us. Since that day in my office when he dipped his big toe in my personal life, things between us weren't the same—mainly because of his slick subliminal hood comments. I quickly made my apologies for leaving early and then headed for the elevators. I hopped on the first one that opened. The doors were closing as he looked around the room for me.

"You really should be more careful of the company you keep."

I looked over my shoulder and started in surprise at a uniform policeman standing behind me. I arched my brow and eyed him before I turned to face forward. We were the only two in the elevator and he *had* to be talking to me.

Those twenty-two flights were the longest elevator ride of my life but I maintained my composure and kept my face emotionless in case he was stalking my profile. When the elevators finally slid to a stop, I took a step forward before the doors even opened and my foot was damn near off the floor getting ready to take the second step off that motherfucker as soon as I saw a big enough opening in the metal doors.

He didn't say anything else to me and I never looked back at him as I walked out the towering glass building like I owned it. The downtown street was empty save for a couple of police officers standing together outside the building. There were a few marked and unmarked police cars parked in front of the building and I knew the presence of the mayor was the reason for it.

I felt more at ease as soon as Dane pulled up in our convertible Jag. The sounds of Young Jeezy's "Leave You Alone" played from the car. As he hopped out the car and came around to open my door, I noticed he had already removed his bow tie and opened the first couple of buttons of his shirt. I slid onto the butter soft leather and kicked my heels off as Dane closed the door.

As soon as he climbed into the driver's seat I lowered the

volume. "That black cop with the short 'fro was on the elevator with me and he told me to be careful of the company I keep," I told him, reaching over to run my fingers lightly over his thigh.

Dane chuckled as he checked for oncoming traffic before he pulled away from the curb. "Fuck him," he said without a care in the world. "Matter of fact, fuck all of them."

"The cops on you?" I asked as the night wind blew against our faces and he pulled to a red light.

"Nah, I used to talk to his daughter back in high school. He never liked me," Dane said, reaching over to turn the volume back up.

I eyed him suspiciously. Some chick's father still mad after all these years? Or was this some new shit that went down *after* we got together?

"'She said I know you bad but I want you bad,'" he sang along with Ne-Yo's hook, off-key as hell.

I reached up and took my hair down, running my fingers through the thickness and trying to act like I wasn't doubting Dane's loyalty to me.

"That's how you feel, Suga? You gotta leave me alone?" Dane asked over the music, leaning his head back against the headrest as he pulled to a stop at a red light and looked over at me.

I had other shit on my mind but my struggle to get Dane to go legit.

"Be my backbone . . . every nigga need a spine," he rapped along with Jeezy's raspy voice.

The light turned green, but Dane still sat there, eyeing me and waiting for an answer.

I shook my head and licked my lips as I took in his face

and got lost in the actual questions and uncertainties I saw in his eyes. Seems like Dane had some doubts about me too. "I'm your backbone," I assured him, leaning over to hold the sides of his face and taste his lips.

"And I'm yours," he promised me against my mouth.

The sound of a police siren filled the night and I opened my eyes to see red and blue lights flashing against our faces and the interior of the car. We both looked over our shoulders at a police car parked behind us and the driver's door opening.

We faced forward.

My stomach filled with bubbles. I didn't know a soul who grew up in cities like Newark who was calm about interacting with the police. There were plenty of stories of shit going to the left—whether you were innocent or not. I usually lived life trying to stay the fuck outta their way.

"The most they can get me for is no seat belt," Dane said, his eyes locked on the rearview mirror as the officer walked up to the driver side of the Jag with his flashlight beaming bright.

I glanced up expecting to see the old boy from the elevator but this was a redhead white dude that was tall enough to dunk on Lebron. You could tell he was used to stooping over because his body was damn near in the shape of a question mark.

"Shut the car off," the officer said, his voice all hard.

Dane did that and then placed both his hands on the steering wheel.

"License and registration," the officer said, standing near the driver side door.

"Would you like me or her to get it out of the glove

box?" Dane asked, sounding more college educated than me.

Dane didn't take any chances with the police. When it came to unarmed African American men, some police officers seemed to have a trigger finger. Racial profiling wasn't no joke and Dane said he'd handle a pull-over by a cop politely and hope to drive away to live another day. He plainly said he wasn't trying to become the next Amadou Diallo, Abner Louima, or Sean Bell. Or Yusuf Hawkins and Trayvon Martin—no police involvement, but the racial profiling leading to their deaths was just the same.

"Let the passenger get it," the officer said.

Suddenly the beam of a flashlight hit the right side of my face. Out the corner of my eye I noticed another police officer standing just beyond my door with one hand on his sidearm. I opened the glove compartment and pulled out the small leather billfold holding the info. Slowly I raised it into the air as I closed the glove compartment. A bullet didn't have a name or a gender preference so I knew to take it easy as well.

Driving While Black wasn't a joke. Shit, depending on who you came in contact with, living while black could be risky as hell too.

Dane and I said nothing as we sat there and waited while one of the cops kept watch and the other ran the info. Cars passed by and you could see them slowing down to see who the cops had hemmed up in the middle of the street. I glanced in the side mirror and my eyes widened to see three other police cars behind us with their lights flashing as well. *Like, really?*

After about twenty damn minutes, the beam of the flash-light disappeared.

"A green light means go," the officer told Dane as he handed him two citations. "Next time do that."

Dane said nothing as he took the tickets.

"Those are for not having your seat belts on."

Dane nodded. "We're going to put them on now," he said, sounding Ivy League as hell.

That shit almost made me smile.

We both put on our seat belts.

The officers turned and walked back to their cars.

Dane's eye's stayed locked on his rearview mirror as he started the Jag. Each and every one of the cruisers turned off their lights and did a U-turn and went back to park in front of the Gateway Building.

I unclenched my ass and relaxed my pose in the seat. Dane moved the CD back to the start of "Leave You Alone" as he waited for the traffic light to turn green. "You think your father-in-law sent them?" I asked, very aware of my sarcasm.

Dane cut his eye at me and smirked like he knew I was a smart-ass. "The only thing I know for sure is I'm glad they didn't find an excuse to check the car," he said, reaching between his seat and the center console to pull out his gun and using his free hand to steer as he accelerated forward down the Newark street.

7

One month later

Fall was my favorite time of the year. It was just early September and still a little warm but not too hot and the coolness of the air felt good as hell against the skin. It was a
break between the heat of summer and the brutal cold of
winter on the East Coast and a chick like me wasn't really
checking for either one. Now that the sun was gone there
was just enough chill in the air to turn on my heat in the car.

After a meeting that ran over, I was happy to pack my
briefcase and head home. I had almost made the turn by
Weequahic Park to head to our house but I drove to my
father's instead. I parked behind Luscious's parents' black
Cadillac and climbed out my car, careful to avoid putting my
heels in a puddle of water.

I hadn't seen Luscious since the morning she got out of
jail and had no clue what she was up to with her life. Thinking of her, and of how quickly everything spiraled out of
control for my former childhood best friend, made me think
of Johnica. My job had begun the mentor program again and
I went to the afterschool meet-up, but this time I didn't sign

up for a new mentee. I was too disappointed that Johnica was not there. I even questioned a couple of girls who went to her school but they said they Johnica didn't come back to school in September.

It was weird because in that moment I thought maybe she had gone on another of her damn adventures looking for love and was hurt or missing or dead. I dared to ask if she was okay. My knees almost gave out in relief when one of the girls said they saw her one day. I was thankful she was alive and if she'd moved on from wanting me as a mentor, then it was her choice. She knew my number and she knew how and when to reach out to me.

God bless her. That's all I say at this point.

And my thoughts on Luscious? *Fuck her.* That's all I say on that either.

Locking my car door, I looked up and down the street as I stepped up on the curb. It felt odd not having the Tahoe and whoever Dane had on watch to protect me. About two weeks ago the Tahoe disappeared. I assumed whatever threat he felt there was had been eliminated and I honestly didn't have the heart to ask Dane about it. We never spoke about the end of my security detail. Not once.

Climbing the steps of my father's house, I noticed a few of the bricks was loose and made sure to avoid them. I knocked on the door and looked around. The house needed a paint job and the windows were cloudy as hell.

"Come in," he called out.

I opened the unlocked door and walked into the house. It always felt like stepping back in time. Whatever decorating my mother did back in the eighties before she passed is the same way it's been for years, making it dated as hell.

And when he did buy something new for the house he didn't try to make sure the shit matched. My father had to know that an art deco rug clashed like a motherfucker with that flowery-ass furniture. And then everything looked gray from the layers of dust he didn't fuck with.

The house smelled like an old mix of food and alcohol and stale air.

"Hey, Daddy," I said when he glanced over at me from his spot in his brown recliner in front of the television.

"Hi, Sophie," he said, actually smiling at me before he turned back to watching *Wheel of Fortune* and sipping from an oversized mug that said WORLD'S GREATEST DAD. I saved up all my change to buy that for him for Father's Day when I was ten years old. I didn't feel all warm and sentimental about it though. The house was proof positive he didn't throw a damn thing away. Sentimental feelings ain't had shit to do with saving it.

"How's your leg?" I asked, pressing one knee of my blue linen pants into the sofa to open the windows overlooking the front porch.

He just grunted.

I side-eyed him. He wasn't that tipsy because he only was talkative when he was lit. "You worked as a janitor for twenty-five years but you just sitting back and letting dust and old age tear up your house," I said, wiping my hands against each other as I rose back to my feet.

"I was paid to do that shit," he said.

I side-eyed him again, noticing a slight slur to his voice. Another hint he was into a bottle. That was my hint and a half to be out. My daddy was a mean drunk. "Did you have something to eat?" I asked, crossing my arms over my chest as I walked over to stand by his recliner. I frowned at the dinner tray in front of him holding the shattered pieces of something porcelain that he was trying to glue together.

"I'm not hungry," Victor said, his hands shaking as he tried to put glue on the edges of one of the shards.

He's gonna fuck around and glue his damn hand to that shit.

"Why are you trying to fix that?" I asked, reaching down to take the glue and the piece of flowery porcelain from his hand.

"DON'T TOUCH IT!" Victor roared.

I jumped back from his quick-ass anger and the spittle that flew from his mouth. "It's not even that serious, *Papi*," I told him, feeling a pang of hurt. "You obviously have lost your mind. Call me when you find it."

"Don't be disrespectful, Sophie," he said, his voice low but hard.

I paused on my way out the door. I shook my head at myself. I was my father's child. This man loved his liquor as much as he loved me but he had taught me to have respect for him. That's all I knew as Sophie "Suga" Alvarez, the daughter of Victor Alvarez. *"Me disculpo para ser irrespetuoso a usted, el Papá,"* I said, my hand on the doorknob of the front door.

He grunted.

I left.

This was nothing new between us. Nothing new at all.

I drove the short distance to my house but I called and paid for pizza to be delivered to my father's house. *Maybe the smell of it would make him eat.*

As I parked in front of the house, I spotted someone rolling a rack of clothes through the open front door. Barely taking time to scoop up my briefcase and oversized woven tote, I made my way up the stairs. The front door was closing but I put my hand out and pushed back, stepping inside. Lil Wil looked up at me in surprise. "Don't play with me," I joked, looking past him to all the hustle and bustle going on in the living room. My precious, expensively decorated, no-one-ever-sits-in living room. *The fuck?*

"I didn't see you, Boss Lady. My bad," Lil Wil said.

I shooed him away with a wave of my hand on my way past his little ass. I eyed Dane, Hunga, Keno, AaRon, and a few more of Dane's runners lounging and laughing it up while Armina and one of her staff from On Your Back were removing the garment bags from two racks of clothing. "What's up, everybody?" I said, sitting my things on the chaise lounge in the corner by the entrance to the living room.

All eyes turned on me.

Dane came over to me looking fine as ever in a deep purple V-neck silk sweater and stiff denims with a pair of leather Prada sneakers. He pressed a quick kiss to my lips as he steered me out the room to the kitchen.

"Can you get tomorrow and Friday off?" Dane asked me, walking to the fridge to take a six-pack of Heineken.

"For?" I asked, moving past him to remove the chicken breasts, sausage, and shrimp I put in the fridge that morning to cook for dinner. Dane loved home-cooked food and my jambalaya was his favorite.

"Jamaica."

I damn near dropped everything that was in my hands

as I eyed him. Dane and I loved to travel and see the world, but it had been a minute since we left the city, far less the dang-on country. "Really?" I asked.

Dane nodded as he opened one of the bottles and took it to the head. "You take off work, go in there and pick out whatever you want from your favorite store, and in the morning we're flying to Jamaica. You good?" he asked, looking smug as hell.

"Why the rush? Something wrong?" I asked, feeling like we were running from something.

Dane shook his head. "Nope. Just time for a vacation, man. You good?" he asked again.

I came over to where he was leaning against the granite countertop. I straddled his legs and placed my hands on either side of his warm and muscular body. "I'm damn good," I whispered against his mouth.

He brought his free hand around to slap my ass. "Go shopping. I gotta handle some last-minute business with the fellas," Dane said. "Don't worry about cooking. I'll bring something back to eat."

"A'ight," I told him, moving from in front of him with a stroke of his square jaw. "What's my limit?"

"It's just a weekend, Suga," Dane said, picking up the six-pack container.

"A long motherfucking weekend and I'm ready to smoke up some Jamaican weed," Hunga said as she strolled into the kitchen in skintight jeggings and an off-the-shoulder sweater.

I shot Dane a hard-ass look.

"Armina asked me to see if you was ready," Hunga said. "I already picked out my shit so I'm headed somewhere fun.

No offense but its dry as a motherfucka 'round this bitch . . . as always."

She turned and left.

Bye, bitch.

Our vacay included Keno and Hunga? "Oh, sky's the limit, Boo-Boo," I warned my fiancé before I followed Hunga's wide-hip ass out the kitchen.

Jamaica was beautiful but the dopeness of our suite at the Sandals Resort put our trip over the moon. Dane went all out. First-class seats on the airline. A huge swim-up suite with a personal butler who served us meals on the patio leading into our private access into the river. Full views of the turquoise ocean, white sand beach, and emerald-green palm trees. The decorations were luxurious as hell and our bed put us out with a quickness.

I can't front that the four of us had fun all weekend between all the scuba diving, windsurfing, snorkeling, just lying out on the beach, hanging out at local clubs that native Islanders put us onto, and all the spa treatments.

I was going to miss it all.

I pressed a kiss to Dane's shoulder as he slept on his stomach, before I climbed naked from the bed and stretched. I took a quick shower to wash off our sex from late the night before and pulled on a strapless bright yellow bikini that showed off my breasts and rode low on my curvy hips. Leaving my hair wet, I pulled it up into a topknot before I ordered breakfast and moved out across the living room to the patio.

The sun felt good as hell against my skin as I walked

down into the water and then swam out to the beachfront lagoon. I turned over onto my back and floated in the water, enjoying the feel of the heat against my body. This was the motherfucking life. True, it was a by-product of the life I wanted Dane to give up but damn it was some real boss-type shit to travel in style. This wasn't even touching the lives of celebs, but I knew damn well there was plenty of motherfuckers who would never experience this shit.

Extending my arms above my head, I stretched before I did a few more backstrokes and then swam back across the lagoon and into the swim-up access. As I stood up and emerged from the water, I noticed Dane, Keno, and another dude I didn't recognize sitting in the living room talking. The stranger had that smooth dark skin like Morris Chestnut's fine ass and dreads that were long and thick and looked matted on some Rastafarian shit.

I squeezed some of the water from the ends of my hair before twisting it back up. I opened my eyes to see the Rasta staring out the door at me. He said something. Dane and Keno looked over at me as well. Dane said something . . . just before he stood up and came over to close the patio doors.

What the fuck is that about?

All of their faces were serious as hell. Intense. Focused. Doing business?

Couldn't be. *Better* not be.

Dane said this was just a quick vacay. No parts of his slick ass coming to Jamaica to handle business was a part of the equation. I shoulda known there was a reason for the last-minute shit.

Lying down on one of the rattan patio chairs, my stomach grumbled and I wanted my shades, but I waited. I didn't want Keno or the Rasta eyeing my plump-ass pussy pressed against my bikini bottoms. I didn't want to know shit about their business dealings anyway.

Tomorrow we would be flying back to Newark and all this beauty was staying behind. Out of all the places we've been, this was one of my favs. *Maybe we can come back for our honeymoon,* I thought, looking down at my engagement ring. The sun's rays hit the diamond and it glittered strong enough to blind me for a second.

We'd been engaged for years—definitely on the LaLa and Carmelo Anthony engagement blueprint. I was ready to plan my wedding, wear my dress, and sober my daddy up long enough to walk me down the aisle to Dane. I was just as ready to have a child. I loved him and I knew he loved me. I knew it.

Yeah, we was young and we been together forever but I believed in us. And I believed that Dane was going to keep his word and go legit. I had to, because if I didn't, that made me his fool and *that* didn't sit well with me. So I stuck to my word to myself not to walk the aisle and have the baby until he kept his promise to me first.

But how long was I willing to wait?

The patio doors opened and I leaned up to look over my shoulder at Hunga strolling out in a bright red strapless bikini top and a long wraparound skirt with a red straw hat covering her waist-length weave. It's the best I ever seen the bitch look. Random tattoos and all.

"I thought we were going sailing?" she asked, sounding grouchy as she dropped down onto the patio chair next to mine.

"That'll be nice," I told her, closing my eyes and tilting my head back to eat up more of the sun.

"I'm having a good time but I'm ready to see my son," Hunga said.

I popped one open and looked over at her in surprise. "You have kids?" I asked.

Hunga used her four-inch nails to pull a bag of weed and a blunt from her bikini top. She bust the cigar down the middle. "Yup. Just one. He's not Keno's. He live wit my mother because he got shit wrong with him and I couldn't handle taking care of him," she admitted.

Shit wrong with him?

"He ain't right in the head," Hunga admitted, looking off in the distance at the lagoon. "I can't take care of him twenty-four/seven. My mama got way more patience than me. But I go see my baby every day and I make sure I get whatever he need. So don't judge me, Suga."

I never thought I would feel sympathy for this chick . . . but I did. "What's his name?" I asked.

Hunga looked over at me in surprise before she pulled a lighter from her top and lit the blunt she finished rolling. "Mason. He's seven," she said. "Don't do that math. I had him when I was young. Fast, fucking, and not giving a fuck."

Hunga held the blunt with the tips of her nails and took a deep drag that she held.

I pulled my knees up to my chest and rested my chin atop them.

"This some *good* shit," she said as she exhaled a thick stream of smoke through her nostrils. "This shit right here will have your lightweight ass thinking you see pink dragons licking your pussy or some shit."

I frowned at her as she took another hit.

"Keno won't let me take none back but if I got to smuggle a bag in my pussy, this ganja gone see America, believe that shit."

Trust me, I believed that bitch.

We were in the middle of turquoise waters that were so clear we could see fish swimming near the top of the water. I stood near the railing in a strapless wide-leg jumpsuit in bright white. My shades were in place and the champagne I sipped from a crystal flute was Veuve Clicquot. Keno, in his aviator shades, cargo shorts, and wifebeater was lounging on the padded seat with Hunga laid out between his legs as they sipped champagne as well. Dane walked up to me with his flute in his hand looking fly as fuck in all white—from his V-neck tee, linen shorts, white diamond–banded watch, and kicks. He would not wear flip-flops no matter the name brand.

Dane was really delivering the hip-hop video reenactment when the sound of Ne-Yo's "Champagne Life" suddenly blasted from the ship's surround system.

"Yes . . . it's a beautiful day. It's gonna be a beautiful night."

"Oh!" Hunga and I both roared at the mid-tempo salute to the good life.

"Break out the champagne," we all said in unison with Ne-Yo.

Dane raised my hands in the air as I worked my hips back and forth in front of him. He knew that was one of my fave songs.

It was perfect.

The beauty of being surrounded by nothing but miles of water. The feel of the sun. The easy ride of the sailboat under the direction of the captain. The champagne. The music. We were just enjoying life. Fuck it.

"Let's toast it up," we all sang together, raising our champagne flutes to the clear blue skies as the sailboat sped across the tranquil waters.

It wasn't easy leaving Jamaica behind—especially for Hunga, after Keno found her trying to live up to her promise to push a bag of weed in her pussy—but the long plane ride back made me care about nothing but getting home to my own bed. It was after ten when we landed and close to eleven by the time we got our luggage. Lil Wil and AaRon picked us up from the airport. Midnight was coming on stronger than a motherfucker when the Tahoe pulled to a stop in front of our house.

Between the long trip back and the thick cloud of weed smoke giving me a contact, I was beat. I opened the passenger door. "Bye, Hunga. Bye, Keno," I said to them from where they sat together in the third-row seat.

Keno gave me a head nod and Hunga snored in her sleep.

Stretching and yawning, I came around the Tahoe. The street was quiet as hell. There was never anyone just chilling outside on my block. And at this time of the night I knew it would be graveyard still.

"I got the luggage, baby," Dane said, coming around to open the rear door.

I nodded and kept it moving up onto the sidewalk and

then our stairs. I was checking our mailbox when I looked up and spotted a blacked-out Chevy Caprice turning the corner with its lights off.

I didn't hear shit but the sudden hard ass beat of my heart as I turned around to spot Dane still fucking with the luggage. In slow motion my eyes shifted back to the Caprice just as the windows lowered and the barrels of guns flashed in the moonlight.

"NOOOOOOOOOOOOOOOOOO!" I screamed, dropping everything I held just as the first explosive gunshot filled the air with a flash of fiery light.

POW!

The windshield of one of the parked cars on the street shattered.

Everything—absolutely everything—moved in slow motion.

The windows of the Tahoe lowered as AaRon and Lil Wil prepared to fire back. I could see Keno cover Hunga's body in that third-row seat. I stooped down but my eyes stayed locked on Dane as he sidestepped the Tahoe. "Back up, Wil!" he shouted through the open rear door, kicking our luggage out the way.

The Tahoe was thrown in reverse.

The bullets flew until the air was nothing but sparks and tiny explosions. The sound of bullets crashing glass and piercing metal echoed like cazy.

POW. POW. POW. POW. POW. POW. POW. POW. POW. POW.

I laid flat on the porch and covered my head with my arms as I screamed.

"Damn!"

POW. POW. POW. POW. POW. POW. POW. POW. POW. POW.

Through the hail of bullets I heard Dane holler out. He sounded close.

I jumped to my feet.

Dane was lying on the sidewalk and street between two parked cars in front of the house. He was holding his thigh, his face tight with pain. He got shot trying to get to me. He coulda just jumped in the back of the Tahoe but he tried to get to me.

POW. POW. POW. POW. POW. POW. POW. POW. POW. POW.

I crawled down the stairs and across the sidewalk to him.

The sound of police sirens entered the fray.

"Go back, Suga," Dane said, trying to push my arms from around him.

"Hell no," I told him. Even as my heart beat like crazy, I took off my jacket and pressed it to the blood pouring from his thigh.

POW. POW. POW. POW. POW. POW. POW. POW. POW. POW.

The sound of the sirens got louder.

The shooting stopped.

In the sudden silence after the steady gunfire I heard the squeal of tires.

I eased up long enough to look through a shattered car window to see the shooters were gone. I turned my head to the left. The Tahoe was shot the fuck up. "Oh my God," I said, feeling hysterical tears fill my throat. I raised my hands and pulled at my hair as I shook my head in denial.

I checked the street again just as some of the doors to

our neighbor's home began to open. I raced toward the Tahoe but all I heard was my own heartbeat. This shit was crazy and after everything I was glad that motherfucker was still beating. It sounded good as hell to me.

BA-DUM.

"Suga!" Dane called out behind me.

BA-DUM.

Hunga and Keno sat up before they lowered the third-row seat and came out the Tahoe through the rear door.

BA-DUM.

The passenger door opened and Lil Wil fell out with his hand pressed to his neck as blood poured through his fingers. Keno snatched his shirt over his head and pressed it to Lil Wil's neck. His mouth was moving but I didn't hear nothing they said.

BA-DUM.

I eyed the driver side door. I waited for it to open and for AaRon to climb out. It didn't. I walked closer to the truck and I cried out at the sight of a bullet through AaRon's head lying back against the headrest. His eyes were wide open with no life in them. No life at all.

BA-DUM.

Part Two

I'm just trying to get mine,
I don't have the time to knock the hustle for real.

—Jay-Z and Mary J. Blige, "Can't Knock the Hustle"

8

I was numb.

I couldn't get over that night. I couldn't forget.

The sound of the bullets. The taste of fear. The sight of blood. The look of death.

The vision of the casket suspended on the metal contraption above the six-foot-deep hole in the ground blurred as my eyes filled with tears that raced down my cheek. I shook my head at the end of a young life. For the world it was just another young African American man from the hood killed far too soon. It's a damn shame it was a familiar story. A goddamn shame.

AaRon was dead.

The sound of a woman wailing out with her soul in pain echoed through the graveyard. I shifted my eyes forward to AaRon's mother rushing forward to drop to her knees at the graveside and press her hand to the shiny black casket.

"Why you leave me?" she cried as other family members came forward.

I thought they were going to pull her from the edge of the grave but instead they knelt with her and held her while she cried as she should—like a mother who lost her child.

I closed my eyes, feeling weak even as I tried to imagine her pain. A mother should never have to bury her child.

Never. I stumbled back in the grass and Dane's arm came up to surround my waist and steady me.

And for the first time ever I was filled with the urge to push his hands—his touch—off me. But I resisted because he was mourning the death of his friend. It wasn't the time to step away from him or to remind him that if he had just left this life when I asked, all of it might have been prevented: Lil Wil wouldn't need a talk box to speak. Hunga wouldn't have a permanent scar on her cheek from where one of the bullets grazed her face. Dane wouldn't be at risk of walking with a permanent limp. And AaRon would still be around, smiling with the face of a baby and the body of a bear.

I thought of the day he stepped in front of me when I went to those abandoned buildings to get Johnica. He would've taken a bullet for me.

My shoulders deflated as the funeral attendees started moving forward to place flowers on his casket. I crossed my arms over my chest as the October wind sent a chill through my body and we followed Hunga and Keno to the front to take a rose from one of the funeral home employees.

"We miss you, brother," Keno said, tossing his flower before he stood there for a long time looking down at the casket from behind his shades.

Hunga placed her flower as well before she wrapped both her arms around one of his and pressed her face against his upper arm.

I'm sorry, AaRon, I thought as I leaned forward to place my flower as well.

I looked up just as AaRon's mother's glanced up. I saw her body stiffen. Her eyes shifted from Keno to Dane. Her face tightened and you could see all of her true feelings for them on her face.

My pulse raced as I continued to watch her from behind my own shades.

Dane tossed his flower and then stepped back, his head hung so low that his chin damn near touched his chest. I stood close to him and I felt his tears rack his body even as I watched AaRon's mom rise to her feet and come around the grave with her eyes locked on Dane.

Keno and Hunga spotted her. They stepped back.

"Dane," I said softly, nudging him with my shoulder as he continued to stare at the casket.

The woman's eyes were red-rimmed from her tears and sorrow but they blazed with anger as she took one large step and slapped Dane across his face just as he turned to look at her.

WHAP!

Everyone surrounding the graveside gasped in shock right along with me.

She never said a word and just turned to walk back into the waiting arms of her family. Dane shook his head as another of his tears fell. I finally slid my hand into his and squeezed it tight. "Let's go, Dane," I whispered up to him as the murmurs and whispers of the crowd overtook the wails and cries.

His jaw was stiff as a motherfucker when he bent to press one hand to AaRon's casket before he finally turned and walked away from the graveside. Hunga climbed into Keno's car and I climbed into our Benz as Dane and Keno quickly exchanged a few words before the men climbed into their vehicles.

"Damn, Miss Roberts ain't said shit square to me all week," Dane started as he loosened his tie and undid the top few buttons of his black shirt. "Especially when I paid for the whole funeral Monday."

"She's just hurting," I said, reaching over to pat his thigh.

He placed his hand on top of mine and I let it rest there for a few before I eased my hand from under his and turned my head to look out at the window at the passing landscape of the city . . . at life continuing on for so many others.

AaRon's death symbolized so much other shit for me.

We were ambushed in front of our house. Those dudes were gunning for Dane. That could have been his body in that casket and my knees pressed into the cold dirt as I mourned the loss of the man I love. That shoot out was a helluva wake-up from the fun and fabulousness of the Caribbean . . . like nothing back in the real world mattered.

We rode the rest of the distance in silence.

It wasn't anything we weren't used to. Since that night, we barely said shit to each other. We hadn't fucked. We were just two people coexisting in a house together with unspoken words hanging heavy as hell in the air.

As Dane turned onto our block, I shook my head at the bullet holes and shattered glass of some of my neighbor's cars. It all just went down less than a week ago. And the neighbors were still side-eying me and Dane like a motherfucker. The who, what, when, where, and whys were still flowing . . . even if Keno rushed to hide the guns that weren't registered. We all gave our statements to the police about arriving from the airport and suddenly being hit by bullets from an unknown car. There was no lie I could tell about that. I never thought we were coming home to a fucking ambush.

The story ran on the news for a couple of days right after it happened, but more stories of local crime or national politics knocked it right off the radar. The police and news cameras were done on our block but the neighbors were now suspicious as hell . . . and I couldn't blame them. Fuck the dumb shit. I was embarrassed as hell.

Dane turned onto the drive and hit the overhead button to open the garage door. The interior motion light came on as he drove in and parked. I was already picking up my oversized crocodile clutch and making plans to strip out of my black wide-leg pantsuit.

I climbed out the car and smoothed my hands over my hair.

"You ready to talk to me, Suga?"

I stopped at the rear of the car and turned to eye Dane in confusion. "Huh?" I asked, undoing the loose knot of curls at the base of my neck and running my fingers though my hair.

"You barely had ten fucking words to say to me since that night," Dane said, coming around the car to stand over me. "You don't even want me to touch you."

I shifted my eyes away from him as I licked the neutral gloss from my lips.

Dane reached out and lightly grasped my chin. "You want to slap the shit outta me too, Sophie?" he asked, his voice low and hurt.

I looked at him and jerked my head back a bit to free my chin as his grasp tightened. "No, I don't want to slap you."

Dane chuckled scornfully. "Then say what you have to say, Suga. Say it!" He finished with a slash of his hand through the air before he rammed it into the pocket of his pants.

I shook my head but even as I fought not to say anything the words came. "I asked you to get out. I asked you to leave it behind," I admitted, my throat tight as hell with emotion as I looked at him with watery eyes. "No jail. No funerals. That's all I asked. No jail. No funeral, Dane."

He walked away from me and turned right back to face me. "So you're blaming me for what happened? You think I want AaRon dead and Wil walking around with some shit in his neck so he can talk?"

"No . . . nope. I don't think that at all, but the fact remains that it is what it is, Dane." I sat my clutch on the trunk. "I asked you to take the money and open a business. Use your smarts to make the same money and not have to fucking deal with thugs and goons and gamblers and motherfuckers who got to borrow money to make ends meet. Niggas with nothing to *lose*!"

"Sophie—"

"No, no, no, Dane," I said, holding up my hands as I stepped back from him. "See this shit right here—me and you—is everything to me and I haven't come across a *motherfucking* thing yet to make me risk losing this. Nothing. Like, we're good. You feel me?"

Dane released a shaky breath as he turned from me again.

I leaned forward against the car as I swiped the tears from my eyes.

"You don't understand, Suga," he said. "You don't know—"

I threw my hands up in the air and fought the urge to literally fling something at the back of his head. "I don't know what?! What don't I know?"

Dane looked at me over his shoulder. His eyes were so

intense and the lines in his face so severe. I felt completely shook by it.

"Who killed AaRon, Dane?" I asked him, my voice soft.

His brows dipped as he worked his wrist to shift his diamond watch. "I don't know," he said, turning to face me.

"Liar," I said, my voice sharp.

That took him by surprise.

"You *know* who killed AaRon. You *know* who robbed you. And I wouldn't doubt if it's the same motherfucker so you keep lying to yourself or whoever else but don't lie to me, Dane," I told him.

"I'm not lying to you."

"Just like we went to Jamaica for vacation only, right? That's what you said, right? No business, *right*? Huh? Fucking lie about that too. Go ahead." I smirked at his silence as I grabbed my clutch and shoved it under my arm. "What more has to happen for you to wise the fuck up?"

"I didn't want AaRon to die," Dane insisted.

I walked over to him and cupped the back of his head as I pressed a kiss to his cheek. "I know that," I admitted to him softly.

I felt the wetness of his tears against my cheek and my heart literally ached. "I know that, Dane," I said again in a soft whisper and stroked the back of his head. "I know."

Trust and believe, I was not done with my one-woman crusade to get my man—my fiancé—up out of the game. I wasn't done at all. But in this moment I decided to leave it the fuck alone when we could talk without anger and accusations. I don't know how long we stood there in that garage with me trying to soothe the pain and guilt he felt. It really didn't matter. I got what I had to say off my chest and those words that I held were no longer forming a wall between us.

"I'm your spine, Dane," I promised him, recalling that night in the car when the police stopped us.

He wrapped his arms around my waist and held me so fucking tight that I thought he would break my ribs. Still, I held him and let him hold me. He pressed kisses to my neck and my cheek. Nothing sexual. Just comforting. Loving. Reassuring.

I got you and you got me.

He released me with a final kiss to my forehead and we walked out the garage together. The October winds seemed to filter through my suit. I was glad when Dane unlocked the back door and we entered the house through the mudroom.

"I'ma cook," I told him as we came through the doorway into kitchen. "What you feel like?"

"I ain't really hungry." Dane removed his suit jacket.

"You gotta eat," I reminded him, kicking off my five-inch heels.

Dane chuckled as my height dropped like I stepped in a hole. He bent down to kiss my lips as he passed me. "Whatever you make is good for me, *shorty*," he teased.

BOOM-BOOM-BOOM-BOOM-BOOM!

Dane and I looked at each other in shock seconds before the front door burst open and the house was flooded with Newark police officers with their guns drawn. "Hands up," they shouted just as the back door burst open and more police rushed in to surround us. To ambush us. To take over our home.

This right here was my nightmare.

I couldn't do shit but shake my head as one of the female officers led me to the hall outside the kitchen and forced me to sit down on the bottom step. "Are you Sophie Alvarez?" she asked me.

I nodded as I looked around at the officers literally tossing our shit aside like it was trash as they searched our home. Violated it. Disrespected it.

But what the fuck could I say or do but hope they didn't find shit.

Dane's going to jail.

The thought of that made me sick and I brought my knees up to drop my head on them. I didn't even have tears left in me to shed. This day had been a huge emotional mind fuck already and I honestly didn't know how much more I could take.

Dane's going to jail.

We hadn't even made love all week.

Dane's going to jail.

What are his charges? Will he get bail? How strong is the evidence? How much time will he serve?

Dane's going to jail.

No jail. No funerals. AaRon's funeral and now . . .

Dane's going to jail.

I could just imagine what the fuck the neighbors were thinking. First the shooting last week and now a police raid.

As soon as they left I was calling our lawyer. I didn't give a fuck what it cost.

"We got guns," one of the officers yelled from somewhere in the house.

As far as I knew all of the weapons in the house were registered.

"And weed," another officer added. "Just enough quantity for personal stash though."

Dane didn't sell drugs. Never did.

Dane's going to jail.

"They're finished at the other house?" one of the officers asked.

"Oh yeah," another cop said with much too much satisfaction.

Shit. Shit. Shit.

I kept my face expressionless but deep down I felt like a man in steel-toe boots gut-kicked me.

Dane's going to jail.

Two officers breezed past me to head up the steps. I raised my face to wipe it with slightly trembling hands. Something crashed upstairs and I flinched, hoping like a motherfucker that it wasn't something that was irreplaceable.

Opening my eyes, I looked out the doorway where our front door barely hung on its hinges. Some of my neighbors were already beginning to gather and stare and point from across the street.

I just got my father to stop talking shit about Dane for the shoot-out and now this? Somebody was probably already on the line calling him and spreading the news. *Once these mofos clear out the house, I'll go talk to him . . . after I call our lawyer.*

I looked up as they led Dane out the kitchen limping and in handcuffs. He looked down at me and I had to fight the urge to jump up and wrap my body around his. "Wait for the attorney," he said, before the officer jerked him around and led him through the door.

My eyes shifted to the detective handling Dane and they opened in surprise to see one of our neighbors from down the street, Jonathan. We've been to his house for his huge Fourth of July cookout every year. His wife always made sure to send us cards for every holiday.

But I barely had time to ponder that when Dane's words came back to me strong as hell: *Wait for the attorney.*

Huh?

Wait for the attorney? Wait to call the attorney? Wait for the attorney to call me? What the hell was Dane talking about?

"Please stand and turn around," the female detective said to me.

My eyes got big as shit when she reached for her handcuffs. For a few moments I looked at her. "Bitch, you done lost your motherfucking mind."

Wait for the attorney.

I was going to jail.

What the fuck was going on?

What are my charges? Will I get bail? How strong is the evidence? How much time will I serve?

I stood and turned around. I can't front. Those tears I thought I was done with for the day rose like a flood but I fought like hell not to let them fall.

The first feel of the cool metal against my wrists buckled my knees but I locked them motherfuckers.

"Hand me her shoes," the officer said.

And when she eventually sat them in front of me, I stepped up into them and tossed my hair back over my shoulder like I wasn't scared. Like I'd been to jail before. Like I knew what to expect.

Like this wasn't a fucking nightmare.

"You have the right to remain silent . . ."

They led me out onto the porch and I paused at the sight of the police cars, officers, news truck, cameramen, and neighbors flooding the street like a fucking block party.

"This is Natalie Bond standing outside the home of Sophie Alvarez in the Weequahic section of Newark where the Vice and Narcotics Squads have conducted a raid looking for Daniel 'Dane' Greenley. Greenley is suspected of running a major loan-sharking and underground gambling enterprise. Another home in Newark was also raided in conjunction with this investigation. This is also the home where a shoot-out occurred just last week and a young man lost his life. No word if the raid and the shooting are related incidents . . ."

As soon as I bent my head to slide onto the backseat of the police cruiser, they closed the door and the rest of the newswoman's words, observations, and speculations was blocked.

Great—now my name and face was splattered all over the news again. I let my head drop back against the seat and closed my eyes. "Damn," I swore, unable to fight the feeling of doom settling around me.

9

Judge not, that ye be not judged.

It's amazing what thoughts come to your mind when you're sitting in a police station for hours on end. And I suddenly remembered me looking down my nose at Luscious for getting arrested and now here I am. Hell, she got out the next morning. Would I?

About an hour ago they brought me up from one of the temporary holding cells to an interview room and left me. I tried to stretch the cramps from my body from sitting up all night. I refused to lie down and sleep and get comfortable in that motherfucker. There was nothing about this whole fucking process that I wanted to be comfortable with. Nothing at all.

I never so much as got a fucking speeding ticket. I didn't even jaywalk and now my ass was in jail being charged with promoting gambling, possession of gambling records, and maintenance of an illegal gambling resort. The fuck?

What about my father? I ain't had the nerve to call him yet.

My job? Would I have to call in from jail and take a fucking sick day or two?

The house? Did they secure it or were crackheads and

dope fiends—and maybe even some of my neighbors—looting our shit out the house?

I felt like screaming out in frustration. That all was minor shit compared to me spending time in jail. Day after day in a cell?

And what if bitches tried me and I wound up getting shanked in that motherfucker for not toeing the line? What if I became the pussy bitch of some big-backed chick? What if a gang of chicks raped me with a broom handle or some shit?

I was about to lose my motherfucking mind.

I am not cut out for fucking jail. No way. No fucking how.

No lie, my hand itched to slap the shit out of Dane like AaRon's mama.

He got me into to this shit. *His* bullshit got *me* caught up.

I told that motherfucker to quit. I told him.

I had been worried about his ass going to jail and not me. I couldn't do shit but call myself a dumb-ass bitch. Twisting and shifting in that chair that had my ass numb, I put my hands over my face as I tilted my head back causing my hair to fall back. I felt like I was on the edge. My thoughts were all over the fucking place. I felt more panic than I did the night we got shot at.

What the fuck my life done become?

I'm the good girl. I got good grades. I never got in trouble in school. Never. I never skipped school. Never made out in the stairwells with a boy. Never even smoked a cigarette in the bathroom. Same at college. I didn't experiment with shit. I didn't even take the time away from my studies to fucking pledge a sorority. I got more good grades and graduated magna cum laude. I got a good job. I worked. I paid my taxes. I paid my bills on time. I have good credit. I mentored Johnica's wild ass. I didn't go to church but I watched T. D. Jakes on TV. I said my prayers.

What did I do wrong? Fall for a motherfucking criminal. And I fell hard.

I dropped my head on my arms on top of the table. Making a fist I pounded the desk. *I told that motherfucker to quit. I told him.*

I never even got in Dane's business though. I'd been to that fucking gambling house less than five times. I'd never seen paperwork. I didn't know his clients. I never handled money. I never dropped off or picked up cash.

I sat the fuck up.

Wait. Why am I in this bitch?

Running my fingers through my hair, I stood up and paced back and forth behind the table in the center of the room. I was still pacing damn near twenty minutes later when the door finally opened. I straightened my back and turned to face the two detectives who took a seat at the table. The door opened again and a tall black dude in a suit came in to lean in the corner of the room.

This was bigger than I thought because nothing in the world would convince me that old boy in the corner wasn't the feds.

"Have a seat, Suga," the short Danny DeVito–looking one said.

His use of my nickname made me pause. When they were taking my info the officer asked if I had any nicknames or aliases and I told them no.

I smoothed my trembling hands over my pants before I

did take a seat and cross my legs as I prayed I didn't faint from my heart beating too fast. I was suited for facts and figures and fly shoes, not *this* shit. I never fronted and acted like I was a thugstress—real chick—ride or die chick like Hunga. Never.

Wait. Did Keno get picked up too? And Hunga? Her ass was around their shit way more than me.

"Suga, you and your fiancé are in a shitload of trouble. I won't lie to you," the black detective with big-ass marks on his face said.

My eyes shifted to all three of them.

"I'm sure a young woman like you with your career ahead of you realizes you made a mistake and the best thing to do is to get out of this before it's too late."

I did the eye shift again.

"The more info you can give us on Dane's enterprise, the more the prosecutor would be willing to give you immunity. No jail time," the black cop offered.

I was confused as hell. I thought everybody in the streets claimed the feds didn't come for you until they were ready. Like, they would investigate a motherfucker for years to get airtight evidence. So . . . why are they asking me to snitch on Dane for evidence against him?

And a sweet deal to be a fucking snitch is exactly what the fuck they set on the table for me.

"We have reason to believe that the shoot-out outside your home is directly related to Dane and his crew retaliating against a man known as Poppi for robbing that gambling house he owns."

I kept my face neutral but on the inside of me it all made sense. These motherfuckers were sniffing on the right trail;

they just needed a guide to get home. This wasn't about the loan-sharking and gambling. They were gunning for Dane for more charges.

"Anything you've witnessed, know, or overheard would be helpful."

I knew what they were sniffing for. I knew exactly what these motherfuckers wanted me to reveal. They didn't know what I knew but they figured I knew something . . . and I did:

Dane and Keno beating the fuck out of Poppi's ass outside Club 973.

All that money Keno was counting at the gambling house the day it got robbed.

Dane putting security detail on me after those cars blocked me in the street.

AaRon revealing to me the robbery and some other sketchy shit going on.

Dane on the phone in our basement: *"Keno, when y'all catch up to that grimy punk-ass motherfucker, you make sure that fuck ass nigga know he don't walk away with fifty stacks of my money and live to spend it."*

Yes, there was plenty I witnessed, knew, and overheard that would be helpful as evidence that Dane had *something* done to Poppi. I wanted to ask was Poppi in fact dead, but I didn't crack my mouth.

I blinked and looked down at my engagement ring missing from my finger. The cops had taken and inventoried it along with all my other possessions. Including my locket with my mom's picture. I missed them both. I felt lost without them. And now they wanted me to help send Dane to jail for murder/attempted murder/assault . . . whatever.

"Let's be clear, Ms. Alvarez."

I swung my eyes to the man in the corner. His voice was hard and clipped like he was never in the mood for bullshit. Never ever.

"We have enough evidence where you can't sit there all pretty and try to play dumb to how your man made his money. Not when you've been to the gambling house. Not when you went with him out of the country to conduct business. Not when we have you on the phone trying to convince him to *go legit*," he said, making air quotes with his fingers.

I begged Dane to get out the game before it got him . . . and now it had the both of us. I had to be honest that the thought of Dane being a murderer or even someone to order a murder didn't set well with me. Never did. And then he knew I was getting arrested before I did.

Wait for the attorney.

Did he overhear they were taking me too or did he know he was being investigated?

"You don't understand, Suga," he said. "You don't know—"

Do I walk away from him and go on with my life? Or do I take a chance on being that ride or die chick that would do a bid before she flipped on her man? Fuck around and be one of them dumb asses sitting in jail gathering pussy cobwebs and that nigga on the streets and straight free-falling into pussy.

But Dane wouldn't do that to me.

This wasn't a new relationship. We put in years. We built shit together.

That night of the shoot-out he was trying to get across the street to check on me—to protect me—instead of running for safety. Instead of looking out for himself.

Wait for the attorney.

I've watched enough people on *The First 48* give up their rights that it was ridiculous. Me? Nada. Regardless of anything I wasn't saying or signing shit without my attorney sitting front row to the show. "Has my attorney arrived?" I asked.

"This offer for immunity comes off the table eventually," the black detective said.

I looked down at my bare finger. I didn't say shit else.

Eventually the fed left first and then the two detectives followed behind him.

As soon as the door closed my shoulders slumped. I knew there was no way I could flip on Dane and so the weight of what the future held for me was great.

"You thought I wouldn't fix this, Suga?"

I turned in Dane's embrace and eased my hands up around his neck and kissed him. His hands came up under the short silk cover-up I wore to undo the strings of my bikini on each hip. I suckled his neck and spread my legs when the bikini fell to the floor. The first press of his fingers to my clit made me shiver. I held him tighter until my breasts flattened against the hard contours of his chest.

He picked my body up with one strong arm around my waist and I bent my legs to clench his waist with my thighs. One strong hand eased down the middle of my buttocks and down to stroke my pussy while my lips pressed against his face until they found his mouth. He swallowed my moan of pleasure and I tasted his tongue.

Dane braced his body against the railing of the boat as he used one hand to snatch his trunks down until they fell on top of his bare feet. I forced myself to relax as he grabbed his dick and probed the moist opening just a millisecond before I felt him inside me. Bracing my knees against the boat, I worked my hips until my pussy had swallowed every inch.

"Yes," I sighed at the feel of the heat and hardness of it against my walls.

Dane brought one hand up to wrap in the length of my hair and tugged until my head tilted back as I continued to circle my hips, work my walls and ride that dick.

"Get that motherfucking dick," he said thickly.

I smiled and bit my bottom lip as I opened my eyes and looked up to the blue skies. I was glad to be with him. To be on him and for him to be in me. To be free.

I never wanted any part of jail again. Fuck that.

The thought of my freedom made me fuck him harder until he was hollering out.

"Dane," I cried out as I felt my nut coming on strong. "Dane . . ."

"Miss Alvarez."

"Dane," I sighed.

"Miss Alvarez."

"Dane . . ."

My eyes popped when I felt someone shake me. I closed them again at the sight of the same fucking wall of that interview room in the police station. I glanced up at the clock on the wall. An hour had passed and I had fallen asleep.

What a whack-ass dream.

Wiping the drool from the corner of my mouth and the table where it puddled, I sat up and seen this fine-ass white dude sitting across the table from me in a three-piece pinstripe suit and paisley tie. He was white boy fine like the blond dude from *The Fast and the Furious.* Paul Walker.

He smiled at me. "I'm Hunter Garrett. I was retained to be your attorney," he said.

Wait for the attorney.

"But Anthony Barton is our attorney," I said, looking at him skeptical as hell.

He reached in the inside pocket of his blazer and withdrew a thin gold case holding his business cards. He handed me one between his index and middle finger.

I took it.

"Anthony and I both work for the same firm. He is officially representing Mr. Greenley and because they are trying to leverage you against him it would be a conflict of interest for you two to share an attorney. I assure you that we are on one team concerning this matter, Miss Alvarez."

I nodded as I pressed the card onto the table under my hand.

"Mr. Greenley also had me contact your father. I sent a car to his home and he is here waiting to see you," Hunter said.

And *that* piece of news made me tear up all over again. As much as my father and I weren't close, he raised me. He was my *papi*. And I never wanted to let him down. Never. But even more than that, sometimes I was still the little girl who would sit quiet as a sneaky roach to keep my father from showing how disappointed in me he could be. Especially when he was drinking and mean and uncaring of what came out his mouth. And in this moment I was that little girl. I couldn't handle it. I couldn't.

I shook my head adamantly. "I don't want him to see me in jail. Tell him . . . tell him I'm okay and then have the car take him home. *Please*," I finished with emphasis as I sniffed and blinked away my tears.

Hunter nodded.

"I wonder if they are trying to wear me out on mental warfare type shit by leaving me in this empty-ass room," I said, trying to shake off all the emotions beating me the fuck down. "No window. No TV. No nothing. Just four walls. Now I know why people just get on the floor and go to sleep on *The First 48*."

Hunter just smiled and I wondered if he knew what the hell I was talking about.

"So I did speak with the assistant prosecutor handling your case and they are offering you immunity in exchange for your testimony against Mr. Greenley," he said, moving on to business.

"They came in and explained that to me," I said.

"Did you say anything?" he asked, his blue eyes on me.

"I listened to everything they had to say and then asked if my attorney was here," I said.

He nodded.

"What charge are they trying to make against Dane?" I asked.

"Manslaughter."

My gut clenched.

"So Poppi is dead?"

Hunter nodded. "My understanding is he was injured in

a hit-and-run a few weeks back and has since passed away from the injuries."

I winced.

"So what are your thoughts about the deal?" Hunter asked

"No," I said adamantly.

"I have to stress to you the risk you're taking by not taking the deal. With the charges you've received, if you're found guilty, you could face anything from probation to five years' incarceration—"

I jumped to my feet and almost stumbled on my heels. "Five years!"

"That's *if* you're found guilty. I haven't seen the evidence or had time to review anything they have to make a fair assessment on your case," Hunter said, motioning with his hands for me to sit down.

I did.

"Right now the focus is on getting bail and I don't think that will be a problem," Hunter said. "Your arraignment should be in the morning, so you are in here for the night."

Fuck it. At this point I just wanted to sleep and maybe resume my dream.

"How's Dane? Have you seen him?" I asked.

Hunter smiled. "He is worried about you and wanted to make sure I got in to see you tonight to check on you."

"He knows I am not cut out for this but please tell him I'm good. I'm straight," I lied.

Hunter smiled like he wasn't even trying to believe that shit. "He wants to also let you know that you do whatever you have to do to get out," Hunter said, leveling his bright blue eyes on me again.

My face filled with confusion as I sat back in the chair. "He knows about the deal?" I asked.

"Yes."

"And he wants me to take it?"

Hunter nodded and crossed his hands atop the desk. "Yes, if it comes to that. Yes."

"No, I won't flip on him. I won't do that. I can't," I said.

"I don't think it will come to that."

I massaged the bridge of my nose. "Do you think he'll get bail?"

Hunter rose to his feet, picking up his briefcase, which I recognized as Ferragamo. "He should," he assured me.

I ran my hand through my hair and had to fight not to pull every thick strand out at the root. First the funeral, then my argument with Dane, then the raid and my arrest. I just wanted this particular night to be the fuck over.

"You okay?"

I took my eyes away from the front door of my home haphazardly hung with that yellow POLICE LINE DO NOT CROSS tape across it. I looked over at Hunter as we stood on the sidewalk. "Yeah, yeah, I'm good. I'm alive. I'm free."

Early that morning I was released from jail. I was just as surprised by the news of the charges being dropped as I was by the arrest in the first place. And I was even more surprised when I discovered the cost of my freedom.

"Damn it," I swore. "I have never cried so much in my fucking life and that's saying a lot with *my* father. Trust me."

Hunter chuckled lightly.

I released a heavy breath.

Dane pled to the fed charges of loan-sharking and running a gambling enterprise in exchange for the charges against me being dropped and a three-year prison term. Without my cooperation the chances of them charging him with manslaughter were done. They hammered the deal out late last night after Hunter let Dane know I wouldn't flip on him to go free. Hunter assured me of all that this morning when he arrived for my release and to give me a ride home.

"Let me go in first and just make sure everything's okay," he said, placing a strong hand on my elbow.

"You don't have to do that," I told him, wincing as a cold snap of air sandwiched our bodies as we climbed the stairs. "You probably ready to get the hell out of the city."

"Why? I live in Ivy Hill," Hunter said, his eyes twinkling. "I have all my life."

Like Weequahic, Ivy Hill was another section inside the huge city of Newark. It was located on the other side of South Orange, New Jersey. "No wonder I like you," I teased as we came to stand in front of the door that was barely on the hinges and damn near swinging in the fall winds.

They wrong for this shit.

"So what am I supposed to do without him for the next three years, Hunter?" I asked him with a sad smile. "Any advice?"

"You be grateful that it's not fifteen years or even life."

True.

///

$\mathscr{M}$y house looked like a tornado went through that bitch. They tossed everything.

Hunter had stayed with me until the carpenter I called finally showed up to reframe and hang the front and back doors. But now I was just left alone to put together my house and my life. Without Dane. Every time I let the idea of that rest on my shoulders I either broke down crying or felt so anxious that I started biting my nails.

Once he posted bail and came home, we would only have the time until his sentencing to spend together. I was just waiting on a call from either of the attorneys on just how much it would take to bring Dane home . . . even if for a little while.

Three motherfucking years.

I stepped over and around the drawers on the floor of the kitchen to get a goblet. There was a bottle of red wine in the fridge and I poured it up until the goblet was filled to the rim. I drank down a big gulp of it and then refilled the glass. Fuck it. If the cops hadn't taken whatever weed stash Dane had around this bitch I woulda smoked me one.

I went still and paused at the sound of something vibrating. Setting the glass on the counter, I squinted my eyes and poked out my chin as I listened for it.

Bzzzzzzzzz . . . Bzzzzzzzzz . . .

"My cell phone?"

When they raided the house yesterday I had just set my purse on the counter and they damn sure didn't ask me if I wanted it when they hauled my ass to jail. I was lucky the female officer thought of my shoes. I shifted all the shit they pulled from the drawers that covered the countertops—takeout menus, utensils, plastic bowls, odds and ends—until I found my oversized clutch.

It was my cell phone.

Bzzzzzzzzz . . . Bzzzzzzzzz . . .

They rummaged through my shit but left it behind. There was nothing on my phone. Not even contact numbers. I traded them out so often that I didn't bother storing info in them. And they didn't need my cell to pull my phone records.

"Shit," I said, tucking the clutch under my arm. I had over fifty missed calls.

Dane was in jail. My father knew I was home. Everybody else could wait.

As I grabbed my wine and walked out the kitchen, I looked around at everything that needed to be set straight. I just felt tired. "This shit can wait too. I'm going to wash my ass and then take a nap before I tackle it," I said aloud to myself, turning to head up the stairs, still in the suit and heels I wore to AaRon's funeral.

And on the second level more chaos reigned. I stepped over all the towels and sheets they'd pulled from the linen closet and walked into my bedroom. The mattresses were on their sides. The closet doors wide open. All our clothes were tossed into a corner. Every drawer in the dressers were open and everything once in them hung out—including my bright pink dildo. *Jesus.*

I know it was the police who been all up and through my shit but it still felt just as violating as a burglar invading my home.

Finishing the wine with a Sheneneh-like tip back of my head, I stripped naked, pulled my hair up into a ponytail, and walked over whatever was on the floor to get to the bathroom. Them motherfuckers had tossed all kinds of shit from the medicine cabinet and the countertop into the tub. But the real kicker was seeing a big-ass footprint of someone's damn boot in my tub. Like really? Who does that?

And that shit defeated me. That one thing just fucked me all up.

All I wanted to do was wash my ass. That's it.

I turned from the tub and caught sight of myself in the mirror over the sink. I looked tired. Way older than my twenty-four years. Haggard. Beat up and beat the fuck down. Way down.

I left the bathroom as my cell phone sounded off again in my purse. I ignored it.

I fought the mattresses to put them back on the king-size frame. Grabbing one of the pillows they'd flung to the floor, I climbed onto the middle of the bed and pulled my knees to my chest as I buried my face in the softness. I could just barely make out Dane's scent on it, and I buried my face deeper.

Three years.

The tears fell.

I never felt so lonely in my life.

• • •

BAM-BAM-BAM!

I shot up in the middle of the bed with my heart pounding and looked around. The sunlight streaming through the windows was glaring to my eyes as I blinked and tried to get myself orientated.

BAM-BAM-BAM!

I jumped again at the sound of something banging on the front door downstairs. It sounded way too similar to the front door getting rammed in yesterday. I climbed off the bed and was halfway across the room before I remembered I was naked. Turning around, I dug through one of the pile of clothes until I found a sequined tank and a pair of Dane's sweats. A mess? Yes. But it was all I could find that wasn't work clothes.

BAM-BAM-BAM!

I rushed down the stairs and rose up on my toes to look out the glass square at the top of the door. My father stood there with his cane raised and ready to knock out chips of wood. I jerked it open and then jumped back as the cane came down. I took it from him. "Hi, *Papi.* I—"

"So you're free," Victor said, stepping into the house and then turning in the foyer to face me. "Where's the other jailbird?"

"Dane has his bail hearing this morning," I told him, closing the door. "How'd you get here?"

"I walked," he said, holding his hand out for his cane.

I gave it to him and then stepped back. He'd never hit me, but I could tell he was hot and I wasn't trying him.

"I didn't raise you to be a liar, Sophie," he said, his accent so heavy. I didn't know if it was from drinking or his anger.

"Or to be the mule of some dope dealer."

I frowned. "Dane never sold drugs. They are accusing him of loan-sharking and running an illegal gambling enterprise."

"Don't give me the answer you would give on the stand," he spat, his eyes glassy and blazing. "I'm your father and you will tell me the truth, Sophie."

He took a step forward and I stiffened my spine. "The truth is that all you should be concerned with is that I am free with no charges filed against me," I told him.

Victor laughed.

It surprised me.

"You think you are so fucking smart, Sophie. Always have and always will."

"Am I supposed to think I'm dumb?" I clapped back.

His face got hard.

"If I don't praise me, who will?" I asked him, getting courage by the minute. "My whole life you made me feel like I was in the way of your drinking."

He waved his hand at me dismissively. "Don't sing me no sad songs," he said in disgust.

"Trust me, I wouldn't waste my time," I said.

Victor turned in a circle to look around the house. "I don't want that boy back in this house," he said.

I made a face and ignored him. I wasn't even arguing with him about that. This was *our* home—mine and Dane's. Me and the house would be right here waiting for him when he got out . . . today *and* when he finished his three-year bid. *Fuck whatever Daddy's drunk ass talking about.*

"Daddy, I gotta clean up and take me a bath," I said, my hand already back on the doorknob. "You want me to take you home?"

"*Sí*," he said, switching to Spanish. He always did that shit so random as hell, like he remembered he was Puerto Rican in spurts.

"Let me get my keys."

I jogged up the stairs. My cell phone was kicking up dust again and I dug it out my purse. The missed call count was up to over a hundred. Sitting down on the edge of the bed, I started going through all the call, texts, and voice mails. Most of the missed calls were from Leo.

"What the fuck he want?" I muttered, deleting all his calls from my log.

Some people just sent texts or left voice mails trying to get the scoop on what happened. *Um, we got locked up, duh . . .*

A few called just to say they were praying for us.

I frowned at about a dozen calls from a number I didn't recognize. I checked the voice mail: *"Humph. You ain't 'round this motherfucka looking down your nose at me now, are you? What kind of mentor are you and your ass on the news getting arrested? Good thing I stopped Johnica from fuckin' with you. My gut told me you wasn't about shit. Dumb bitch. Don't drop the soap, ho."*

Johnica's mother. Her laughter was mad crazy before the voice mail finally ended. The only thing her fucking gut could tell her was to stop eating. Fuck her, and at this point I didn't even have the time of day for Johnica, so a mini-fuck you for her too.

The phone vibrated in my hand. I looked down at it. Johnica's mother. I answered the call.

"Oh, so you out?" she asked before I could even open my mouth.

"How you get my number?" I snapped.

"From Johnica's old cell phone. Why?"

I triple blinked and looked down at the phone. "I'm trying to figure out why you stalking me? Like, what's your purpose playing on my phone? You ain't got shit else to do but sit on your wide, sloppy ass eating and playing on the phone?"

"NO THIS BITCH DIDN'T??!!"

"Oh yes, I did," I assured her. "Your slow ass needs to enroll your daughter back in school and get up off my shit. You know?"

I can't lie. It felt good to snap on a bitch. I needed to vent. She asked for it and there the fuck it was.

"Don't worry about my daughter, you bougie convict bitch. My daughter is being homeschooled while she get ready to have her baby!"

She said that shit like she was giving a speech on some shit. Dumb ho.

"If you keep your face out the fucking fridge and your eyes on your daughter instead of a bucket of chicken, she wouldn't be pregnant, Biggie Smalls," I told her, jumping up to my feet.

"BIGGIE SMALLS?" she shrieked into the phone. "No you are not disrespecting the dead."

"You gotta problem with me calling you Biggie. Well fuck it . . . how about Fat Joe, Rick Ross, Chubb Rock? All you need is a fade and a mic, bitch!"

"See, a smartmouth trick like you need to pop all that shit face-to-face. You real strong over the phone."

"Well, you know where I live. It's all over the news. Roll

your mentally touched ass on over here," I told her. "And then I'ma physically touch that ass and help you get your thoughts together."

Brrrnnnggg.

The house phone. That had to be the attorneys. I hopped on the bed and reached down on the floor to scoop it up. I hung up the cell phone and answered the cordless. "Hello."

"Hi, Sophie, this is Anthony Barton."

"Yes."

"Dane did receive a bond of seventy-five thousand without the ten-percent option."

Damn.

That meant I had to pay the entire seventy-five grand in cash for him to be released. I have ten grand in the bank and I could have easily posted the ten percent. Where the hell do I get another sixty-five thousand dollars?

"Sophie, you there?"

"Yeah, just trying to figure out what to do. When can I see him?"

"He's going to call you as soon as they get him back into lockup but he asked that you don't do anything until he calls you first."

I nodded as if he could see me. "Okay."

I wasn't even sure when he ended the call because I just sat there shell-shocked and lost as hell as to what to do. I fell back on the bed and held the phone pressed to my chest as I waited for that motherfucker to ring. Waited for Dane to call and tell me what the fuck to do. Waited to not feel like everything about my life had changed and would never go back to the way it was. Waited to not feel panic or fear or anger or disappointment.

Somewhere during the hour I waited I heard the television come on downstairs and I knew my father had set himself up to wait for me. I wouldn't doubt if the bar in the living room didn't help him feel a little more at home. Whatever.

Brrrnnnggg . . .

"Hello," I said into the phone.

"You have a collect call from . . ."

Relief flooded me as I waited for the message to end to accept the call. It took far too long to hear Dane's voice on the line. It felt like forever plus another day.

"Suga, I'm sorry, baby. I thought I protected you."

"I'm okay. I just want to know what to do about the bail. It's seventy-five grand."

The line went quiet.

"Dane," I called out to see if he was still on the line.

"Suga . . . I don't want you to pay the bail," he finally said.

BA-DUM.

Was it possible for a heart to jump through a rib cage?

"Why the fuck not?" I asked. "You have to come home because that's all the time we got together until you leave to do three years."

"The judge has to accept the plea for sentencing," he reminded me. "And because I'm pleading guilty everything confiscated during the raid is gone. The house, the club, the cars, the guns, the jewelry—

"The cash too," I added, my voice as dead as I felt on the inside.

This shit just got real as hell. Too real.

"I'm tapped out, Suga," Dane admitted. "They got everything."

My attorney did tell me I was lucky to have the house and car in my name with mortgage payments made through my checking account. My job paid substantially enough to cover it. All of Dane's shit was paid in cash and was in his name. It all belonged to the feds now. They would eventually auction off all the shit and who knows what they would do with the cash. I hated to ask how much he had stashed that they found. I hated to ask.

How much could my shoulders bear? How fucking much?

"I love you, Dane. I do. And you know I do. But I was hoping for at least a month or two to spend with you before your sentencing and now you're telling me I don't even get that?"

"I can't really talk like I want."

He was right. Either the feds were still tapping my end or the jail was listening in on his. Either way, it was time to shut the fuck up. Period.

"I'm getting transferred out of here soon. As soon as I find out where, I'll add you to my visitation list. You coming to see me, Suga?"

And that's the thing. I could hear the uncertainty in his voice because he knew I never wanted to have to see my man in jail. He knew that. He knew that was one of my biggest fears. But this man just copped to charges to free me and there was no way in hell I was turning my back on him. Love and loyalty over everything.

"You know I'm coming . . . and you know I got a lot to get off my chest," I warned him.

Dane laughed a little. "I know."

I dropped my head into my hand and massaged my eyes with my fingers.

"Suga, I love you."

"Yes, you sure do," I told him, trying to remember the feel of his lips on my forehead in those seconds just before the police raided our lives.

"And I know you love me too."

"Yes, I sure do," I swore to him as I tilted my head and closed my eyes as the tears came on strong.

"We been together a long time, Suga, back to the days your father had that old-ass Nova."

"You right. That was a lot of years and twenty pounds ago," I agreed, with a soft smile.

"We'll get through this."

"Yeah, but it would've been better to float through it than have to crawl over broken glass on our knees."

"I know."

We both got real quiet. I was thinking about all the blows we took and how the hell we were going to recover from the knockout. I wondered what was on his mind. Looking at three years behind bars couldn't be easy, especially on top of everything else.

If only he had listened to me.

"I gotta go, but I'll call you back later. Okay?"

"Yeah. Okay. Love you."

"Love you too."

Click.

What was so crazy about it all was I didn't have time to wallow and have those "Why me, Lord" moments. There was too much shit popping off to go crazy.

"Sophie!"

Allowing myself one last deep inhale of breath, I left the room and made my way back downstairs.

"Sophie!"

I leaned against the doorway of the living room. My father was sitting on the living room sofa without the cushions. I know his ass hurt. "I'm right here," I said, surprised at how happy I was that he was there—even with one of our bottles of Paul Masson brandy opened and sitting by his sneakered feet.

"No need crying over spilt milk," he said.

He glanced at me for one second and then turned back to the flat-screen on the wall.

Crying? I felt like crawling in a fucking hole and burying myself. I turned and walked toward the kitchen to start putting my house and my life back together.

"You ready to take me home?" Victor called out behind me.

"No," I called back, pausing at the entrance to the kitchen for him to have a tirade about going to his house. I didn't want him to go home. I didn't want to be in the house alone.

He surprised me.

"Okay," he called back just before the volume of the television went up.

11

*T*he next morning work and getting back to my normal routine stared me in the face. I had no choice but to get my ass up and make it happen. No choice at all.

It took all of yesterday to put my house back together, wash all my towels and linens—and I do mean *everything* in the house in and off the beds and towel racks—and cook a stew for my father before I finally took him home later that night. I was used to Dane being the type of dude not to sit around the house, and you would think being home alone wouldn't feel so empty . . . but it did.

And so I was glad to have somewhere to go and something to do. Work.

I took my time with my appearance. If nothing else, I figured Leo knew about my arrest and I refused to show up looking like life was whipping my ass like Floyd Mayweather.

I washed and blow-dried my hair, then pressed it bone straight with one of my ceramic flat irons. Neutral makeup. Glossy lips. Cream silk shirt. Wide-leg, high-waist linen pants. Five-inch, pointy-toe crocodile shoes with a gold heel. Long gold chains of various lengths. My heart locket. Diamond stud earrings. No rings except the one Dane gave me when he vowed to marry me. It was all I needed.

I reached for it and twisted it on my finger as I gave myself one last check in the mirror before I left the bathroom and scooped up my trench coat, clutch, and briefcase.

When I stepped onto my front porch and closed the door securely behind me, I was surprised to see a cop car sitting in the middle of the street in front of my house. I paused and started to run my ass back inside until I glanced up the street at two uniformed cops searching about five teenage boys on the corner.

Taking a steadying breath and flexing my shoulders, I came down the stairs and climbed into my car. During the entire ride downtown, my stomach was filled with nerves. What would Leo have to say? Would some of my other coworkers know about the raid and Dane's arrest? And if they did, would they smile in my face and whisper behind my back or boldly shun the black girl from Newark who wasn't shit but a criminal like all the rest—in their eyes?

As I strolled into the building with my head held high, I flashed my badge and signed in. My stomach was a knot because I swore the guards would yell out, "Hey, that was you on TV!" But they didn't.

I rode the elevator up, thankfully alone, and stepped off to head across the black polished tiled floor to my small nondescript office with my name plaque on the door:

SOPHIE ALVAREZ
Senior Account Specialist

"Good morning, Miss Alvarez," the receptionist said, carrying a cup of coffee as she made her way to her station directly across from the elevators.

"Morning," I said to her. I doubted she even heard me.

In my office, I put my things away and started my day. Facts and figures. Reports and files. In my head this 1980s song, "Manic Monday," played.

"It's just another manic Monday. I wish it was Sunday. 'Cause that's my fun day . . ."

Or something like that. Fuck it.

Knock-knock.

I barely had time to look away from my computer before the door to my office opened and Leo stepped inside. *I knew this shit was coming.*

"Good morning, Leo."

He made a fake-ass sad face as he sat on the edge of my desk. "Well, good morning to you, Sophie. I sure wasn't expecting you today," Leo said.

I leaned back in my chair and eyed this slick motherfucker. "Really?" I asked.

He shook his head. "No reason. I just had a gut feeling."

Yeah, right.

"Is it okay if I sit here, I don't want to offend anybody— oh, but wait, I don't have to worry about Thug Life coming through telling me to go find something to do around here. Do I?"

I eyed this smug motherfucker. I couldn't jump across my desk like Evelyn on *Basketball Wives* and then scratch up that smooth brown skin on his face. Not at work. "How's your fiancée, Leo? I would think you would be more focused on her than me. Right?" I asked him, leaning my head to the side to eye him.

He reached over and tapped my engagement ring. "I would think a woman like you would understand that this ring doesn't mean you're locked down anymore. You're just with somebody *on* lockdown."

I slapped his hand away. WHAP!

Leo just laughed and stood up to smooth his tie. "I'm sorry. Okay. You all right?"

I gave him a stiff smile and nodded.

"And we're still cool?" he asked.

This motherfucker had just joked about my man being locked up and he thought shit between us wasn't more awkward than ever? "Of course," I lied, forcing myself to sound laid-back.

"It was a bad joke and I apologize," Leo said, his voice and eyes serious.

Some of the tension left my shoulders. Some . . . but not all. "We're good, Leo," I told him, leaning forward to resume my work.

He didn't say anything else before he turned and left.

Whack-ass. Bounce with your bitch ass.

I got up to come around my desk and close the door. I felt resistance and looked around it to see my supervisor, Kelsey Walker. "Sorry about that. I didn't see you," I said, stepping back and opening the door wider.

"No problem, Sophie," he said.

I felt confusion at his sudden appearance at my door but when Vickie, the Human Resources director, followed him inside and closed the door, shit got a little clearer.

"Have a seat, Sophie," he said, as he and Vickie took the chairs in front of my desk.

Wow. Really?

"I'm good, thank you," I said, giving them both a tight smile.

"I cannot begin to say how proud we have been of your work and your advancement in this company since you first started. We had a lot of faith in you and you have proven that we weren't wrong," Kelsey began. "But in light of your recent arrest—your *highly* publicized arrest—things have changed . . ."

These motherfuckers were here to fire my ass. Plain and simple.

One thing I could respect was that he looked me dead in the eyes as he spoke. Never once did he flinch or glance away. No stuttering. No weakness. Not at all.

I stiffened my back and stood up taller. "All of the charges against me were dropped yesterday," I said, not explaining or begging, just stating fact.

I looked at Vickie and her green eyes shifted. *Punk ass.*

See, it didn't matter what I said. My ass was grass at this job and these two were the lawn mower.

"That's good news for you," Kelsey said.

Translation: I don't give a fuck.

"We still believe that with the type and size of investments we deal with, having an employee who is closely affiliated with someone involved in federal crimes such as loan-sharking could make some of our clients feel the firm is being used for money laundering with or without our knowledge." Kelsey rose to his feet and buttoned his blazer. "We are not willing to take that risk."

Translation: *Go on. Get. And take your problems with your ass.*

I moved over to my desk and slid open the bottom drawer.

Vickie literally jumped a millimeter up out of her seat.

I eyed her as I took my wallet from my clutch and removed my security badge and expense card to hand to her, which forced her to rise from her seat to take them from me.

I took my photo of Dane and me from the top of the desk and slid that into my briefcase. I tucked my clutch under my arm before I took my trench from the coatrack behind my door.

"We have forms that you need to sign describing the reason for your dismissal," Vickie said, sitting them on the desk.

"I don't sign anything without reading it first, and since I am no longer being paid to be here, then I'm ready to leave. So please FedEx those to my home address and I will read them over, sign them, and send them back to you before the end of the week."

Kelsey looked annoyed. "Sophie—"

"It's been a pleasure," I told them both with a wave of my hand.

I opened the door and sure enough, two security guards waited to escort my fired ass from the building. Many of my former coworkers stood in the hall waiting to see it all unfold. The walk of shame. If they thought I would leave with a box of my shit, crying and hugging everyone like Neil did last month when they booted his ass . . . they were mistaken.

I flung my hair over my shoulders and held my head high. "Let's go, fellas," I said to security, leading their rent-a-cop asses to the elevator.

It was quiet except for the sound of my heels beating against that tile. As soon as the door opened I stepped into the elevator and turned and struck a pose like I was a model at the end of the runway. The security stepped around me and stood behind me.

Just before the door closed, I spotted one of my coworkers smiling and waving good-bye.

"Fuck you," I mouthed.

I didn't panic until I left that building and climbed my ass behind the wheel of my car. "Fuck, fuck, fuck, fuck, FUCK!" I screamed, banging my hands against the steering wheel as I sat at a red light at the corner of Mulberry and Market Street. Hell, it could've been the intersection of Fuck You and Kill Yoself, the way I felt.

"Fuuuuuuuuuuuck!"

I dropped my head on the steering wheel. *Fuck my life.*

I spent the rest of the day in the middle of bed, alternating between sipping wine and eating ice cream while I watched a marathon of *Mob Wives*. I figured I should get lost in somebody else's reality since mine was about to make me lose my mind. I was on the edge and I could see me straight sitting in a corner rocking and drooling with a thumb up my ass. Like fuck the world. Fuck reality. Fuck it all.

Brrrnnngggg . . .

I eyed my cordless phone lying beside me on the bed. I started not to answer it. Honestly, I didn't even feel like talking to Dane. He was still in county and there were no visitations on Mondays. I wanted to see him face-to-face. I wanted to tell him that not only did he get knocked on his ass financially, I also lost my job. This shit was getting worse and worse.

Brrrnnnggg . . .

Plus I wasn't sure just when the combo of the liquor and the ice cream was going to send my ass to the bathroom with the runs. I was just asking for the bubble guts and I wasn't trying to handle my business while I was on the phone.

Brrrnnnggg . . .

I picked the phone up and pushed it under the stack of pillows on the bed. I wasn't ready to talk to Dane, not yet. If I had to deal with him being in jail and losing everything, then he just had to twerk it out with not being able to reach me every time the mood hit him to call. Even for the next three years he had three hots and a cot. If I didn't find another job soon he would be doing better than me.

With my savings I had about three months of bill money put away. And then what? Three months wasn't that long. I'd file for unemployment but the benefits were just a portion of my regular salary. Plus, on top of my normal bills, Dane would need money for his books, care packages, and the phone bill was going higher without a doubt. Shopping sprees? Out. Weekly doobies? Done. "I love me" spa days? A wash. Vacations? Forget about it.

No man. No dick. No job. No extravagances.

I was fucked.

Brrrnnnggg . . .

The sound of the phone ringing was muffled by the pillow but I still heard it.

Brrrnnnggg . . .

I dug the phone from under the pillows and answered the call. "Hello," I said, before I went through all the motions to accept Dane's call as I flopped back against the pillows.

"Whaddup, Suga."

"Nothing," I lied. I wasn't going to drop my firing on him. Not today. Not yet.

"I just wanted to tell you that I'll be transferring to the fed prison in Fairton tonight or tomorrow and I won't be able to get any visits until I get the forms to do my list and then they have to approve them. It could take like a week from whenever I get there."

"Fairton? I never heard of that, so it must be in the boondocks," I told him, shifting my eyes to look out the window.

"I ain't gone lie. It's a ride. It's down by Atlantic City."

I picked up my cell phone and searched the distance from Newark to Fairton. *One hundred and twenty-two miles.* "It could be worse," I admitted, dropping the phone to the bed as I pulled my knees to my chest.

"I know."

"Who are you putting on your list?" I asked, just to talk about anything but how fucked up we felt about everything. "What about Keno?

"You ain't heard?"

"Heard what?"

"Keno on the run."

So the feds *had* come for Keno too.

"You know I'm not up on shit like that. You was my connect to shit going down."

Dane laughed. "Yeah, you right. But I thought Hunga woulda hit you up."

I shook my head. "I haven't heard from her."

I had to bite my mouth to keep from questioning why Hunga's ass wasn't arrested. She was way deeper into Dane and Keno's business dealings than me.

"Do me a favor . . . go check on her for me? See if she still around," Dane said.

I jumped from cool to shitting in less than a five count. *Check on her? Who the fuck was going to check on me? The hell?*

"I just want to check something. Cool?"

Why would he care if Hunga was on the run with Keno?

"Was you fucking that trick?" I asked, my face straight twisted as my stomach twisted into a knot.

"Hunga? Hellllllllll no," he said with emphasis and a little bit of disgust. "Fuck outta here."

"Then what the fuck you checking on her for?"

"Keno is my boy and he on the run. He would do the same for me, Suga," he explained.

"I'll see," I said, not even sure I would keep that much of my word. I wasn't trying to see a damn thang. *Fuck Hunga and Keno.*

"You good?"

What the fuck you think? "I'm getting there."

"How your pops? You been by his house to check on him?"

I frowned. Dane knew how me and my father went. Was jail making him sentimental? "He was over here yesterday with me but I haven't seen him today."

"Oh."

He sounded disappointed.

"Just be sure to check on him more often. You only get one father and before you know it he'll be old and forgotten about like an old car."

I nodded. "It was cool having him here that day while I cleaned up. He drank up all the Paul but that's no shocker."

"Well, just don't forget about him like that Nova."

"Okay, I heard you."

Dane released a heavy breath that echoed in the phone like a harsh wind. "I gotta go. I love you. And just make sure you stay focused and pay attention and be on the lookout for *everything* because I'm not there to look out for you for a while. Okay?"

"O-kay," I said, scrunching up my face. "I love you too."

Once we ended the call I picked up my bowl of rum raisin ice cream but it had already started to melt. I took it downstairs to slide back in the fridge to refreeze. I spotted the open bottle of wine in the fridge, but I passed on it. If I had some weed stashed around here, I woulda definitely rolled me one up and relaxed my nerves.

But I knew where I could get some *and* kill another bird with the same stone. I jogged back upstairs and grabbed a black leather jacket to pull over the black leggings and fitted tank I wore around the house with black sequined flats. I felt like I needed to get out the house anyway and maybe a trip to crazyland would make me feel better about my shit.

Brandy and Chris Brown's "Put It Down" played on the radio as I drove through the Newark streets just as the sun was starting to set. It was early November and I had the heat on to knock the chill off in the car. Fall would be over soon and winter in the Northeast was no joke.

And I was going to fight the cold and the holidays all by my lonesome.

"Time for an electric blanket and a new fucking dildo," I muttered out loud as I looked out at the street signs. "Just me, my rubber dick, some lube, and a fresh pack of batteries for Thanksgiving and Christmas. Yippeee!"

I stopped at a red light and looked over at a bar on the corner. The door burst wide open and a big-ass bald-headed dude threw another man out into the street. A car coming up to make a right at the corner had to swirl to miss hitting him. Crazy.

At the next light two drunk women were fighting in front of a liquor store. Them chicks looked every bit of fifty or sixty with those wet, reddened bottom lips that let you know they drank heavy and straight from the bottle. One moved to slap the other but lost her footing and fell facefirst into a puddle. Fuckery.

Half a block down, I had to slam on my brakes when a car came out of nowhere and drifted down the street. It just missed slamming into me before it straightened up and went speeding away with squeal of tires and smoke drifting up into the night air. It probably was stolen. Bullshit.

This was definitely the type of hood where shit *stayed* popping off.

I started to turn my ass around and head home but I pressed ahead, parking outside a small brick house off of Eastern Parkway. The last time I been there it was summer and every porch on the block had been filled with people. Tonight the porches and streets were empty.

I looked out the window at the house. It was a Monday night and every window in the house was lit. *That bitch gots to be home.*

I got out the car and climbed the stairs to ring the doorbell. Hunga opened the door in nothing but an open silk robe and a red thong, smoking a blunt. She eyed me up and down before she stepped back, motioning with her long fingernails for me to come in.

"I just came to check on you after everything that went down this weekend after the funeral," I said, walking inside her home.

The floors and walls were painted black and the furniture was all red and black. Even the lights in the lamps were red, giving the house a real crazy vibe. Don't get me wrong, the house was laid with good shit but it looked like hell—literally.

"I'm straight," Hunga said from behind me.

A short and curvy Asian chick with long black hair came walking into the living room naked as the day she was born, like she didn't have a care in the world. I could've done without seeing everything from her tits to her twat. She bent over to pick up a lit cigarette in the ashtray before she sat down on the red leather sofa and propped her leg up on the edge, exposing all of her pussy to me.

I looked away.

That Sandra Oh–looking bitch had the nerve to laugh. "She scared of pussy, Coko," she said, sounding more black than Asian.

"Coko?" I asked, turning around to eye Hunga.

She blew a thick stream of silver smoke at me as she came around to press the blunt between the other woman's lips. She was repaid by the Asian chick reaching behind her to slap and then squeeze her ass. "I used to strip under the name Coko but I quit all that shit out when I met Keno," Hunga said. "Ming stills calls me that though."

Ming reached up to pull Hunga's robe down until it fell to a puddle around her feet. A name tattooed in scroll and surrounded by stars on Hunga's lower back damn sure spelled out *Coko*. "She'll always be Coko to me," the Asian chick said, standing up to wrap her arms around Hunga to stroke her tramp stamp and then ease her hands down her ass to massage the fleshy brown cheeks.

My eyes got big as shit when they started kissing like I wasn't standing there. I'm talking moans, tongue flickers, smacking, sucking lips. All of that. These bitches was on one.

"I'm just curious what Keno thinks," I said, glad when they stepped apart.

Hunga turned to face me and I had to look away from two hard nipples with piercings in them. Way more than I needed to know or see or have burned into my memory. "Keno cool with it. Believe me. We pop pills and the three of us get in bed together and that nigga is *so* gone," Hunga said, reaching out to drag her finger between Ming's pussy lips before she sucked the juices. "Long as he helping me to take care of my son and pay my bills, he can play in the pussy. Shit, I don't give a fuck."

"You heard from him?" I asked, watching Ming pick up a small can from under her chair to take out a pill that she tossed back into her mouth.

"I don't know," Hunga said with an attitude and a shrug as she dropped down onto the leather sofa. "Why?"

How the fuck you don't know if you talked to somebody? I shook my head and fought the urge to point out what should be common sense. "Dane just wanted me to check on everybody," I told her.

Ming moved to squat in front of Hunga's open legs as she leaned back against the chair and smoked the blunt. Ming pulled her thong to the side and unrolled her tongue. "You tell him we good," Hunga said, her eyes squinted against the smoke that came from both sides of her mouth.

Yeah, good and fucking crazy.

That shit killed my desire for weed with a quickness. I didn't want none of whatever these freaky-ass hos was smoking.

I turned and left them to their issues.

12

Two weeks later

I left the office building and tied the leather belt around my cashmere trench coat. I gave myself a long moment to stand on the street and look around at the towering buildings that I badly wanted to work in. This was the hub of Newark's own corporate America, and I belonged among my peers. I was hustling my ass off to get back on point. I got up bright and early every day to search for open positions. I reached out to the few contacts I thought I had at other companies. I sent out the résumés. I even had a couple of interviews. More would come. I would be back in the world of finance.

I believed that. I was willing to hustle even harder for that.

Pulling the collar of my coat up around my ears, I decided to kill some time downtown before I headed home to do the same shit I'd been doing all week: job hunting.

Dane was moved to Fairton just like he said and now he was just waiting on the paperwork to do his visitation list. Even after he turned it in he had to wait on approval. Translation: They were running background checks.

I'm straight. The arrest was on my record but no convictions.

As I walked down Halsey and window-shopped, I spotted a trio of women laughing it up together as they browsed the clothing store. It was clear they were friends. It hit me that I had never really put in time making female friends once I cut Harriet loose in college. I met up with Dane not too long after that and we became each other's shadow from that point on. My life went from Dane and college to Dane and my career. And now that I had lost both, I wished I had some girlfriends to chill with and confide in.

But, no, not a one.

"It's just me, myself, and I, that's all I got in the end . . ."

Beyoncé's chorus came to me like she sang it into my ear as I turned from the window, but I pushed the song and my lonesome thoughts aside. Digging my hands into the pocket of my coat, I moved on up the busy street, eventually pausing to look at the designs displayed in the window of a stylish boutique on Halsey Street, when I spotted a red car stopped in the middle of the street behind me. I looked over my shoulder just as the car accelerated forward.

It reminded me of the car that blocked me in the street that day.

I'd assumed, with the police attention from the major shoot-out and Dane's arrest, that I was safe again. But was I? Poppi was dead, but was there anyone out there looking to avenge his death? Was Dane safe in prison? Hell, was I safe out here in these streets?

Or was I being paranoid?

Fuck living my life looking over my shoulder. Once I

could sit down and talk shit out with Dane face-to-face and not worry about the feds or anybody else still ear hustling on the phone, I could get answers to a lot of questions. Did fucking Poppi up that night outside Club 973 start the whole ball rolling toward his downfall? Was it worth it? I heard him give the order to handle whoever robbed him, but did that order truly lead to Poppi getting run the fuck over or was it just an accident and coincidence? Did he see that he lost so much more than whatever money his former friend stole?

I didn't even realize how far I walked as I came upon the seated Lincoln statue outside the Essex County Courthouse. Following a whim, I climbed the five stairs, checked the empty bench portion of the statue for bird shit, and politely sat my ass down. People eyed me as they walked by on the street or was making their way into the courthouse. I didn't give a fuck. I felt like sitting down and I figured sitting next to President Lincoln was as good a spot as any.

"Abe never looked so good."

I turned my head to see this fine-ass bald-headed brother in a tailored suit and open wool coat with a briefcase paused at the base of the stairs looking at me. *Probably an attorney.* I smiled. "I agree," I said, crossing my legs and pretending to strike a pose.

"You have a good day," he said with a smile, continuing on his way to court.

"You too," I called to him.

I watched him until he disappeared inside the building. I love Dane. Loved him. But I couldn't help thinking that if I put all of my time, energy, and love into a brother hustling hard legitimately, I would not be jobless, manless, and on the verge of being hopeless.

Shit, if I don't find a job, my ass will be homeless.

Blowing a deep breath that was visible in the November cold, I stood up and made my way back across the long, congested downtown streets. The thing about Dane was, everything about his laid-back vibe drew me in. I was a college girl, but there was something about a dude's "I don't give a fuck attitude" that I liked even in high school. I had never really checked for the fellas who loved their books and their band instrument a little too much.

There was just something about a bad boy.

That shit was clichéd as hell but true.

Bzzzzzzzzz.

I jumped, startled by the sudden vibrating of my cell phone in my pocket. I pulled it out and checked the caller ID. The sight of Johnica's old cell phone number surprised me. *What the fuck she want?*

After the way her mother took time out of her life to call and bash me for getting arrested, I washed my hands of her and Johnica. I hated that she was fifteen and pregnant, but I wasn't rocking and raising *my* teenage daughter's baby, so I was good. I sent the call to voice mail and slid the phone back in my pocket. Dealing with Johnica meant dealing with her whack-ass mother and that was not happening. Fuck the dumb shit.

Once I made it back down by Penn Station and to the parking lot, my feet were screaming *Get off me, bitch* when I climbed behind the wheel of my car. I took the gorgeous leather and suede booties off, threw those mothers over my shoulder onto the backseat, and drove barefoot. Fuck it.

Bzzzzzzzzz . . .

I drove with one hand and reached for my cell with the other. It was Johnica again. I sent it to voice mail, tossed it onto the leather passenger seat, and turned the volume up on Beyoncé singing all about Jay-Z on "Love on Top."

Humph. Something about them bad boys. And being a big-dick bad boy *really* fucked a chick's head up. One of them video chicks from his past claimed Jay-Z was toting a dick like one of those old Pepsi Big Slam bottles. Beyoncé needed all those hips to handle that monster. "I don't need *all* that," I said, making a face.

Still, every time I saw him in a photo or video, I wondered: "Is that dick as thick as those lips . . ."

Bzzzzzzzzz . . . Bzzzzzzzzz . . . Bzzzzzzzzz . . .

I pulled to a red light and leaned over to eye the phone. Johnica. She was really messing with my ability to distract myself from my own problems by focusing on celebrity BS. The best way to avoid your own business was to stir in someone else's.

Bzzzzzzzzz . . . Bzzzzzzzzz . . . Bzzzzzzzzz . . .

I snatched the phone up but my thumb moved from hovering over the button to end the call and over to the button to answer it. "Hello," I snapped with attitude, not sure if it was Johnica or her dodo-bird mother.

My face softened at the sound of crying. Johnica.

"What's the mat—"

"My mother fighting me."

"Open this fucking door, bitch!" I heard in the background.

I pulled over onto Broad Street and double-parked. "Johnica, what happened?"

"She mad 'cause I asked her not to blow her weed smoke in my face and I'm pregnant," she said, her voice trembling with tears and emotions. "We got in an argument and she boxed me in my face and kicked me. I ran in here."

"Come out that bathroom!"

I had come in contact with her mother's particular type of crazy and I wasn't sure what this chick might do. But why call me? "Where's your aunt?" I asked.

"She stayed at her boyfriend's house last night."

BOOM! BOOM! BOOM!

I knew the sound of a door being knocked in all too well.

"Call the police, Johnica."

"I can't—"

The sound of the door crashing in echoed through the phone line. Johnica cried out.

A piece of me died on the inside.

"Who you on the phone with?!"

WHAP!

"Stop, Mama," Johnica wailed.

A second later the line went dead.

I dropped my head on the steering wheel as I clutched the phone. I had to do something. Neeci wasn't fit to be a mother. Hell, I wasn't sure the bitch was fit to be free on the streets. There was a bed in a crazy hospital with her name on it that needed her ass in it! I lifted my head and dialed 911 as I pulled out into traffic and looked both ways before I ran the red light and sped toward King Court.

"Yes, there's a fifteen-year-old pregnant girl being beaten by her mother," I said, my eyes darting from the rearview and side mirrors as I zoomed in and out traffic.

My heart was pounding. I didn't know what the hell I was going to do when I got there, but I knew I had to go. I finished the 911 call, giving as much detail as I could, just as I whipped into the parking lot. I reached behind me for my booties and jerked them back on before I flew from my car and rushed over to the building. *I wonder if I'ma have to fight that big bitch.*

I looked around for a stick or something metal to use to beat that ass as I climbed the stairs to the building. The door was back in place. The same damn door. *Who owned this motherfucker?*

The slit in the door opened and the gun barrel appeared.

I rolled my eyes. This shit was wild and unbelievable like we were on *The PJs*.

"Not you again," a male voice said.

A set of eyes replaced the gun. They looked left and right.

"Where's big boy?" he asked.

I wouldn't dare let them gloat about AaRon's death, so I ignored the question.

"There's a little girl getting her ass beat up upstairs and the cops are on the way. I advise you and whoever else is in that stairwell to haul ass. O-kay?"

The door suddenly pushed open and banged against my side, pushing me into the railing on the stoop as dudes and a few women flooded out the building. One was running with his pants down around his ashy ass and his hard dick bouncing like a diving board. Sick of being door-fucked I pressed against the metal with both my hands and pushed back hard. Somebody hollered out. *Fuck 'em.*

I came around the door, stepped over a little Kevin Hart–looking fool, and raced up the stairs in my heels just as I heard the police sirens. I came through the door of the stairwell and my heels beat against the tile, echoing along with the sound of raised voices. An older woman a few doors down from Johnica's door was standing in the hall, her face filled with concern.

I banged on the door.

"It's a damn shame," the old lady said, waving her hand like "fuck it" before she went back inside her apartment.

It really was a shame but her old ass was disgraceful too, willingly living in a building run by dope boys and standing there listening to a mother beat the shit out of her child but didn't pick up a hand to do a damn thing.

"Stop, Mama!" Johnica cried out.

I could hear the kids crying and something crashing to the floor—or someone crashing into something.

The door suddenly swung open and a stream of kids pushed passed me to run into the hall. All of them were crying. I pushed right past them to run into the apartment, ready to kick off my heels to straight fuck Neeci up if I had to.

A horrible scream of pain filled the air and my knees gave out as I came to stand in the doorway of the kitchen as Johnica dropped a bloody steak knife to the floor. "Mama," she whispered as a tear raced down her face.

My own blood ran cold as my eyes shifted over to see Neeci fall back against the stove with her hand pressed to her side. Blood spread against the cotton fabric of her T-shirt and pooled from between her fingers. Thick and fresh and far too much to mean any good for her.

Johnica dropped to her knees and fought like hell to keep Neeci from falling to the floor even as her lips moved and her eyes began to roll back in her head. Neeci gasped with her last breath.

She looked up at me with tears in her eyes, her lips and cheeks already swollen and bruised. "She was punching me in my stomach. I couldn't let her hurt my baby," she whispered.

I averted my eyes from the sight of her mother's eyes wide open. Just like AaRon. There was nothing left in the depths but death.

"I couldn't let her hurt my baby," Johnica kept whispering, even as the police rushed into the apartment and past me to pull her to her feet. "I couldn't let her hurt my baby."

I've seen more violence in the last month than in all the years of my life. And for damn sure, it's more than I ever wanted to see again. I wasn't cut out for this shit. Not at all. I turned away from the detective who was taking my statement outside the building. I didn't want to see the coroner rolling out the black body bag.

First chance I got, I had left the apartment and the smell of death behind. I didn't know if I would ever erase the memory of Neeci's death. I didn't know if Johnica would ever settle down with the fact that she held the knife that pierced her mother's gut and punctured her organs . . . causing her death.

It was bitter cold outside but King Court was filled with people watching on as if it was a case on *Law & Order* or *The First 48*.

But this shit was real.

Neeci was dead.

Johnica was in handcuffs in the back of one of the police cars.

DYFS workers had just arrived to scoop up all the kids.

Detectives were taking statements.

And I didn't want to do shit but get the hell away from the whole scene.

This shit was real. Changing the channel wasn't going to take back everything that went down. Johnica would forever go through life having killed her mother.

I shook my head to free it of the image of Neeci's dead body.

"Thank you, Miss Alvarez, if we have any further questions for you, we'll be in touch," the detective said, closing his notebook.

I nodded. "Can I speak to Johni—"

A yellow cab turned into the parking lot and before it could come to a full stop, the back door opened and a taller and somehow wider version of Neeci fell out onto the pavement. She hopped to her feet and came at a full run toward the stretcher.

Uh-oh.

"My sister!" she screamed at the top of her lungs . . . just a second before she knocked the body and the stretcher over onto its side.

Everyone—including me—gasped in shock. *What the fuck?*

A few people were heartless enough to laugh.

"Oh shit!" someone hollered from the surrounding crowd.

I couldn't do shit but shake my head as the police officers dragged her from the body when she bent down and
started to unzip the bag. My mouth fell open at this fuckery.
I understood she was grieving her sister, but unzipping the
body bag. Really? What the fuck was next? This dumb bitch
was going to do mouth-to-mouth or some shit?

"NEEECCIIIIIIIIIIIIIIIIIIIII!" she screamed as they
fought to turn the stretcher and the attached body back
upright. "Why you leave me, NEEECCIIIIIIIIIIIIIIIIIIII?"

What was even crazier was how the detective who had
questioned me didn't move from beside me to help out one
bit. He stood looking on with an expression like he needed
to shit. His ass was completely unaffected by the whole
scene. And that was the cherry on top of the entire bizarre
day.

Neeci's sister turned and spotted Johnica in the back of
the cop car. She went running that way like a bull who spotted red. "You killed my sister. Why you kill my sister?" she
roared, pounding her fists against the glass.

Johnica just sat there with tears wetting her cheeks and
looking up at her aunt like she wanted the glass to crash in
on her face . . . to hurt her . . . to punish her. That shit broke
my heart.

The same officers who dragged Neeci's sister off the
body moved quick to pull her away from the police car. She
started crying like a baby and her big fleshy body crumbled
to the ground.

"Damn, Reeci. It's gone be a'ight, girl," someone hollered
from the crowd.

Reeci . . . and Neeci. Twins?

The police cruiser with Johnica in it pulled out of the parking lot. Some of the neighbors came over to take care of Reeci. The coroner's van eventually rolled out with the body. I climbed into my car and left King Court as well. In my rearview mirror I saw the DYFS workers release the children, who all came running to surround Reeci where she still lay crying on the ground.

What a day.

I went to the police station to try to see Johnica but they refused me. I made sure to stress again that she felt like her mother was going to hurt her baby and they assured me they had my statement. Leaving that station without laying eyes on her had been one of the hardest things I ever did. I felt like she didn't have a soul in the world to rely on and in her scariest moment she reached out to me.

By the time I headed home I felt more tired than when I put in a full workday.

If I wasn't sick of crying about everything going on in my life I would boo-hoo cry about Johnica and even her mother. But I was all cried out. For real.

Bzzzzzzzzz . . .

I reached on the console for my cell phone. It was my father.

"Sophie, I'm hungry."

No greetings. No good wishes. Just a demand.

"Okay—"

"I want those little burgers."

My hand tightened on the steering wheel as I slowed

down to make a left turn. "White Castles, *Papi*," I said. "I'm on the way."

Click.

He was drunk.

Dane seemed to think I needed to try a little harder on my relationship with my father. For some reason incarceration had him feeling some kind of way. Maybe because his own parents were gone? Who knows. Every chance he got he was pushing me to go to my father's house.

I drove to the White Castle on Elizabeth and Hawthorne for a sack of sliders and onion rings. My father loved everything that wasn't good for him. Liquor and greasy food.

I can't front. I mostly did it to get Dane the hell off my back.

"How your father? You been by his house to check on him?"

It wasn't like my father and he ever really hit it off. Dane always showed respect and my father was always polite but Victor Alvarez didn't trust *any* man around his daughter. It's been that way since I was a little girl. That's why Luscious always spent the night over at my house but I hardly ever stayed at hers.

Just be sure to check on him more often. You only get one father and before you know it, he'll be old and forgotten about like an old car.

I wasn't gonna sit and chill with him in that dusty-ass house all damn day but I would drop him some dinner off before I headed my behind home to update my résumé and get on my hustle to find a new job—another truth I was not sharing with my father. No way in hell.

I parked my car in front of his house and grabbed his bag of food. The feel of a late-night fall wind beat through my clothes like they were paper thin. "Shit," I swore, shivering as I raced across the street.

I started to climb the stairs but stopped and looked down the long drive leading to my father's garage in the rear. With a soft smile, I headed up the drive and opened the garage door. Dane remembered things I forgot.

We been together a long time, Suga, back to them days your father had that old-ass Nova.

I flipped the switch to turn the ceiling light on and sat the White Castle paper bag on the trunk of the rusted red Nova. I was like six or seven when my father drove this death trap home. He drove it, patched it up, and drove it some more until it finally gave out when I was a freshman in high school . . .

I hesitated, shaking my head to maintain my train of thought. Dane never saw this car. By the time we got together it'd been broken down for like years.

What the fuck is he talking about?

But Dane's memory was always on point. Like, he didn't forget shit. He wouldn't make a mistake like that. Hell, I'm surprised he even knew about the car. But he did. Hell, he kept mentioning the old rusty motherfucker like he wasn't dead-ass wrong.

Well, just don't forget about him like that Nova.

The Nova. The Nova. The fucking Nova. What about the Nova?

Did he . . .

I used the side of my hand to make a clear circle in the middle of the thick layer of dust coating the car before my common sense finally kicked in and I just opened the unlocked door. The interior of the car was musty and a spiderweb hung from the roof. I checked the front and back seats.

Nothing.

Maybe I was looking too deeply into his words.

"Sophie!" my father called out. "Is that you in the garage?"

"Yes," I called back, opening the trunk. I snatched the carpet back.

"What are you looking for?"

I gasped at the sight of the plastic-covered money belt taped to the underside of the carpet. I had to fight not to scream like I won the Mega Millions. "Nothing," I answered even as I tore that motherfucker free, ripped the plastic, and locked the belt around my waist under my shirt.

I rushed to put everything back the way it was, but as soon as I did, I gave in to the shaking weakness of my legs and dropped to my knees. Dane looked out for me even when he was away. He looked out for me. He planned ahead for me. The feds hadn't found *this* money and he made sure of that. Fuck them.

Thank God Daddy never sold the car.

I pressed my hand to the money belt under my shirt. It didn't matter how much it was, just knowing he didn't let the feds do a *Survivor* move to "outthink, outlast and outplay" him made me proud as hell of him.

I loved him so much in that moment that my heart felt like it would burst wide open in my chest. "Thank you, thank you, thank you," I whispered.

More of his words came back to me.

*And just make sure you stay focused and pay attention
and be on the lookout for* everything *because I'm not there
to look out for you for a while. Okay?*

"Okay, Dane," I said aloud, climbing to my feet. "Okay."

13

One week later

I never wanted this moment to arrive.

Never.

That morning my alarm woke me up at 4:00 a.m. I showered and dressed, being real careful not to wear anything too revealing. Nothing khaki or orange or army green. Nothing sleeveless or with too deep of a vee in the neck. No skirts.

I decided on a causal look. Hair in a ponytail. Denims. White tee. Burnt orange leather jacket. I removed all the jewelry I usually wore. No diamonds. Just my engagement ring. This wasn't the time to be flashy.

The sun hadn't even come up yet when I left the house and climbed into my car. I programmed the address into my navigation system, slid in an oldies but goodies CD and headed out toward the New Jersey Turnpike. And I rode with nothing but the music and my thoughts. I stopped just once for some coffee and a pack of gum. I was trying to eat up those miles, not sightsee.

This shit boring as hell . . . but the end justifies the means.

It was a little after 8:00 a.m. when my navigation finally led me into the parking lot of the Fairton Federal Correctional Institution. I parked and slumped back against my seat for a few before I pulled the cheap little plastic Dollar Store change purse from inside my Gucci. I double-checked for my ID and some singles for the vending machine.

I was a nerd. I was happy and I knew it. So I read all the rules and regulations Dane mailed to me about what to expect for my visits. I was ready. No hold-ups. No bullshit.

I was ready for every step of the process, from walking through the metal detector and filling out forms with my ID to the black-light stamp. Still, the thought of that two-hour ride and the whole checking-in process made me annoyed. I couldn't lie.

Dane could have prevented all of this shit.

My father was pissed at me for coming to a prison to visit him. Especially on Thanksgiving Day. Love or no love.

Last year I cooked a big-ass dinner and my father came over. We all spent the day together. Not this year. Hell, not for a while. "He did the crime, let his ass do the time . . . alone," Victor said.

I understand what he meant. Trust me. It was almost like I was on lockdown too. Many of Dane's friends were out and about and ready to report any sign of impropriety on my part. See, a wifey whose man was on lockdown wasn't supposed to be in the club or up in some Negro's face for too long or even look like life was so fucking fabulous while their man was doing a bid. It's like she had to prove to this man—

who left her lonely and horny—that her life (and her pussy) was on lockdown too.

But after the escorting officer took me back to the visiting room and I stood at the officer's desk waiting for Dane, all of my anger melted like ice on a hot sidewalk when he walked up to me. And even in his plain khaki shirt and pants looking like a fucking janitor or some shit, Dane was still milk-chocolate fine. I teared up because I knew when I left here I was leaving him behind. For seven years of my life every day had included him.

Shit was so different now.

"Whaddup, Suga?" Dane said, with a smile, taking my hands in his to squeeze tightly as he pressed his lips to mine for a kiss that was too quick.

As we made our way to our table, I kept licking my lips, hoping to reclaim some taste of him. I missed the feel of his tongue stroking mine. The pressure of his lips. The heat of his hands on my body as he kissed me.

And the kissing was just the appetizer. I didn't even want to fixate on the sex. On THE DICK. *Oh Jesus!*

Three motherfucking years of this shit . . .

Dane leaned in toward me as we walked to a table. "Listen, go to your father's house and look in the trunk of the Nova—"

"I got it. Finally," I said with emphasis looking over at him. "Thank you."

He looked relieved. "I was like, damn, how long before she gets it. You know I didn't want to risk talking over the phone. It ain't much but it'll help."

Twenty-five grand *wasn't* much to Dane but now it was everything to me.

"You got the money in your commissary?" I asked, setting my change purse on the table as we sat across from each other.

Dane nodded and just kept staring at me. "I got your letters and the pictures," he said.

"Don't nut 'em up," I teased, surprised at how nervous I felt in his presence as I wondered if I looked as good to him as he looked to me.

"You can't even jack off in peace in this mo'fucker," Dane said. "I'm not tryin' to turn another dude on listenin' to me go for mine. You know? Fuck *that* shit."

"Don't flip on me in here," I said.

Dane eyed me hard.

I laughed. "I'm playing. There ain't an asshole made that can beat out this pussy."

"You dumb," he said, his eyes smiling again.

We both looked around at the men visiting with their families or girlfriends. Loving from behind a prison wall. Maintaining a relationship was hard enough with the luxury of seeing and feeling and fucking the one you loved every day. Trying to make shit thrive when he was on lock? Trying to be a daddy by phone? Trying to stay relevant on visiting days only? Shit was bananas.

And now it was my life—our life—and we wasn't no better than anyone else.

"You want something out the vending machine?" I asked, needing something—anything—to break up my thoughts.

"Nah, I'm good," Dane said, looking at me. "I'm just waiting for you to say it."

My gut clenched. "Say what?"

Dane leaned back in his chair and crossed his arms over his chest as he eyed me. "Whenever you ready, Suga," he said.

I made a face like I was confused but I wasn't. At. All.

Dane just waited.

Fuck it. Wanna hear it? Here it go. "Okay, fine. I told you so. I told you so. I told you so," I said, hitting my fist on my other palm.

Dane opened his hands up like *There it is*.

I leaned forward. "I *had* to get that off my chest."

Dane leaned forward. "I know and you're right," he said, his eyes searching mine.

"Hindsight is always twenty-twenty."

Dane sniffed the air. "Damn, you smell good as fuck, Suga."

"I do?" I asked, my voice all soft and my memory wiped of my *I told you so* rant.

"Hell yeah," Dane said his voice deep and sexy as shit. He shifted in his seat.

"I smell like that everywhere," I whispered over to him.

"See, now you fucking with me," he said back in a low voice.

"I wish I was fucking you," I said.

Dane's eyes got heated. "My dick hard as hell right now. Shit."

I licked my lips. "Fuck around and do a Tiny in this bitch."

He dropped his head and laughed.

Shit, I was serious. I could see why TI's wife was willing to risk giving her man a hand job to get him through.

"If we get caught they might yank your visitation," Dane said, licking his lips as he looked up at me again.

I fanned myself and leaned back from him. "What the hell we gone do for three years?"

"Build up pressure like a motherfucker."

I got up from the table to walk across the room to get a bottle of water from the vending machine. I drank half of the bottle down before I made it back to my seat.

"You *know* I ain't fuckin' nothin' in here," Dane said as soon as I sat down. "Do I have to worry about you out there?"

My back got stiff and my eyebrow shot up. Way up. "If you were that worried about how I manage my pussy you shoulda stayed out there to watch it," I snapped back.

Dane lounged back in his chair. "But I am in here and I can't watch it. So what's up?" he asked.

I was offended and my face showed it.

"Hell, mo' fuckers gone try you, Suga," he said. "Hell, you walked across the room just now and I caught about a dozen of these fools checking you out."

I laughed. "Please. Right about now a dude with long hair and some lip gloss would fuck up a lot of worlds in here."

Dane's face said he didn't think that was funny.

I bit back my laughter. "Look, am I happy all my fears and worries came true? Hell no. Did I enjoy getting up out of my bed at four in the morning to drive down here just to be watched and monitored like I'm a fucking criminal? Hell no. And do I want to live alone and not have my man in our bed every night making love to me? Hell no. But I accepted the arrest. I made the drive. I'm putting up with the restrictions and I'm not about to become a ho just because you're not home."

Dane looked doubtful.

"If I have the utmost faith you not about to become somebody's booty bitch in here then give me that same respect, playa."

He chuckled. "I miss you, Suga," he said, shaking his head.

"I know."

We fell into a comfortable silence.

"The police told me that Poppi died."

I saw his jaw get tight as he turned his head to eye me. "Yeah, they told me too," he said, his eyes cold.

"That was the first you heard about it?" I asked, studying his face.

Dane sat his elbows on the table and massaged his forehead with his fingers as he bit his bottom lip and kept looking at me. "Do me a favor and take some flowers out to AaRon's grave for me," he finally said.

I nodded and shifted in my seat. Translation: The only dead man that I give two fucks about is my friend AaRon or did you forget?

I knew my man. Well. I decided to leave it alone.

I got home from the prison about a quarter to five. I stayed until visiting hours were over. It was hard to share just one last kiss at the end of the visit before we all left our loved ones behind in the visiting room. They wouldn't be taken back to their cells until all the visitors were cleared from the building.

I started to get a motel room and drive back home in the morning but even with my savings and the money Dane put up, I was unemployed and trying not to waste a damn thing. Plus I just wanted to be in my own house and my own bed, so I hit the road.

The ride home was always quicker than going. Thank God.

I didn't want to do shit but take me a shower and a nap. My father told me not to darken his step if I went to see Dane. I am an obedient child. So fuck it.

But once I finally dropped on the middle of the bed, I couldn't sleep. I sat up in bed and crossed my legs Indian-style. I had so much shit on my mind.

Johnica was being charged with the murder of her mother. They weren't charging her as an adult though, and she was being held in the Essex County Juvenile Detention Center. She was facing twenty years to life.

"I couldn't let her hurt my baby."

I couldn't get the sound of her voice saying that out of my head. I just couldn't.

A vision of the crime scene flashed before me and I squeezed my eyes shut as the echo of Neeci's scream played inside my head.

Ding-dong.

The sound of the doorbell made me tense. I wasn't up for company. I looked down at the shorts I wore with a sports bra. I grabbed one of Dane's beaters from his drawer and tugged that over my head as I made my way downstairs.

Ding-dong. Ding-dong. Ding-dong. Ding-dong.

"I'm coming. Damn," I hollered down the stairs.

When I reached the door I eyed the bat I kept leaning in

the corner. I wasn't a killer but I was willing to handle some-body's head like a cantaloupe if they tried me. Rising up on my toes, I looked through the glass at the top of the door.

Hunga.

What the fuck she want?

I unlocked the door and opened it.

Hunga took a drag from her cigarette before she dropped it on the porch and pressed it out with the thigh-high boots she wore over skintight jeans with a black turtleneck and short leather trench tied at the waist. "Hey, bougie," she said before she strolled past me to walk into the house.

"Whassup, Hunga?" I asked, closing the door and flip-ping the switch to turn on the metal chandelier in the ceil-ing of the small foyer.

"I was in the hood taking care of some business and I decided to come through and see if you wanted to hit the club with me later tonight," she said, running her long color-ful nails through the long length of her bone-straight weave.

I shook my head. "Nah, I'm good."

Hunga rolled her eyes. "Look . . . my man on the run and yours locked the fuck up. I know we never really clicked or whateva but I was just tryna be nice and get you out this house. A few drinks. A few laughs. That's it."

I started to shake my head again.

"Look, I done went through a nigga being on lockdown and you have to do more than sit in the house and wait for his motherfucking call," Hunga said, walking up to me.

I flinched when she reached out to lightly pluck my pony-tail and tug softly at my shirt. That shit made me uncomfort-able as hell. This chick was a lesbo. I could care less about that if she hadn't been bold enough to let her bitch eat her pussy in front of me like they was trying me to see if I was down. *Do you . . . just don't try to do me.*

"Do your hair. Beat your face. Put on a fly outfit and I'll scoop you up 'bout eleven," she said.

I could smell the weed and Doublemint on her breath. "I'm not gay, Hunga," I told her, my voice insistent as I stepped back from her.

Hunga eyed me and then laughed. "Bitch, please. I know *that.* You are way too tense and fucking uptight to be getting your pussy licked right," she said, with a wave of her claws. "No offense to Dane, but ain't shit he could do to compete with this."

My eyes got big as shit when she uncurled her tongue and nothing but the pointy tip quivered like it was having a seizure.

"You ain't my type anyway. I don't do beige . . . as in boring," she said once she put her tongue away.

"I'ma have to pass, Hunga," I said. "But thanks. I just got a lot on my mind with Dane and some work shit and this little girl I know killed her mother—"

"In King Court?" Hunga asked, reaching in an oversize studded Gucci bag for her soft pack of Newports.

"Yeah." No need to lie; the shit been all over the news.

"I heard about that. That's some wild shit," Hunga said, tapping the tip of her long fingernails against the plastic. "Is that true the mother was beating her and knew the girl was pregnant?"

"Yes, I was on the phone with her. I heard it."

I couldn't let her hurt my baby.

Hunga turned and walked into the living room to the bar. She grabbed the bottle of Red Berry CÎROC. "You got some cranberry juice?" she asked, walking past me to head into the kitchen.

I was still standing in the foyer when I heard the ice machine on the fridge sound off. I eyed my bat for a long-ass time before I finally turned and headed into the kitchen behind her. Hunga was rummaging in my fridge. All I could remember is her scooping up Ming's pussy juices with her finger nails. My face twisted in disgust. "You wash your hands?"

Hunga eyed me. "My house cleaner than your house," she said, setting oranges and a bottle of cranberry juice on the counter. She turned and grabbed a knife from the wood block near the stove.

The knife reminded me of the one Johnica held in her hand the day her mother died.

I couldn't let her hurt my baby.

"You know what's fucked up 'bout your friend that axed her mama?" Hunga asked, slicing the oranges in half and squeezing the juice into the glass pitcher she filled with ice and the CÎROC.

"She didn't ax her," I corrected her. "It was an accident."

Hunga rolled her eyes. "Okay. You know what's fucked up 'bout your friend that accidentally axed her mama?"

"What's that, Hunga?" I said, leaning against the counter to watch this chick take over my kitchen.

"Them public defenders so swamped that her case gonna get pushed right through or they gonna plead her out and that child ain't gone see the light of freedom until she 'bout forty," she said.

When I called to talk to Johnica's public defender, the woman wasn't even familiar with the case offhand and had to call me back. And even that took two or three days. Johnica was just one card of many getting shuffled through the system.

"True," I agreed.

I couldn't let her hurt my baby.

Hunga stirred the cranberry juice into the mix. "Glasses?"

I turned and reached into the cabinet to pull out two highball glasses to hand her.

She filled each one and added a slice of orange to the rim like she was a bartender before she handed it back to me and took off her jacket to sit at the island. "My son in the hospital," she said all of a sudden. "My moms just called me."

"Why don't you go to the hospital?" I asked. "Why you trying to hit the club?"

Hunga looked up at me. Her eyes were sad. "My mother understands me but the rest of my family is up there and they always make me feel like what am I coming around for? Like I don't give a fuck about my son. I didn't say I didn't love him. I just can't handle him," she admitted, taking a deep sip of the drink as a tear rolled from her closed eyes.

I didn't know what the fuck to say. I didn't even really know why Hunga came here. I felt for her but I was lost like a motherfucker.

"I miss Keno being around. Like for real," she added to the air. "He would go with me to the hospital and dare somebody to say sum'n. You know?"

I sipped from my drink. "I know," I said softly, thinking of Dane.

"We had fun in Jamaica," Hunga said, emptying her glass and pouring another drink. "That was the best trip ever."

And then I got it.

This chick had no more use for me than I had for her but she was trying to reclaim the days we all chilled together and maybe being around me reminded her of that. If I opened myself up a little bit, being around her could remind me of that too.

"Remember when we went jet-skiing and Keno flipped over?" I said.

Hunga laughed. "He hollered out a like a *bitch*."

I nodded and laughed. "Yeah, he did."

For the longest time we sat there drinking and reminiscing. It did make me feel closer to Dane. When Hunga left after an hour or so to go see her son, something she said stuck in my head.

Them public defenders so swamped that her case gonna get pushed right through or they gonna plead her out and that child ain't gone see the light of freedom until she 'bout forty.

I ran upstairs to my closet for the suit I was wearing when I got arrested. I reached in the pocket of the wide-leg pants and pulled out my attorney's business card. I grabbed the phone and dialed his number. It went to voice mail. "Hunter, this is Sophie Alvarez and I need your help with something. Give me a call as soon as you get this. Please."

I couldn't let her hurt my baby.

I dropped the cell phone but it rang as soon as it bounced on the bed. "Damn, he fast," I sad aloud, picking it back up. "Hunter—"

"No, Sophie. This is Ms. Jordan. Your father is on his way to the hospital—"

BA-DUM.

"What happened?"

"He was walking from the store and passed out. I think he had a heart attack. I called an ambulance."

BA-DUM.

"What hospital?" I asked, already snatching off my shorts to pull on jeans and a pair of flats.

"UMDNJ."

"Thanks, Ms. Jordan."

I ended the call, tossed the phone and grabbed my keys and coat before I flew down the stairs and out the house.

Click.

My diamond-encrusted locket sprang open in the quiet of the hospital room. I took my eyes off my father sleeping in his bed to look down at the picture of my mother and me. I smiled a little even as I wished she was here. I stroked her face with my thumb. The photo was hardly enough, but in moments like this it was all I had. I wished I could lay my head in my mother's lap.

Click

Standing up, I forced my head and spirits up—or at least I tried—as I grabbed a pair of gloves from the box the hospital staff kept in the room. Visiting hours were almost over and I needed to handle my father's bag of belongings before I left for the night. I frowned as I opened the small closet. The smell of shit hit me in the face like a punch.

"Damn," I swore as I opened the bag.

Victor shit himself up either before the heart attack or during it. I shook my head. There wasn't a worse shit going than that of an alcoholic or drug addict.

Holding my breath, I avoided the obvious shit stain as I rushed running through his pockets. The clothes were going in the trash. I would buy him an outfit to come home in. Fuck washing shitty clothes. I wasn't even built for that.

Tucking his wallet, a chain with a small key on it with the initials FSL, and some balled-up receipts into a used Burger King bag, I was glad to tie that clothes bag tight and drop it into the garbage can along with the gloves. I didn't take a breath until the lid dropped down on the tall can.

I washed my hands and moved to stand by his bed. Victor looked so much older and thinner as he lay there. *If it ain't one thing it's another.*

I didn't even know I was crying until one of my tears dropped down onto his cheek.

My father almost died. That shit about fucked me up. I just couldn't take another loss.

Part Three

I want the finer things in my life . . . So I hustle (hustle)
N*gga you get in my way while I'm tryin get mine,
And I'll buck you (buck you)

—50 Cent, "Hustler's Ambition"

14

Two months later

Shit was getting real as hell.

I sat with my hands on my head and just stared at my online banking info on the computer screen. I had just paid all my bills for the month of January online. It was the third month in a row that I drew from my savings to make up what my unemployment check didn't cover. My balance was at under four grand and the unemployment wouldn't last forever.

Slamming the laptop screen shut, I rolled off the bed to pull the metal cash box from it. I counted the money, even though I knew damn well what was in it. Twenty-two grand. Hiring Hunter to take Johnica's case cost me close to three grand but at least he promised to make sure she didn't get railroaded.

Still, that money was a huge chunk when I didn't have a new job and didn't even have any prospects for an interview. Something was definitely up. The finance world was just as incestuous as any other industry. Had the word spread about my arrest? Was my rise up the corporate ladder done?

Six or seven more months without a job and my ass was

broke. I could take a lower-paying job but making sixteen hundred a month wasn't gonna cut it when I had over three grand in bills. I needed the inside scoop so I could plan my shit accordingly.

I was used to being on my grind. I hustled just as hard as those in the game. My goal? A high-ranking position in corporate America. A six-figure salary and an expense account. Traveling all over the world on business. My bio in the career and finance section of *Ebony, Essence,* or *Black Enterprise.* Prestige. Respect. Clout.

That's what I was hustling for, but these last three months my life were just about visiting Dane, spending time with my father as he recovered from his heart attack, sending out résumés that went no-damn-where, and hanging out with Hunga's crazy ass.

No business meetings.

No talk of finance.

No mention of politics and current events.

I can't even remember the last time my ass slid into one of my fly-ass suits.

Like, whose life was I living? Not the one I carved out for myself.

"This some *bull*shit," I screamed at the top of my lungs as I punched the air like my most hardcore enemy stood before me.

I want my job back. I want my career back. I want my fucking life back.

Holding my hands up in the air, I walked into my bathroom and double-checked my appearance in the wood-framed full-length mirror behind the door. Ming was hell with some rollers and wrap lotion, so my normal straight and thick jet black hair was soft and curly. Once I made it clear to her that I didn't want to replace her loving Hunga/Coko/WhotheFuckEver's pussy long-time, she was pretty chill the few times I was around her. Most times them chicks smoked they weed, got right off that Molly, and had me dying about their past escapades stripping at private shows. Pouring candle wax on some dude's balls, though? They crazy.

Shaking my head, I had one more glance at the leather leggings I wore with matching heels and a silvery off-the-shoulder sweater before I left the bathroom.

Brrrnnnggg . . .

I picked up my cordless. It was Dane. I didn't like to lie to him and I damn sure wasn't telling him where I was headed. I left the bedroom and eventually the house to the sound of the phone endlessly ringing. It was bad enough I still hadn't told him about getting fired.

Downstairs I used the remote to automatically start my car. By the time I got in it, the heat would be good and toasty. I just had to stay by the window with my eye on it to make sure no one broke the glass to unlock the doors and hop in my shit for a joy ride.

"Oh shit," I swore at the sight of a few snowflakes floating to the ground. Hopefully it didn't keep going until we had snow up to our ass. It was nothing for a snowstorm on the East Coast.

Hell, Dane usually did the shoveling or paid somebody to do it.

I sighed as I climbed behind the wheel and headed out toward the neighboring city of East Orange. The long strip of stores on Central Avenue was still lit up even though it was after eight. I maneuvered through the traffic and was glad to turn off the major road onto a side street lined with houses.

I double-parked in front of a stone-faced house on the corner. Picking up my telephone, I dialed. "I'm outside," I said.

"Come in."

"You said dinner. I figured I would follow you . . . to the restaurant." I bent my head to look though my windshield at the wooden front door of the house.

Click.

I parallel-parked in between a Benz SUV and an old-ass Chevy station wagon, trying my best not to let my annoyance get the best of me. When I finally made my way up every step of the two stories of stairs, I was thinking, *I know I'm going to regret this shit . . .*

I knocked on the front door and it swung open under the light pressure. "Hello," I said, stepping inside.

My mouth fell all the way open at seeing Leo butt naked on his sofa with his dick and balls hanging over the side. I screamed and whipped back around. "Put some fucking clothes on, Leo! Or I'm out!" I snapped over my shoulder, my eyes closed. *I knew I was going to regret this shit.*

"Damn Thug Life been in jail for three months and you're already scared of dick," Leo called out from behind me. "I thought you would be ready to pounce on it."

I frowned. My face was straight twisted at the thought of that. Leo did nothing for me and I couldn't believe he was really pulling such a perverted-ass stunt with me. I thought we were cool. "I'm leaving," I told him, stepping out onto the porch.

"A'ight, a'ight, a'ight."

I wanted to haul ass but I needed this fool, so I stood waiting on him to find some clothes and his fucking mind as I fingered my keys. I looked down at the small can of Mace swinging between my keys. I never used it before. *Humph, fuck around and he gonna get all of this shit tonight.*

I should've known when his ass pressed so hard for me to meet him at his house before we went to dinner that he was up to something. Still, I wasn't expecting to see all of his business on display. And he was proud like he was toting around a log. He was a'ight but Dane's dick would shadow his shit. *Poor thang. Somebody been gassing his head up.*

The front door swung open wider and I turned to see Leo now dressed in denims and V-neck sweater. "*Much* better," I said, giving him a hard eye as I passed him on the way inside his home.

"Yeah, right," he drawled.

Leo's house looked just like I thought it would. Masculine and edgy and real contemporary. "Thanks for agreeing to meet with me," I said, accepting the glass of wine he handed me. "But let's be clear that I called you to talk business—"

"But you could use some pleasure," he said, all smooth and cocky.

"I don't mix the two."

"We don't work together anymore."

I took a sip of the wine. "And that's a part of what I wanted to talk you about," I said, trying to steer his mind right. "I wanted to know if you heard anything about me being like blackballed."

"Truthfully?" Leo asked, moving to sit down on his sofa. He patted the seat next to him.

I arched my brow at the spot where he'd just had his raw

ass. He could cancel that shit. I eased down onto one of the two ottomans on the other side of his low-slung glass table. "Real talk. What's up? Tell me."

"Can I eat your pussy?" Leo asked suddenly, his eyes locked on my pussy print between my thighs.

I snapped my knees closed. "Leo, me and you were so cool until you got it in your head to fuck me," I said, my voice sounding disappointed.

Leo shrugged. "Oh, I wanted to fuck you the whole time. But since I don't have to worry about sexual harassment in the workplace, I finally said just go for it. Fuck it. You know?"

I shook my head.

"I want to *demolish* your pussy. I want to lay up in it and just die. Fuck it. Kill me now. Right now. In that good ass pussy," he said, with emphasis as he sipped from his drink.

I couldn't help but laugh. The way he said the shit was so shot out.

"I'm serious as hell," Leo said, sweat beading up on his bald head. "Look."

He stretched his legs out in front of him and his dick looked like a snake in his jeans. *Oh, he's a grower,* I thought, seeing the tip damn near reach mid-thigh.

"Leo—"

"A'ight, just touch your pussy and let me lick your fingers?" he asked, moving to sit on the edge of the sofa.

"Where's your fiancée?" I asked.

"Don't know. Don't care," Leo said with the utmost seriousness.

"Look, I'm 'bout to go," I said, sitting my glass down on the table and standing up.

He unzipped his pants. "Just let me beat this mother-fucker while you look?"

I threw my hands up in the air. "What the fuck is *wrong* with you?" I exclaimed, making a face before I turned and headed to the door.

Leo caught up with me before I could open the door. "A'ight. I'm sorry," he said, turning me around.

I rolled my eyes at his dick hanging out his open zipper. "Could you put your gun back in the fucking holster?" I snapped, surprised and annoyed as hell that he was coming on so strong. This pervert was not the motherfucker I knew at work.

"I thought we use to be friends and look out for each other," I said, shrugging his hands off.

"A'ight, a'ight, a'ight," Leo said, lowering his hand to fight his hard dick inside his pants.

He caught all kinds of hell getting that zipper up over it and I stood right there enjoying the comedy. *It ain't half bad . . . once it grew.*

Did my clit jump a little at the sight of a dick that was hard and ready to fire off? Yes.

Was I horny as hell and tired of the steady hum of my vibrator? Hell yes.

Was I even going to think about letting Leo blow through my coochie cobwebs? Definite no.

He walked back over to his bar to pour himself another drink.

"I wanted to know if you heard anything about someone at the firm stopping me from getting a job anywhere else in the city."

Leo sipped from his glass before he looked over his

shoulder at me for a second. "I did hear that Vickie from Human Resources got a hold of the news reports on your arrest and was showing it to people on her iPad," Leo admitted, turning to walk back over to me with his erection still leading the way.

"That ugly, no-ass-having, flat-tittie, stank-breath bitch," I said, hot with anger.

"Plus there was a big Human Resources conference with all of the big companies in the Northeast not too long after you got arrested, and Vickie can't hold water. Word spreads fast."

That wasn't what I wanted to hear. How the hell was I gonna book a management position at another firm when my name and arrest was the talk? "Damn it," I swore.

My career meant everything to me and in that moment it felt like with every second my dream was dying. I didn't know if I needed to start going to church or buy some fucking lucky charms, but nothing but bad blows were hitting me left and right. I felt a migraine coming on. "Thanks, Leo. I appreciate the info," I said.

"No problem," he said, wrapping one strong arm around my shoulder to hug me close to his side.

"Don't make me Mace you," I threatened with a mean side-eye.

He held up his hands and I sidestepped right out of his embrace and then his front door before he got back on his "I want to fuck Sophie" campaign.

"What about dinner?" Leo called behind me.

"Rain check," I lied.

I was already headed down the stairs among the falling snowflakes when my cell phone vibrated. A picture text.

From Leo. I didn't even bother to open it. I had seen enough of his dick to last me a lifetime.

Plus I had other shit on my mind besides Leo, his dick, or his desire to fuck me.

I had always held out hope that I would find another position. In this economy, with rumors and gossip swirling like trich, how the hell was I going to get back on?

Would I need to move to another state or just wait it out?

Bzzzzzzzzz . . . Bzzzzzzzzz . . . Bzzzzzzzzz . . .

I didn't even bother to check to see who was calling. Fuck 'em. Fuck it. Fuck everybody.

Bzzzzzzzzz . . . Bzzzzzzzzz . . . Bzzzzzzzzz . . .

I turned the volume on the radio up. 2 Chainz's "Spend It" blared through the speakers. "Ain't that a bitch?" I muttered, picking another channel.

In any other moment that was my jam, but the last thing I gave two shits about was some dude bragging about "ridin' around gettin' it and spendin' it."

I made my way across East Orange and back into Newark. My stomach grumbled but I couldn't picture myself sitting down and eating a plate of food. Plus I had plenty of food for thought.

Fuck protecting Dane. It was time to let him know that I lost my job—*my career*—because of him. What if I couldn't get my shit back on track? *Then what?* The feds snatched all of Dane's shit that was left after the robbery so he didn't even have the cash flow to start a legitimate—or illegitimate—business when he got out.

We were fucked and a dick called the "hard knock life" was digging deeper and deeper.

I picked up my cell phone. The missed calls were from Hunga. *I'll call her later.*

I called my father. Since he was released from the hospital after recovering from his mild heart attack Thanksgiving night, I'd been spending more time at his house. I cooked for him every day, dumped his hidden bottles of liquor, and even started cleaning up some. I swore the dust would kill him.

"Yes, Sophie," Victor said, sounding annoyed.

"How you feeling?" I asked, turning the corner on my block.

"I'm good. My heart is good. My appetite is good. I'm good."

"Good," I said with emphasis and cheerful sarcasm.

Spending so much time with him the last two months, I was learning my father's bark was worse than his bite and so his little tirades and smart-ass comments rolled off my back like water. "I'll come over tomorrow," I told him, placing the phone on speaker as I set it down to parallel-park directly in front of my house.

"Oh, the warden is setting the prisoner free tonight," Victor snapped.

"Yup," I agreed, shutting off the car.

Click.

I just laughed as his dial tone echoed. Snow had already coated the steps and the sidewalk in white. I looked up to the sky and under the reflection of the streetlight the snowfall looked heavier. A chill hit me that sent me racing up the stairs and into the house.

I turned on the light and brushed off the melting snow that had landed on me as I jogged up the stairs.

"Whaddup, Suga?"

I froze halfway up the staircase. Every hair on my body felt like it stood on end as I turned to look down into the dark living room. The flicker of a flame from a lighter flashed just before the lights came on in the room.

Keno was sitting on my sofa smoking a Newport and sipping on some clear liquid in the glass. He was comfortable too. His leather bomber was lying on the sofa next to him as he lounged in a sweater and jeans and boots. "How's Dane?" he asked.

I turned and came down the stairs with my heart still pounding and my pulse racing. I eyed the bat and I wondered if I needed it. "He's good. How are you?" I asked, slowly coming to stand in the doorway.

"Could be better," Keno said, holding his cigarette in the circle he made with his index finger as he eyed me.

"How you get in here?"

Keno smiled and leaned forward to flick his ashes inside an ashtray. His sweater rose up a little in the back and I spotted the handle of a gun. "There ain't a lock I can't pick," he admitted.

The sight of the gun had my heart thumping like a motherfucker. I stayed posted up in the doorway. It wasn't but a turn and two large steps to grab my bat. "It's some creepy shit coming home to someone sitting up in the dark," I admitted.

"I'm real low-profile these days," he said, drinking from his glass.

"So I heard," I told him.

He shrugged and laughed in his glass again before settling back against the sofa like he didn't have a care in the world. Like he didn't break into my house. Like I wanted him here. Like his ass wasn't wanted.

"Why are you here, Keno?" I finally asked.

"Business."

I frowned. "Is there something you need me to talk to Dane about?"

"Nope. I'm talking about you fronting me the money to pick up where Dane had to leave off and we split the profits," he said, standing up to his full over-six-foot height and walking over to the bar to refill his glass. "I know all the connects that need to borrow money. I can find a new spot to play cards and charge them ten percent of the winnings. A lot of the crew ready to make this money too. Nobody filled the gap Dane left. It's time."

"What makes you think I have money to front—"

"Dane left twenty-five grand in your father's car," Keno said. "You can go get it . . . if you haven't already."

I was completely mind-fucked that he knew he was a step ahead of me. *Thanks, Dane.*

"You not working and that money ain't gone last long," Keno said, standing up again to finish his drink and reach for his coat. "Let Hunga know what's up."

"Hunga?" I asked. "So she knows how to find you?"

Keno zipped up his coat and then pulled a skully from the pocket to put on his bald head. "She always did."

Okay, more than one step.

He passed me to head toward the kitchen. I turned to follow him. He walked through the mudroom and out the back door. By the time I made it to the door to open it and look out, I didn't see shit but footprints in the snow leading to the back fence.

Bzzzzzzzzz . . . Bzzzzzzzzz . . . Bzzzzzzzzz

I checked my vibrating cell phone. It was Hunga. I sent that slick bitch straight to voice mail.

Upstairs in my bedroom, I lay across the bed on my side and looked out the window at the snow falling. The TV and lights were off, the room was darkened, and the only light shone into the room from the streetlight. That was straight with me.

My thoughts were all over the place and I had enough noise in my head and I didn't need anything extra to distract me. Dane's incarceration. My father's health. Johnica's murder charge. The death of my career. My coochie growing cobwebs. The shrinking of my bank account. Hunga's phoniness. Leo's freakiness. Keno's offer.

My mind ran over a dozen different scenarios that I could make a comeback in my career. I fought for my advancement at that firm and now my slate was wiped clean by some bigmouth Human Resources chick that I wanted to straight choke out until she was as blue as Hpnotiq.

I couldn't let her or whoever else was blacklisting me win.

But while I was busy plotting my comeback, that didn't change the fact that I would feel hella stronger and more confident in my business moves if I wasn't counting every dollar spent. I couldn't focus on my business hustle because of my fears of going broke eventually. Money matters. Forever and always.

And that brought my thoughts back to Keno.

First and foremost, was he to be trusted with my money? Would he haul ass and live on the run with it? *But he could have gotten the money out the car himself . . . and he didn't.*

Keno wanted to be partners off my dime and his time. Was I crazy even to consider that shit? If the risk was on him and I stayed clear of his dealings, was I wrong to flip some money real quick?

Hypocrite.

I reached out to turn on the beside lamp and sat up in bed to eye my reflection in the large leather-framed mirror hanging above the eight-drawer dresser. I ran my hands through my hair and studied myself as I released a heavy breath.

It had been hours since Keno reappeared in my life, and during every possible second since he left, I kept coming back to just how badly I could use some steady, heavy cash flow. Maybe just enough for a helluva cushion for my bills and start-up money for whatever business Dane chose to get into it when he got out. Then Keno could have at it all on his own . . . because I knew damn well Dane wasn't trying to fuck it up by risking another jail bid.

I still had plenty of questions but I couldn't help asking myself: How could I not take the chance?

Fourteen days. Three hundred and thirty-six hours. Too many fucking minutes to count. I spented every last one of them going back and forth about this hustle. This illegal hustle. With Keno. The majority of the time, my fears made me say "fuck him," but there were plenty of moments that I wanted to risk it.

Make that money.

I didn't know the ins and outs of Dane's business but I knew that there was money to be made. Big money. Nothing to take lightly . . . especially in between this rock and a hard place.

Hypocrite.

I did a lot of growing up in those days too. Everything wasn't quite rose-colored no more. Life wasn't all black-and-white, and lots of people lived in those shades of gray,

"You don't understand, Suga."

The day of AaRon's funeral and the raid on our house, Dane had said those words to me with such conviction. I could still see the look on his face. He felt he was making the only decision he could and he wanted me to understand that. I didn't. Not then.

I released a heavy breath and pulled my knees to my chest as I sat in the window of the empty room I planned to turn into my office. In the days that I struggled with my decision I found myself in this room. Would I have a need for it anymore?

I reached down into the ashtray with my bare feet and took out the lit blunt. I could count on one hand the number of blunts I smoked my entire life, but I really wanted to feel the smoke in my lungs. People claimed it eased your nerves. And my nerves was shot.

Releasing a stream of smoke, I looked out the window at the snow covering the neighborhood. A cold and icy beauty covering the mess that sometimes lay beneath. I needed the peace and serenity of the scene because I was contemplating letting chaos into my life.

One week later I was sitting in my car and checking the rearview mirror as I tried to stay patient. I'd been waiting for forty-five minutes already. Cracking my knuckles to relieve the irritation I felt rising. It was hard to focus though. The last place I wanted to be was sitting in a parked car on an empty street like a duck. I was tense as hell.

Ten minutes later, Hunga's car finally turned the corner and pulled up behind me. I climbed from the car. She did the same. We met halfway.

I barely took the glance to take in the leather form-fitting dress she wore beneath a floor-length faux fur. It was cold. True. But it wasn't that motherfucking cold.

"I thought we was done hearing from you," Hunga said.

I dug my hands deeper into the pockets of the ivory wool pea coat I wore as the bitter winter winds whipped around us. "Oh so it's *we* now?" I asked, squinting my eyes as I eyed her.

Hunga chuckled a little bit and shook her head. "You college girls are so fucking emotional," she said, tilting her head to the side. "Y'all take shit way too serious."

"And bitches like you whose most important decision of the motherfucking day is whether to match you eye shadow to your outfit don't take shit personal enough," I snapped back at her, making a face as I pointedly looked at the smoky gray eye shadow above her slanted eyes.

"Look, I don't even have time for the back-and-forth. You. Called. Me. Whatchu want?"

"To look you in your phony-ass face and tell you I would have at least gave you credit for being a bold enough bitch not to front," I began. "To tell you I didn't appreciate you two playing me and sitting back laughing and plit-plotting while Ming ate you out."

Hunga waved her hand like she dismissed me. "Fuck you, Suga."

I watched the bitch as she turned and headed back to her car. "Don't walk away from me, Hunga," I called over to her.

"Bitch, puh-leeze. Who the fuck are you?" she called back.

"I'm the bitch y'all need." Truthfully, I finally decided I needed them motherfuckers too. But I wasn't copping to that.

Hunga stopped in her open car door.

I pointed to the two-story factory on the corner. "You bring him here. Show him this building. Tell him to rent it. The games go down here. It's safer than a house. No neighbors. Not much traffic. If he agrees . . . I'm in for a fifty-fifty split," I told her, reaching in my pocket and pulling out the wad of hundred-dollar bills.

Once I decided to make this money, I thought about where Dane went wrong. And number one was not finding a secure enough spot to hold the poker games. Hindsight was 20/20, but a smart bitch knew to use that hindsight from an old situation for a better foresight on some new shit.

I saw her eyes shift over to take in the factory. I walked back to my car, climbed behind the wheel to do a U-turn, and came to a stop by her car. "I'll be in touch," I said, loving the feeling of control I had as I floored the pedal and sped away.

Two months later

"Thank you so much, Hunter." I watched Johnica through my shades as she walked out the doors of the Essex County Juvenile Detention Center with her DYFS caseworker by her side. Her short, thick frame was swollen with every bit of her eight months of pregnancy. Face fat. Nose wide. Neck darker than anywhere else on her body.

"No problem," he said, as we both stood on the sidewalk in front of his Porsche.

And Hunter put in the work, the hours, and the manpower the Public Defender's office was stretched too thin to handle. Private investigators went back to research Neeci's history, interview her neighbors about her volatile relationship with her child. Psychologists spoke about Johnica's state of mind at the time of the incident. Forensic experts showed evidence that Johnica was on the floor and being attacked at the time she stabbed her mother. Hunter's paralegal staff subpoenaed Neeci's DYFS case file detailing her losing her children on two separate occasions for abuse and neglect.

I couldn't let her hurt my baby.

It all cost me, but when I think of what it could have cost Johnica, it was worth every penny for her to plead to involuntary manslaughter and receive probation. We did it white folks style and now she would not have her baby in a prison.

I smiled as she walked up to me with her longer hair pulled back into a low ponytail and looking cute in the bright pink maternity maxi dress and short denim jacket that I brought for her. "Hi, Johnica," I said, hugging her so close that I felt her baby kick me. I couldn't do shit but laugh. I was so damn happy.

"Okay, Bruce Leroy," I said, releasing her.

But Johnica didn't let me go. She tightened her arms around me. It was then I felt her tears wetting the front of my shirt. I rubbed her back. "Oh, Johnica. It's okay. It's over. It's over. It's okay," I whispered to her, blinking back the rise of my own emotions.

She cried harder. "I didn't mean to do it. I swear I didn't mean to do it," she said brokenly between her tears.

"I know. You couldn't let her hurt your baby," I reminded her.

The caseworker gently motioned that it was time to go and I nodded in understanding.

Johnica was a ward of the state. Her aunt Reeci wanted nothing to do with her and she had no other family willing to step up for her. I couldn't lie and say I was up to the challenge either. I was not ready to be the guardian to a pregnant fifteen-year-old. She was being taken to a group home for pregnant teens down in Toms River. This particular home had a strong focus on therapy.

I knew in that moment that this child I held was a little

girl in the end, mourning the death of her mother—even if it was at her own hands.

It was hard standing there as Johnica slid her wide frame into the caseworker's car, but I had no doubt that I'd done my very best for a child I barely even knew.

"Staying out of trouble?" Hunter asked from behind me.

I froze. *Did he know that I'd stepped into the game the feds pulled Dane out of? Hell, Dane didn't even know—or at least I hadn't told him—so how could our attorney?*

Turning to look at him through my shades, I forced my body to relax. "Yes. You?" I asked, crossing my arms over my chest in the bright yellow cropped jacket I wore with a colorful striped fitted tee, denim leggings, and a fresh bright pink pair of the classic Reebok freestyle high-tops.

"Busy . . . but not too bad," Hunter said, moving around the front of his Porsche to open his driver side.

I laughed as I walked to my car parked in front of him. "Hopefully, I won't be needing you again," I said, as I unlocked the car door and climbed inside. "Bye."

Soon he blew his horn shortly as he whizzed past me to head down the street.

I did a U-turn and headed in the opposite direction. I had to get to over to Hunga's to pick up the package Keno had left there for me. So far I had made the money back I fronted him plus some. Nothing near the money Dane made but I was happy. My bills was paid. Dane had the max on his commissary. I was starting to build our savings back up. I was going to apply for fall entrance into New York University to earn my MBA since I was still coming up snake eyes on getting a new job.

For the past couple of months I studied hard for the

GMAT—the Graduate Management Admission Test. The standardized test was required for entrance into business school. I was scheduled to take the test next month . . . just in time for final deadlines for fall admissions. I just had to pass the test or try again in the spring.

An MBA gave me a two-year verifiable reason for being out of the workforce, plus more education would be a plus for the time I would have fallen off anyone's radar. I planned to come back even stronger. Like I thought, taking my focus off money gave me a clear line on my goal of eventually jump-starting my career.

I pulled up in front of Hunga's house and parked behind her yellow Ford Mustang. It was March and a little warmer now that winter was thawing and besides the chirping of birds, people were back to moving a little slower to get from their cars to the warmth of their homes. Jogging up the stairs, I raised my hand to knock on the door.

What the fuck? My mouth fell open and was as wide as my eyes. "Whoa," I said at the sight of Hunga and Ming butt naked as they tag teamed Keno's dick with their tongues as he lay naked and kicked back on the sofa.

"Well, damn, Keno," I said out loud.

His dick was one of those thick, veiny, dark motherfuckers with a light tip. It was long enough for Hunga and Ming to wrap a hand around it as they took turns sucking the tip and then tongue-kissing each other.

Hunga stood up in a pair of rhinestone heels and reached down to grab Keno's ankles before she pushed his legs straight up in the air. Ming dropped to her knees on the floor and uncurled her tongue to lick and then suck his ass wetly. Keno's legs stiffened and his toes curled.

I was wrong. I know I was dead wrong. But I could not look away from this shit.

Maybe because I never seen a real live threesome.

Maybe because I ain't seen a dick since it seen me.

Either way I stood there fascinated as fuck . . . and turned on. No lie.

These motherfuckers are acrobats.

Ming straddled Keno's head pressed against the back of the couch. Hunga drizzled spit down onto the tip of Keno's dick before she squatted on it, facing him. And then Ming leaned down to suck and lick and bite at Hunga's hard nipples. Keno's chin bobbed as he ate her pussy.

Hunga let her head tilt back until the tips of her hair touched the curve of her ass as she circled her hips, sending her pussy up and down the length of Keno's dick until it was shiny from her juices. His long narrow fingers dug into her ass as he worked his hips up and down on the couch to deepen each thrust inside her.

"Ooh-oooh-ooooooh-ooooooooooh," Hunga moaned, her entire body starting to shiver.

Keno slapped her ass, drawing his hand all the way back before he released it like a spring. WHAP!

Ming cried out as she began to grind her hips against Keno's face. She sat up and grabbed Hunga's face to pull her forward and kiss her deeply, tangling her fingers in her hair.

Keno sucked Ming's clit and then lifted his head between their upper bodies to lick Hunga's nipples. He used his fingers to grip her ass and slammed her pussy down on his dick, sliding out and then disappearing inside her over and over again, his dick more slick and wet by the second.

Ming got down off the back of the sofa to come around on wobbly legs and squat behind Hunga and lick her ass like a cat going to town on a bowl of milk.

"I'm comiiiiiiiiiiiiiiiiiiiiiiing," Hunga cried out.

Keno bit his bottom lips as he looked up into her face all fierce like he enjoyed seeing her pleasure. She cried out and slapped him. "Make this pussy come motherfucker," she said loudly, fucking him harder as she looked over her shoulder and down at Ming attacking her asshole.

I stepped back, afraid they would see me looking through the window at their fuckfest with my nipples hard and my pussy throbbing. It was a real-life porno flick.

Keno must have said something because Hunga jumped off his dick and squatted next to Ming. He grabbed that thick motherfucker and finished jacking the base as they tongued the thick tip and each other. His hips arched up off the couch and his body was as straight as an ironing board just as his dick pumped like a shotgun and his nut shot up against the waiting tongues and mouths and faces.

Them hos was like fuck it.

Hunga deep-throated his dick with her cheeks caved in as Ming shifted to suck his balls.

Keno hit a high note that any woman couldn't fuck with.

I couldn't front. My horny ass was jealous as hell. Not of their threesome. And not because of the sight of Keno's dick. It wasn't the same lubing up with a dildo when you had a hard body to fuck you down.

They all broke apart and I fanned my damn self. My clit was throbbing like I came too. *Damn.*

I turned and rushed down the stairs. Before my foot

could hit the bottom step the front door opened. I just about died of embarrassment as I turned with a fake smile. "I was just coming up to knock and I left something in my car—"

"Bitch, please," Hunga said, barely wearing a bright red kimono-style robe around her nakedness. "Did you enjoy the show?"

I came up the stairs and took the roll of money she had in her fist. "Shut up," I said.

She laughed as she reached out to palm one of my breasts. I slapped her hand away and she laughed playfully.

"Next time we can make room for you," Hunga said.

"No chance because I ain't returning the favor with my man," I told her. "If I ever catch you tag-teaming Dane like that, I have a .357 that will blow a pretty hole in botha you for your boy to fuck."

"Okay, whateva, bougie," Hunga said, waving her hand dismissively before she went back into the house.

Whateva my ass. I was dead damn serious.

I climbed back in my car and undid the rubber band to count the stack of hundred dollar bills. Another ten grand to add to my stash. I pushed the roll down into the leather saddle bag I used as a bookcase.

As I was driving, I thought about how easy I walked up and spotted Keno. The police could have easily done the same thing. A dude didn't stay on the run for over five months by being sloppy. *Fuck around and Ming will have that pussy all to herself.*

Bzzzzzzzzz . . . Bzzzzzzzzz . . . Bzzzzzzzzz . . .

I picked up my cell phone. It was Dane. "Whassup," I said, pushing my shades up on my head as I slowed to a stop at a red light.

"Nothing but time," Dane said. "I just got done with work."

I laughed. "I couldn't get you on a nine-to-five but the feds got you stretched out for less than fifty cents an hour in that motherfucker."

"Oh, so you the King of Comedy now?" he asked sarcastically.

"Jokes. They're just jokes," I told him, sitting up in my seat to scratch my back.

"Where you, on your way from work?"

"Yeah," I said, shaking my head at myself. I changed my mind about telling Dane I lost my job.

I also doubted he knew that Keno had taken over his spot . . . with my help. My gut kept telling me not to tell Dane about my arrangement with Keno, but I knew if he heard it somewhere else, he would be pissed. With Keno on the run I could only assume they weren't lamping on the phone and he damn sure wasn't on Dane's visiting list because of it as well.

I stayed clear of anything to do with it. Outside of handing over the cash, finding that factory was my one and only physical involvement with the shit. So none of his boys could tell him I had partnered up with Keno either.

"That lame-ass dude Leo not pushing up on my pussy, is he?"

A vision of Leo's balls hanging over the sofa flashed in my head. "No, he ain't crazy," I lied, turning the corner onto my father's block.

I frowned at the sight of two police cruisers with lights flashing and an unmarked car parked in the street. One set of cops was talking to the Jordans and Luscious in front of their house and a pair of detectives was on my father's porch talking to him. "What the fuck?" I asked, pulling behind the cruisers. "It's cops at my father's house. Call me back."

I ended the call and dropped the cell phone on the passenger seat, then hopped out my car. Because I was parked down the street, I had to pass by the Jordans to get to my father's house.

"I'll kill that motherfucker," Mr. Jordan said, his eyeglasses tilted to the side on his face.

That shit made me pause midstep because I never heard the man use profanity and it sounded awkward as shit coming from his mouth. Like "shit damn you ass fuck."

"Mr. Jordan, I'm not going to warn you again that making threats against someone's life is a crime," the officer was saying. "You have to let the detective follow up on investigating your daughter's claim about Mr. Alvarez."

"It's not my claims, it's my *truth*," Luscious snapped. "And it's time he paid for what he did to me."

My brows dipped together in confusion. *Claims? Investigation? What he did to her?*

As I came through the break in the parked cars up on the sidewalk and then the stairs, I looked over at my father's neighbors and Luscious's eyes were on me. She stood there posed up with her hands on her hips in a form-fitting ombré bandage skirt in shades of blue, a white tee, and a stretch denim jacket. Aviator shades. Hair jet black and wavy over one shoulder. Lips glossy.

She was looking like she walked straight off one of the sets of the hip-hop videos she started doing last year.

Beats stripping . . . I guess.

"Sophie."

I turned to face my father. He was leaning against the

door frame, his already thin face looking more gaunt and tired than ever. I pushed past the detectives to hold his elbow. *"Papá, estás bien?"* I asked him softly.

"Aquel bastardo me perforó!" he shouted, waving his hand in the Jordans' direction.

"He punched you?" I asked, feeling my anger rise in a flash.

"And you hit him with your cane, Mr. Alvarez," one of the detectives said from behind me.

"He's lucky I didn't shove it up his ass!" Victor shouted.

What in the hot fuck is this shit about?

"Papi, please," I begged, turning to the detective. "What's this all about?"

"Lies. All lies!" Victor said, trembling with his emotions.

"I'm Detective Kotz," the short meatball shaped man with the reddish complexion said, looking eternally bored. "You're Mr. Alvarez's daughter, Sophie?"

My eyes shifted from him to the police officers waiting as Luscious followed her parents up the stairs into the house. "Yes," I answered, looking back at him as the other detective walked down the porch to meet up with the uniformed officers.

"Perhaps we should go inside," he offered.

My patience was wearing thinner than a cheap weave. I followed my father into the house and then held the door for the detective, closing it once he walked in too. Victor flopped down into his recliner as the detective turned in the middle of the living room to face me. "Is there somewhere we can talk in private?" he asked.

"Fucking lies!" Victor spouted again.

I eyed my father as I led the detective into the kitchen.

"What happened?" I asked, leaning back against the fridge.

"My partner and I are currently doing a preliminary investigation of a report made of sexual molestation of Harriet Jordan by your father when she was a minor," he said.

I shook my head and held up my hands. "Huh? What?"

"It's not my claims, it's my truth. *And it's time he paid for what he did to me."*

"We spoke to her parents as part of our investigation and Mr. Jordan got pissed and rushed over here to confront your father," Detective Kotz said, still looking like he'd checked out on giving a single fuck years ago.

My father molested Harriet? *Bitch, please.*

"When did this supposedly happen?" I asked, even as my heart and stomach were flopping like fish out of water.

"She says she was five or six at the time," he said, after looking down at his notes.

"Twenty damn years ago? She's a liar," I insisted. "We were best friends. She was only over here *with me.* Playing *with me.* Spending the night *with me—*"

"And you don't remember seeing anything suspicious or inappropriate?"

"No," I said shaking my head "*Hell* no."

"I know this was a long time ago, Ms. Alvarez, but I just need you to take a moment and think back and be sure?" Detective Kotz insisted. His pale blue eyes suddenly became more intense and alive as he watched me closely.

I shook my head. "Nothing. This *did not* happen, Detective Kotz. I don't know why she's lying or if the dumb bitch is confused, but this did not happen."

Detective Kotz shrugged and held up his hands. "It's our job to investigate this and be sure of that."

Bullshit.

"Is he being arrested?" I asked, opening and closing my hands as I fought off the emotions coming at me like rain on a windshield during a thunderstorm. Anger. Shock. Fear. Anxiety.

"No. She came in with her attorney earlier this week and at this point we're just investigating."

I chuckled sarcastically as I tried to rub the tension from my neck. "My father had a heart attack a few months ago, so please tread lightly with her bullshit. Please," I stressed, the heel of my shoe lightly hitting the chipped tile of the floor as my anger pushed forward and created this crazy energy in me that I had to release by shaking my leg.

The detective reached in his pocket for a card and handed it to me. "I'll be in touch," he said, after taking down my phone number.

We left the kitchen and I spotted the other detective now sitting in the living room with my father. He looked up at me, his jaw tight with anger. His eyes watery with tears. My father looked broken.

That broke my heart.

I wasn't swallowing this bullshit that easily. I walked over to press one knee into the sofa and used my fingers to shift the curtains back a bit. Luscious's Jag was still parked in her parents' driveway. The police cruiser was gone.

"I need some fresh air. I'll be right on the porch," I said, already heading out the front door.

The fates were with me. I was glad for my sneakers . . . and for the bitch picking *that* moment to walk out her parent's door.

Off I went. Fuck it.

She looked up from digging around in her purse just as I ran up and snatched a handful of her weave to jank that bitch off the step. "Fucking lying bitch," I told her, biting my bottom lip as I pushed her head down with her hair in one hand and hammered away on that motherfucker with my other hand in a fist like I was driving home a nail.

Luscious hollered out and dropped her purse before she punched at my stomach. I can't lie, that shit hurt and made me take a step back before I brought my knee up hard against her face. I felt her teeth hit against the top of my knee.

"Ken! Ken! Come quick. The girls are fighting!" I heard her mother screaming.

Two seconds later, Mrs. Jordan was trying to get in between us and get my hands out from where they were twisted in her daughter's hair. I tightened down on my fist and tugged harder, biting down so hard beneath my bottom lips that I thought I would draw blood.

"Let her go, Sophie!" Mrs. Jordan shouted, pushing her elbow against my chest hard.

Luscious started swinging her arms up and a blow landed against my chin.

I felt a strong arm around my waist and then sharp fingernails digging into my wrist. I cried out and opened my hand. Luscious stumbled back and fell against one of the short stone columns of her parents' porch. The top and back of her hair looked like a bird's nest. "You lying slack-ass bitch," I said, lunging for her.

"No, your daddy lyin', you dumb bitch," she said, her eyed blazing and her chest heaving. "Fucking child-molesting, perverted ass."

I spat and it sprayed against that bitch's face.

She came out of her shoes and pushed her mother aside, then kicked at me.

The arm around my waist tightened as someone whipped me around and carried me into the street.

"Enough!" Detective Kotz called out as he came down the porch and into the middle of the fray.

Mr. Jordan put me down on my feet and turned his back on me as he blocked me from coming at his daughter.

"You ain't shit with your lying ass," I spat at her, pacing back and forth with my arms crossed over my chest.

Luscious shook her head and looked at me like she felt sorry for me. "I wish I was lying, Sophie," she said, her voice low, before tears filled her eyes.

"Sophie!" I dragged my eyes off of her to look over at my father standing on the porch. The other detective was blocking him from coming down the stairs. *"Vienen aquí!"*

I gave the woman who had once been my closest childhood friend a hate-filled stare before doing as my father commanded and going to him.

"Do you want to press charges against Miss Alvarez?" Detective Kotz asked Luscious as she accepted her bag from her mother and put her shoes back on. "Keep in mind Mr. Alvarez has the right to press the same charges against you, Mr. Jordan."

"The American justice system at its finest," Mr. Jordan said coldly.

"I'm fine, Daddy. Just forget it," she said, finger-combing her hair as he hugged her to his side.

Nothing like a lie to get some attention from your daddy, bitch.

Detective Kotz spoke to the three of them before Luscious walked to her Jag. She gave me one hard stare and motioned with her fingers to let me know it was far from over between us—like I gave a fuck.

"If there are any more altercations between any of you, I'm personally hauling all of your asses to jail," Detective Kotz said, coming back up on the porch. "Clear?"

I nodded, but I knew I was far from done with Harriet "Luscious" Jordan.

Far from it.

16

Two weeks later

I hadn't laid eyes on Luscious since that day and the police still hadn't made a move forward with filing charges against my father. I was beginning to feel relief that they spotted her bullshit just like I did. I had Hunter on standby if they did charge him, but that didn't stop the fact that he looked weaker and frailer than he did when he had the heart attack Thanksgiving night. I was worried about my father.

I always complained to Dane about my father's coldness and mean comments when he was drunk, and Dane would always say you don't know what it feels like not to have parents. *He ain't the best father but he's your father and he did the best he could.*

That shit was hitting home now.

Brrrnnnggg . . .

The sound of the house phone ringing shook me from my thoughts as I sat on the living room sofa looking out the windows at life while I waited for Hunga to pick me up. Her birthday was a good enough reason to set aside how I felt about her and hit the club for the first time since Dane got locked up. I still didn't appreciate her lying to me about knowing where Keno was but I chalked it up to them making sure I wasn't going to turn his ass in or some shit.

I picked the cordless up from the coffee table.

My heart raced. It was Dane. We talked twice a day if not more and it was sad and cute all at once how happy I got to get a call from him. "Hello," I said.

"I guess you still going out?"

That shit—his tone and rudeness—made all my joy melt right away. "Yes," I stressed. "It's Hunga's birthday party at Club Fabulous. I'm waiting for her to pick me up."

"Man, fuck Hunga's scandalous ass," he said.

I paused. Dane was mad. "What's wrong?" I asked, my face concerned.

"Nothing," Dane said, not sounding like he meant it. "I just miss you. I been in this bitch for almost six months."

"I know. I been out here without you," I reminded him. "I'm the one coming to see you every week just so I can feel close to you and lay eyes on you and smell you—even though I can't kiss you or rub your dick or even give you a good-ass hug. I'm right here doing this time with you and even though it's easier for me . . . it ain't *that* easy, Dane."

"I know, baby. Believe me I know," Dane said. "I don't mean to take this shit out on you."

"What shit, Dane?" I asked, my senses on high alert because I could tell something was fucking with his mind.

The line went quiet. I sat up straighter. Waiting.

"Ain't nothin'. Ain't nothin'. Have fun and you remind any of them knucklehead clowns that try you that I'm in this motherfucker but I can still touch 'em in them streets."

I swallowed back my disappointment. Once again he was keeping shit from me.

And I was too.

"I love you so much, Dane," I told him, making sure everything I felt for him was in my voice.

"I love you too."

He hung up and I instantly felt the disconnection.

The sound of a loud car horn echoed outside and it shook me from my thoughts as I opened the door to peer out. I didn't recognize the bright pink convertible sitting outside my house until Hunga lowered the automatic window and leaned over from the driver's seat to holler out the window: "Tell me this shit right here is not everythaaaang!!!"

I locked my door and came downstairs trying to hide my surprise. I could tell from the gleam of the paint and bigger, rounder body of the car that it was brand new. I opened the passenger door. Ming was sitting in the middle of the back-seat, already sipping straight from a bottle of champagne and floating side to side, singing off-key to Mariah Carey's "We Belong Together."

I climbed into the passenger seat. "Happy birthday, chick," I told her as she pulled away. "Nice ride."

"Keno bought it for me and parked it outside the house today with a big white bow. Yessssssssssss," she said, clapping her hands.

I turned to look out the passenger window and frowned as I eyed the people we passed who walked on the street. "You don't think that's drawing too much attention and Keno supposed to be on the low?" I asked, my eyes focused on my reflection in the glass.

"Oh Lord, bougie, don't be a downer on my birthday.

Damn," Hunga said with a slight hint of attitude. "I don't remember throwing no shade when you was the queen getting all of your gifts."

"And a lot of those gifts got confiscated when the feds arrested Dane," I reminded her with a little bit of attitude too. "But do you boo."

"We belong together," Ming said, leaning between the seats to massage Hunga's nipple in the metallic bodysuit she wore.

Hunga brushed Ming's hand off. "I'm feeling cold in all this shade from you, Suga."

Mariah Carey's "Obsessed" faded in.

"No shade, just concern . . . for all of us," I said, turning to lock eyes with her.

Ming lifted the bottle of champagne up in the air. "Turn that shit up because this right here had plenty of motherfuckers pussy stalk-ing!"

I missed and looked over my shoulder. Ming had jerked the skirt of her silver dress up and pointed between her legs . . . without a stitch of panties on.

"So you just juicy all over the leather seat right now?" I asked her.

Hunga laughed.

"Fuck it," Ming said, looking at me through eyes glassy with whatever she was on.

I just focused my attention outside the window. My thoughts were filled with the madness of Keno lamping up to Hunga's house on the regular and now they were making big purchases. They might as well hang a sign on the front door saying KENO MILLER INSIDE.

Just straight stupid.

The thick smoke of weed stroked the side of my face. I felt it before I smelt it. *Damn, I shoulda drove.* I politely cracked the window.

"Touch My Body" filled the car's crisp and clear sound system.

"Uhm, what's with the Mariah?" I asked.

Hunga held the lit blunt in one hand as she turned the corner with the other one. "It's been all Mariah all day. The hip-hop Mariah—not the pop one," she said, blowing a smoke ring and then sticking her tongue in the center of it before she licked it and broke the ring with a laugh.

"Damn right," Ming said. "Happy birthday, Hunga and Mariah—the bitch I bump pussies with and the bitch I bump pussies to—well, today anyway!"

Her high-ass laugh sounded like she tickled the fuck out of herself.

I couldn't help but laugh with her—or at her. Whatever.

Hunga pulled up in front of the club and the sight of this huge-ass banner on the side of the building made me lean back like Fat Joe told me to do it. *These motherfuckers done lost what little mind they had.*

As the bouncer removed the cones holding her parking spot in front of the club, I mouthed along to what I read on the banner:

KENO AND TOP DAWG ENTERTAINMENT
PRESENTS
HUNGA'S BIRTHDAY BASH!!!

The color graphic of a life-size Hunga in a metallic silver skintight bodysuit like the metallic gold one she wore was madness as well, but I was really head-tripping on the name of a wanted man floating big as ever on the side of a fucking packed-ass club.

"Don't sweat that," Hunga said, pointing up to the banner before she climbed from the car.

The bouncer came around the car to help me and then Ming out before he closed our doors. "Have a fun night, ladies," he said before going back to manage the line of people waiting to get in the club.

"Happy Birthday, Hunga!!!" a bunch of women in the line yelled to her.

She paused and posed in her catsuit on her way inside. "Thank you!!"

When Hunga blew a kiss I had to shake my head. *Did this bitch sign a recording deal and no one told me she was the next Beyoncé?*

We were escorted inside and taken directly to a glass-encased circular VIP section in the center of the club, and there, sitting down already enjoying drinks, was Keno in a black linen blazer, shirt, and pants. Bald head gleaming and reflecting the colorful strobe lights from above as he hid his eyes behind shades and smoked a cigar fat enough to be a dick.

I gave him a smile and waved as I settled down on the leather bench going around the entire section. There were several round tables in the middle of the area that were already covered with bottle service of five different types of liquor and champagne.

Hunga climbed onto Keno's lap and kissed him deeply while he dug his fingers into her ass cheeks, before shaking them up and down until her ass moved in every possible direction. I shifted my eyes to Ming. She slipped something in her mouth before she washed it down with champagne. Then she climbed on top of the tables and started dancing.

I honestly didn't know if she was trying to get Keno's attention or Hunga's or if she just wanted to make sure neither one was that caught up in the other.

At the first flash of bald pussy lips, I turned my head and poured me a glass of champagne. A thick but cute brother in all white leaned over to Keno and said something in his ear. They both looked over at me while Keno shook his head and dragged his hand across his throat like "kill it"—not me, but any idea of stepping to me.

I wasn't wearing a catsuit like Hunga or dancing on table pantyless like Ming, but the black dress I wore with the deep plunging vee, fitted bodice, and short, full bell skirt that just made it mid-thigh was sexy without even trying. I'd pulled my hair into a soft topknot to emphasize my neck, and the diamond necklace I wore with my heart locket sat just a little above my cleavage. Makeup on point. Shapely legs on display. Sky-high heels with lots of black feathery details highlighting the ankles. Felt good. Looked good.

For me. Me and me only.

"Champagne Life" by Ne-Yo came on. It took me right back to that day in Jamaica on the boat. I smiled sadly and missed Dane so deeply in that moment that it felt like he'd passed on.

I looked up. Keno and Hunga held their glasses up to me in a toast. I knew they remembered that day too. One of the last nice times we shared before the feds blew up our world. Feeling myself getting all teary, I stood up and forced myself to move to the music and sing along with Ne-Yo. *Nobody should be sad in the club.*

Keno must've agreed, because when the DJ mixed in 2Chainz's "Spend It," this fool dug in his pocket for a fat wad of cash, stood up on the bench, and started shuffling money over the side of the VIP to rain bills down on the crowd dancing below.

"It's mine . . . I spend it. It's mine . . . I spend it," he said loud as hell.

Hunga stood up and clapped her hands.

The music paused.

"Happy birthday, Hungaaaaaaaaaaaaaa!" the DJ yelled into the air just as he brought the music back up.

People starting snatching the bills from the air and waiting like hungry fish at the top of the tank for him to float down some more.

Luckily he sat his happy ass down, bent his head, and pounded his fist as he rapped along with the song.

Am I in the Twilight Zone?

Still holding my flute, I stood up and moved over to sit beside Keno as he looked up at Hunga dancing in front of him.

"Keno, do you think all of this is a good idea when you're wanted?" I said into his ear, noticing the dude in the white still eyeing me. He had taken his shades off and his eyes were big and gray in his milk-chocolate complexion. "The new car, the club flyers, that big-ass banner. You're drawing too much attention to yourself."

He leaned away from me and fanned his hand like he was shooing away an annoying fly.

I eyed this motherfucker and then held his arm to pull him back close enough to me. "You fucking up, Keno, and you don't even see it. Don't do shit to get me fucked up and fucked over along with you," I told him, my voice hard. "You need to chill the fuck out."

This was business as far as I was concerned, and right now Keno was taking chances with my money and my freedom.

He turned his head and eyed me. His eyes were cold and hard and unflinching. I was so drawn into the depths that the music almost faded to nothing. I knew that whatever the fuck he said next he meant from his guts.

"No, you need to realize who runs this shit, and it ain't you. So sit back and count the money you're making for doing not one thing, because if you think this is *our* hustle, then you're not as smart as *you* think *you* are."

"Oh really?" I asked him, making sure I didn't flinch or blink as I eyed him right back.

Right there in the club was a power struggle.

Keno was smelling his ass and then giving it to me to kiss. He had me fucked up.

"Oh, so you forgot I helped you build your little empire?" I asked him.

He laughed, wiped his hand over his mouth, and then looked back at me. "As long as you understand that it's *my* empire and right now I'm doing you a favor because of Dane."

"Like all those favors he did for you and Hunga for years. Remember?" I asked him, tilting my head back to finish my champagne.

He held up his hand as he reached in his blazer and pulled out his iPhone.

I stood up just as our bottle service waitress came in. Dressed in their uniform of sequined black tee, coochie-cutter satin shorts, and heels she was carrying enough of a new setup for the table to completely wreck Keno's tab. He had to be at two grand or better so far. Fuck him.

A fool and his money are soon separated.

I grabbed a fresh bottle of champagne and topped my flute off before I sat back down next to Keno and crossed my legs.

"Chop one of his fingers off every week until he pays it all back," he said, before he ended the call.

I choked on my champagne and had to cough to get myself straight even as I eyed him. "Are you really about *that* life?" I asked him. "That's how you handling business? That's how you treating Dane's clients that you took over?"

"Mind your business, Suga," Keno said, reaching out to stroke Hunga's ass and then pull her over to sit in his lap.

I felt nauseated. I set my glass down but it tipped over and spread across the table like an amber wave. Getting to my feet, I walked away from them and then squeezed past all these random motherfuckers I didn't know to leave the VIP and press through the dancing bodies to leave the club.

It wasn't until I was outside and spotted Hunga's new pink whip that I remembered I didn't drive that night. "Could you call me a cab?" I turned to ask the bouncer.

"Are you okay, sweetheart?" he asked me, his hand lightly touching my bare arm.

I looked down at his fingers against my skin and a bloody vision of them hacked off flashed. I shook off his touch and reached in my bag for my cell phone but I didn't know the numbers to any cab companies in the city.

"I got you," the bouncer said. "I'll call you one."

I nodded and forced myself to give him a friendly smile. It wasn't his fault that I'd helped unleash a lunatic like Keno onto the streets.

"Chop one of his fingers off every week until he pays it all back."

I fucked up.

///

$\mathscr{A}$ week later I was a wreck. I accepted the money Hunga dropped off and listened to her still talking about how her party was the party of the year, but I was overwhelmed with relief when she finally got the fuck out of my house. I couldn't sleep. I couldn't hardly eat. I wasn't able to focus long enough to study for my GMAT the way I needed to. I hadn't even been checking up on my father the way I should. The news that the police had decided not to move forward with pressing charges against him was the only bright spot.

Was Dane as ruthless and cutthroat as Keno when he ran the business or was Keno running wild without someone else at the helm to rein him in?

It was hard for me to swallow that I gave Keno the start-up money and now he was ordering people's fingers to be chopped. What the fuck?

All week long I scurried the online press for a story about a man being hospitalized because of a finger amputation. So far nothing. But I knew he existed somewhere in this city . . . if he hadn't bled to death.

I had to tell Dane. I had to. I was stalling like crazy, but I had to tell him. All of it.

The guilt of my lies and my role in Keno's come-up was wearing me out.

The pelting of rain on the roof sounded suddenly and I looked out the window at an afternoon shower even as the sun continued to shine bright as ever. Reaching for my iPad, I logged onto my Facebook account.

I frowned. I had a notification for a message. From Luscious. My father said the detectives called and they could not find enough evidence that Luscious's claims were true. No charges were being pressed. Everything was a wrap as far as I was concerned. So what the fuck did she want?

I could see the very first line of her message in the notification box. It read: I stabbed your father in the leg . . .

I pushed the iPad away and sat there with my chin in my hands eyeing it.

I stabbed your father in the leg . . .

I reached for the iPad but then pulled my hand away from it and rolled off the bed, grabbing the GMAT workbook I was supposed to be reading. But I never opened it. My thoughts were on the knife wound that indeed was in my father's thigh. He said he stabbed himself cleaning fish.

But how did Luscious know about it?

From the padded bench sitting in front of the window, I looked over at the iPad sitting in the middle of my bed. "Man, fuck that liar," I said, waving my hand as I opened the book and took the top off my highlighter.

I stabbed your father in the leg . . .

I tried like hell to read the first line of the chapter but that shit never registered and I kept losing my spot because my eyes kept shifting over to land on that iPad. Curiosity was killing me. Closing my textbook, I stood up and crossed the room back to the bed and picked it up. Swiping my finger across the screen, I unlocked the tablet and opened the message:

I stabbed your father in the leg the same night I remembered that he molested me. It's his right thigh and I know I plunged the knife deep. I wanted to hurt him the way he hurt me that night all those years ago.

BA-DUM.

I pinched the bridge of my nose and wiped my eyes. It had been his right thigh that was injured but that proved nothing. She was at her parents the day I brought him home from the emergency room and she could have seen him limping.

I had forgotten about what happened and when some other shit in my life went down, the memory of that night came back from wherever I hid it so it wouldn't hurt no more. It took everything I had to finally go to the police and for them to not even take my case serious really fucked with me. To finally remember and then tell the truth . . . only to be treated like a liar feels like some more fucked up shit.

I know that's your father and it's your job to believe him, but I swear to you that I am not lying. I wouldn't lie about that. For what reason? What do I gain from that shit? Nothing. But I gain a little bit more of my freedom from that night by telling the truth and not living in

*shame. I did nothing wrong. I was a little girl spending
the night with her best friend in the whole world. Not a
little girl who felt so bad about breaking a stupid teapot
that I kept the dirty secret of what happened that night
while you slept upstairs. And for him to keep that teapot even after all these years. What kind of sick shit is
that???—*

BA-DUM.

Teapot? I shook my head to clear it. Something was trying to come forward from my memory . . .

*I was six years old and came running into the living
room from the kitchen with an ice cream pop in my hand.
My father was sitting in the living room with the cracked
teapot on the dusty coffee table in front of him. It was split
in half.*

*"What happened to Mama's pot?" I asked, tilting my
head to the side to lick the stickiness of the melting pop from
my hand.*

"I broke it," he snapped.

"How?"

"I dropped it."

*"Are you gonna fix it?" I asked, coming to stand at his
knee.*

"Go outside and play, Sophie," he said.

"Are you gonna fix it?" I asked again.

*"What does it look like?" he yelled, pressing his face
close to mine as he did.*

*Fat tears filled my eyes. I hated to make him mad at me.
"I'm sorry, Daddy," I said. "I'm sorry."*

BA-DUM.

I pushed the iPad away again. I couldn't read anymore. I didn't want to.

"No," I said, holding up my hands as I hopped off the bed, again fighting the doubts that began to fill me.

I wouldn't lie about that. For what reason? What do I gain from that shit? Nothing.

I left my bedroom as my phone began to ring. Whoever it was would have to wait. *I need to talk to my father.*

I grabbed my keys before I left the house. I didn't even care that the heavy rain instantly beat against my body and soaked my hair until it started to curl up. I didn't even care that I had on nothing but pajama bottoms, a tank, and my fuzzy slippers. I didn't even care that my foot sank into a puddle of rainwater in the street as I climbed into my car.

I didn't care about any of it as I started the car and drove the couple of blocks over to my father's house. My pulses were racing through my body like a car on a racetrack. I had to park down the street on the corner and then run up the block in the rain. By the time I raced up onto his porch, I was drenched.

I knocked. And knocked again. And again. I moved over on the porch to peer through the living room window just as my father came down the stairs. He came over toward the door. Moving slower. Looking still older.

I stepped back from the window.

The front door opened. "Sophie, where is your umbrella? You're soaking wet," he said, stepping back to open the door wider to let me in.

I eyed him as I wrapped my arms around myself and shivered from the wetness.

"What?" Victor snapped, eyeing me back.

A vision of the man he used to be almost twenty years ago replaced the image of the man standing before me. Tall and handsome with dark hair and olive skin that could be mistaken for a fair-skinned African American complexion. He had been married to my mother and over the years some women had passed in and out of our lives as girlfriends.

What could he possibly want from a child?

It can't be true. All of it can be explained. I refuse to believe that.

"What Sophie?" he asked again, sounding annoyed.

I shook my head. "Nothing," I finally answered, looking away from him.

"Did you walk over here?" he asked.

I shook my head as I looked at the coffee table.

I could remember that teapot so clearly. It was white porcelain with a rose pattern and it had sat on that coffee table on a tray for years. But it wasn't there anymore. Hadn't been for a minute. I just didn't notice it until now.

My eyes fell on the dinner tray in front of his recliner. I squinted my eyes, remembering the day a few months back when he was trying to glue together the pieces of something porcelain like a jigsaw puzzle.

Before I reached out to touch it, I asked him, "Why are you trying to fix that?"

He yelled, *"DON'T TOUCH IT!"*

I didn't recognize what the flowery porcelain pieces were that day, but now I was sure it was that teapot my father was trying to patch together . . . again.

Not a little girl who felt so bad about breaking a stupid

teapot that I kept the dirty secret of what happened that night while you slept upstairs.

"How did you stab yourself in the leg?" I asked him.

Victor frowned. "I was cleaning fish. Why?" he asked.

"Harriet said that she stabbed you." I locked eyes with him.

"Fucking bitch," he swore, coming around me to sit down in his recliner.

My eyes widened a little bit. "You called her a fucking bitch the day I picked you up from the hospital for your stitches. I know why you're pissed at her now. Why were you so mad at her *then*?"

Victor sat his tall, thin frame up on the edge of his recliner. It dipped under the weight. "What are you accusing me of, Sophie?" he asked, his voice cold and hard.

I came to stand closer to him. "I'm afraid to say it out loud," I admitted in a whisper.

"And you believe her lies, Sophie? That's what you think of me?" he asked.

"Did. She. Stab. You?"

"No!" Victor shouted, spittle flying from the corners of his mouth.

"Did you rape her? Did you molest her? Did you take advantage of her? Did you hurt my friend?" I asked, bending down to press my face close to his as my throat tightened with emotions.

"NOOOOO!" Victor roared, leaning back from me against the chair.

I stared him down, daring him to look away. "She said *she* broke the teapot that night. The one you glued together that morning after the sleepover."

His eyes shifted.

BA-DUM.

A piece of my soul died.

Victor saw it in my eyes. "She's l-l-l-l-lying," he sputtered.

I shook my head as I shivered, not from the wetness and the slight chill of the air but from pure repulsion at my own father. "No, she isn't," I whispered back fiercely as my entire world spun off its axis.

"The police do not believe her lies but my own daughter does!"

"WHY WOULD SHE LIE?" I roared, feeling myself get light-headed from the strain.

"I don't know and I don't care."

I backed away from him as everything I knew and believed about the man before me changed in an instant. "Are you *fucking* kidding me?" I asked him, notching my chin higher as I eyed him with contempt. "You are a fucking pedophile."

"Sophie, you will respect my—"

"Who else? Did you touch anyone else? Did you rape anyone else?" I asked him, feeling my stomach churn.

"Sophie."

"Should I be grateful you didn't touch me too?" I asked. And that made the dam break. The tears came. The pain flooded over me in waves.

"I would never do that to you."

I laughed bitterly and pressed a hand to my chest. "Oh, not me. I'm the lucky fucking one because I'm your daughter."

"Stop it, Sophie."

The room flashed as lightning filled the sky.

"I can't believe you did that," I whispered with all the pain and disgust I felt clear in my voice.

He struggled to rise from his seat. "Sophie."

"Hmmm. And then you one of them sick motherfuckers keeping mementos? Huh? That fucking teapot was some freaky, perverted-ass reminder of what you did to her? Huh?!" I spat at him, hating that this felt like some *Law & Order: SVU* type of shit.

"Sophie!" he said sharply.

The little girl I used to be would have come to a stop so sharply that my body would have swayed on my feet. I was far from that little girl anymore. I rushed to the door and swung it open.

"No, Sophie!"

He reached out and grabbed my wrist. I looked down at his hand and then up to his face. Midway up my eyes fell on a spot just inside the collar of the plaid shirt he wore. I could see about a quarter of an inch of a chain.

The same chain I took from his bag of personal items in the hospital that night.

The same chain that a key swung from.

Keys opened locks. Locks kept secrets. Secrets were always held close to the chest.

My eyes finally shifted up to his as I reached up, pulled the chain free from his shirt, and then snatched it from his neck in one swift movement.

"NO!" he shouted, spraying flyaway spit against the side of my face as he reached for the chain dangling from my fist.

I shook him off and he stumbled backward, falling onto the coffee table.

I spared him a brief glance that was all of nothing and looked down at the chain and key instead. I lightly rubbed my fingers against the letters *FSL*. "What lock does this open?" I asked in a quiet voice that was almost drowned out by the sound of the rain.

"Sophie, please," my father said. He sounded so weak and pitiful . . . and ashamed.

Of what?

My gut clenched at my father—Victor—still lying on the floor, his skin sweaty and pale, his hand clutching his left arm with tears staining his face.

"Nine-one-one," he gasped, wincing in pain.

"How many children did you hurt?" I asked, feeling the heat of hatred fill me as I stood over his body writhing in pain and actually wished for his death. "You don't deserve to live."

He opened his mouth but no words escaped.

Seconds later his eyes rolled in the back of his head and his body went slack.

"Burn in hell, motherfucker," I whispered before I turned and walked out the house, slamming the door behind me.

I walked to my car in the drenching rain, not even rushing my steps. I was numb to the world anyway. Sitting behind the wheel of the car, I looked down at the key and chain in my hand, then over at the house where I was raised with the man who raised me dead on the floor inside.

He was a monster.

He wasn't fit to exist.

Still, I couldn't become the monster he was. I couldn't do it. I picked up the phone and dialed 911. I barely remembered the words I spoke as I sat in that car and waited for an ambulance to arrive.

• • •

It was hours later when I got the nerve to go back in that house.

Victor had had a massive heart attack and was in ICU at UMDNJ, but I had no plans to lay eyes on him again. I was done with him. There was just one last thing I had to do and I would never walk through the door of this house again.

I searched every bit of the house and tried to push that key into every possible lock I found. From top to bottom and even out in the garage, I tried to find the lock that matched the key. I tried and failed.

I didn't know why I was driven to find out the significance of the key . . . but I was. He was carrying it for a reason. I looked around at the house and everything about what should feel like a safe place just felt depressing and dark and dirty.

I left. I had to.

The streets were still wet and the air muggy from the rain earlier that day. I climbed into my car and from behind the wheel of my car I eyed the Jordans' house. I couldn't do shit but shake my head. My father molested their daughter—my friend at the time.

I fought Harriet because I felt she told lies about my father. I thought I was defending an innocent man. My innocent father.

He sure made me look like a dumb ass.

I drove away from the house with about as much speed and energy as I could muster. I was slow rolling as bad as those dudes who shot at us the night AaRon died. I barely made it two blocks from Victor's house and I was happy as hell for the red light. I shook my head in disbelief as I dropped my chin damn near to my chest and wiped my eyes. The combo of my tears and my stress had them aching.

I felt tears well up again but I swallowed them back down. Tears would not fix or change shit. At this point they were just a waste of damn fluids. And a waste of my fucking precious-ass time.

A horn blew behind me. I raised my head and opened my eyes, leaning forward to look in the rearview mirror at the car behind me before I pulled away from the red light. The car turned into the parking lot of the small strip of stores. "Rushing me to get to that raggedy motherfucker?" I muttered, eyeing the beat-down bodega, a hair care store, a Chinese restaurant I wouldn't let a dog eat from, and an old storage unit that needed to be as abandoned as it looked.

I squinted my eyes at the rotating sign barely turning above the building. My heart felt like it had swollen to the size of a basketball in my chest. "FSL. Franco. Storage. Lockers," I read aloud.

I sat back in my seat and eyed it. And then I eyed the chain and key I still held clutched in my hand like I was afraid the shit would disappear if I released it.

Again I rubbed my finger against the engraved initials.

That strip of stores been there as long as I could remember. So long that it had just faded into the background for me. I never paid it any attention, even though it was a couple blocks from the house I grew up in. Never. Until now.

Checking my rearview mirror, I eased the car over to the next lane and made the turn into the parking lot of the strip mall that was really nothing more than four fucked-up looking buildings and an even more fucked up raggedy-ass parking lot.

I parked in front of the last building on the end. The office was closed. The storage units were in the back. *He wouldn't . . . would he?* It was close enough for him to walk. *He could . . . couldn't he?*

I climbed out of the car and made my way to the two rows of small storage units attached to the last building. My heart pounded and I felt I could find safer places for my ass to be but I tried that key in the lock of every unit. One by one.

Click.

I dropped my head on the metal door with its peeling paint before I stood down to push the roll-up door. My eyes opened in surprise to see old furniture and supplies all gathered along one wall. The rest of the unit empty. Normal shit. Including a few spiderwebs and dust balls.

My eyes searched over every nook and cranny. Whatever was here—if anything—was hidden. My heart pounded as I walked along the perimeter, looking at the items. My foot pressed down onto something and snapped it in half on the concrete floor.

I lifted my foot and stepped back, stooping down to pick up a porcelain piece with a small pink rose on it.

The fucking teapot. Again.

My eyes moved up from the floor to a metal trunk under a blanket. I grabbed the corner and flipped it back. It was the toy chest that used to sit in my room: black with red trimming and clown decals. I opened the trunk's lid and sat back on my haunches to look down into it.

I gasped in horror and fell back from it, the lid slamming shut when I missed and released it. I scrambled to my feet and turned to gag as I got the hell away from the evidence of my father's sins. I slid down to the floor and pulled my knees to my chest as I sat there and stared at that trunk, trying to wrap my brain around the bullshit I saw. The fuckery I just laid eyes on. The sickness. The madness.

There were dozens of ziplocks stuffed with a pair of underwear or a shirt or a piece of jewelry. And taped on each one was a Polaroid photo of some nude little girl and a date scribbled on it. Luscious was on top. Panties and the remnants of the broken teapot were in the ziplock. In the photo she was nude and sitting on the same living room couch in my father's living room with huge tears in her eyes.

Pathetic mementos of innocence lost. Taken, destroyed.

This was some sick shit. Some predator type of shit. Some level of crazy I couldn't comprehend.

One by one I removed the bags and counted them. They were twenty-five in all.

Sitting up on my knees, I pulled my cell phone and a business card from the back pocket of my jeans. "Detective Kotz?" I asked.

"Yes, who's this?"

I dropped my head to my chest and took a deep breath. "This is Sophie Alvarez. You were investigating my father—"

"I remember you, Sophie. I let your father know that no charges were brought against him."

I picked up the bag with the photo of a little girl standing in front of cleaning supplies. Knowing my father worked for over thirty years as a custodian for the Newark public school system, I wondered if the photo was taken at one of the schools where he had worked and how many more victims there might be. How many other lives did he completely fuck up?

"I found some things in a storage unit he had a key for. Things you need to see," I said, letting the bag slide from my fingers back onto the floor as I gave him directions.

There was nothing right about it and I couldn't—I wouldn't—protect him or keep his secrets or pretend he wasn't a monster.

I swiped away my tears and sat up to start putting the bags back in the trunk while I waited for the detectives to arrive. I spotted the corner of an envelope in the side pocket of the trunk. I pulled it out and sat back to open it.

"What the fuck is this?" I said out loud into the quiet of the unit.

There was a school picture of a light-skinned girl with light eyes smiling, with one front tooth missing. Another victim? I turned it over, but the only thing written on it was "South 17th Street Elementary," "2nd grade," and "1995." I flipped the envelope over. "This your daughter Vic in case you give a fuck," I read out loud.

My father had another child. Another daughter. The really fucked-up thing? We were the same age, and that meant he cheated on my mother. "This motherfucker is a piece of work," I muttered, hating him even more.

So not only did he prey and molest and abuse and destroy the daughters of other men, he treated me like I was a pain in his ass, and he didn't even have the balls to step up and claim the one he made on my mother.

I had a sister.

Now ain't that some shit.

18

"*K*eno flipped on me."

Dane and I had barely sat down at our table in the visiting room at Fairton when he dropped that bomb. "What do you mean?" I asked, eyeing the way Dane's jaw clenched and his eyes were so bright with anger that they glittered.

"Lil Wil came to see me and told me all about Keno back running the business, partying it up, and spending money like crazy," Dane said, the tension he felt squaring up his shoulder in his khaki uniform. "So I'm like, yo wait a minute, this motherfucker supposed to be on the run but he high-profiling around Newark? It didn't make sense to me."

I crossed my legs in the denims I wore and slid one hand between my thighs. I knew exactly how the hell Dane felt. It was the same thoughts I had. The same observation I tried to bring to Keno's attention the night of Hunga's party. This fool was not acting like a man who was wanted.

"I had the lawyers put their investigators on it and this motherfucker ain't wanted by the police," Dane said, his hand balled up into a fist that I knew he wanted to drive through something. "That fucking snitch-ass nigga gave me up to the feds and they never charged him. That's why his ass was never arrested. Him and Hunga's ratchet ass put out that lie that he was on the run so the streets wouldn't know he was a motherfucking hating-ass snitch-bitch."

The old folks say when you when you feel a chill run over your body, someone is walking on your grave. In that moment I was chilled to the bone as Keno's words that night in the club came back to me.

No, you need to realize who runs this shit and it ain't you. So sit back and count the money you're making for doing not one thing, because if you think this is our hustle then you're not as smart as you think you are.

Keno's attitude and slick comments made all the sense in the world. That motherfucker orchestrated everything. The fucking puppet master.

Man, fuck Hunga's scandalous ass.

That's what Dane said to me the night of Hunga's party. "You found out about all of this around the time Keno threw that party for Hunga, didn't you?" I asked.

Dane nodded and looked away from me for a second. "I didn't know for sure then. Not like I do now. I'm sorry I kept all this shit secret."

I licked my lips as my heart beat harder. "I've got some secrets of my own," I admitted to him in a soft voice.

Dane's eyes squinted as he eyed me so hard that I could feel the heat of his eyes on my skin.

"I lost my job because of the arrest," I began, easing up to lean my elbows against the table as I whispered over to him. We figured it was safe enough to talk in the visiting room even if the phone lines weren't. Still, I made sure to speak for his ears only. I told him without lots of details about Keno reaching out to me for the start-up money and about the brutality he was showing in handling the business.

"I didn't want you to worry. I didn't want you to feel bad because all the money and everything was gone," I said.

"Shit," Dane swore, rising to his feet suddenly.

"Dane—"

The corrections officers all focused their eyes on him.

"Dane, please. Sit your ass down," I whispered up to him harshly.

And he did, even as he clenched his jaw and kept from looking at me. "You don't understand," he said, shaking his head.

I reached across the table and squeezed his wrist. "Then make me understand. From here on out, you be honest with me and I'll be completely straight up with you. No more of the protecting each other bullshit because in the end we're stronger tackling the bullshit together."

Dane nodded his head in understanding and agreement. "You know I started working with my uncle Stripes when I was in college and he was a runner for these Mafia dudes. I hung around 'em when I was with my uncle, and me and one of the sons got real cool. He's the one who schooled me on the whole loan-sharking and gambling hustle," he said, his voice barely above a whisper. "When he became a boss he set me up with the start-up money, gave me connects, and cleared me to run certain parts of the city with no prob-lem . . . if I agreed to kick back a percentage of my profits and stay completely out of the drug game."

One of the COs walked by our table and Dane said noth-ing more until he moved on to the other side of the room. "One, Keno took over my shit, but I don't know if Keno is livin' up to that arrangement. Two, the fact that you got your ass in the mix could make it seem like I'm working through you from in here."

My gut clenched and I straight up felt like I would pass out. I wasn't cut out AT ALL for no mob shit.

"And three," Dane continued, "I heard about Keno out there being straight reckless and it's pissing people off. There's already been some shoot-outs."

Chills.

Did my involvement with Keno just put me and Dane in the line of fire?

I can't front. I was scared as shit, and knowing Dane was concerned about it didn't help a damn thing. "But no one knows about me," I insisted.

"Don't ever assume what somebody else know or don't know. Never do that."

"Dane—"

He eyed me and the anger I saw in the brown depths was all for me. "You fucked up, Suga. I'm in this motherfucker, how I can protect you? Why would you fuck with that when you rode me so fucking hard about getting out of the game? I catch a bid and your ass is deep in it? What fuckin' sense that make?"

I couldn't say shit. He was right. I was a hypocrite. And for sure there wasn't a bit of street in me and I should've stayed my saddity ass out of it. *I am not about that life.* "I'm sorry, Dane."

"You should be," he said, turning his head to gaze off into the distance.

For the rest of the visit we didn't even speak. We just sat there caught up in our own thoughts. I was so worried about my safety and his that I couldn't even focus on my father's drama or this half sister I had out there in the world. Fuck them. I had to figure out how to fix this mess I caused or at least get me and Dane as far away from it as I could.

Later that night, I was lying on the floor of the basement surrounded by the cool darkness with a wet rag on my head as I tried to fight off one helluva migraine. There was just too much shit going on in my life and all of it was sliding through my fingers and out of my grasp. My appointment to take my GMAT was in the morning and I honestly wasn't sure I needed to fuck with it . . . but if I skipped it, that meant NYU would not even consider my application to start in the fall.

Shit. Shit. Shit.

Hunga was blowing up my phone but I didn't even bother to answer her. I didn't know what to do with her. Cuss her out for her role in Keno flipping on Dane or play along and buy me some time until I figured some shit out. *They played the fuck out of me.*

I could just see them laying around butt naked smoking Ls and laughing at my ass as they celebrated their come-up. They wasn't riding in Dane's and my shadow anymore. They had the spotlight as far as they were concerned.

I still couldn't believe Keno turned on Dane. You see it enough in movies and books and you hear about it on the streets, but I truly thought of them two like brothers. Humph, nothing like a little jail time to turn a so-called hard-core motherfucker into a bird singing away at whoever held the pen to the paper freeing them.

Ding-dong.

I sighed as I moved to my feet and made my way up from the basement to the front door, still holding the damp rag in my hand. I rose up on my toes and looked out the glass . . . at Harriet . . . Luscious . . . whatever. Dropping back down to my bare feet, I stood there for a few moments before I finally stepped back and opened the door.

Luscious turned to face me, looking casual and cute in a silk color-block top and jeans with heels. "The detective told me what you did and I wanted to thank you because I know it couldn't have been easy," she said.

For a second, as I eyed her, she wasn't the tall and pretty dark-skinned woman standing before me but the little chocolate-skinned girl with buck teeth who had been like my sister. For so many years. And my father violated her. I remember the photo of her in that damn trunk and it felt like something hot and sharp pierced my soul. I had to fight the urge to hug the same woman I literally fought not too long ago.

"No, it wasn't easy at all to see or to swallow, but it was the right thing to do," I said, stepping back to open the door some more. "You wanna come in?"

Luscious nodded before she walked through the door and stood in my foyer. "This is nice, Sophie," she said looking around. "You must have spent a lot renovating—"

"I'm sorry," I told her. "I'm so sorry."

Luscious tilted her head to the side as she eyed me. Her eyes got sad. "You didn't know," she said simply, cutting me more slack than I deserved.

"I didn't believe you and then I fought you—"

Luscious held up her palm. "Now *that* you do owe me an

apology for," she said. "I can't lie. I rode by your house every day for a whole week after that shit waiting to see you so I could sneak you with my Taser."

I eyed that bitch to make sure this wasn't that sneak attack. I was hella sorry for what my father did, but I'll be damned if I let someone whup my ass in my own damn house.

Luscious held up her hands and turned to hold up the back of her shirt. "No tricks. Don't get me wrong, that was your one and only chance to fuck me over, but I'm good because I got a couple swings in too."

"True," I agreed, remembering a blow to my chin.

"You want a drink?" I asked her, turning to walk into my living room.

Luscious followed behind me. "Moscato if you have it," she said.

"That's in the fridge." I told her, turning to point her in the opposite direction.

We came into the kitchen and I opened the fridge to pull out one of the blue bottles of the sweet wine I kept stocked. I was looking for a corkscrew in the silver holder of spatulas and other utensils I kept on the counter. When I turned with it in my hand, Luscious was standing in front of the fridge looking at the photo of my unnamed half sister that I put on the door with a magnet.

"On top of everything else yesterday I find out my father has a daughter the same age as me," I told her, removing the cork and pouring two full glasses. "We even looked a little bit alike."

Luscious stared at me. "And y'all still do," she said, before she picked up the glass I gave her and sipped from it.

"Huh?" I asked her.

She reached over to pluck the photo from the door and turned to show it to me. "I know who this is."

"You're lying."

"No, I'm not," Luscious said as she sat the picture on the island and used an acrylic-covered fingernail to tap the picture. "There ain't but one bitch I know with those eyes and that's Goldie."

I looked down at the picture. At my sister. The nickname fit her because of the blondish tips of her hair and her eyes.

Did I really need to add someone new to my life? Someone else with their own issues and expectations? I was stretched pretty fucking thin as it is. "Is she nice?" I asked. "Does she know who her father is?"

Luscious shrugged. "We're not as cool as we used to be. She fucked my man. I fucked hers in return, but we got past all of that and we're cordial, but since I fucked the dude she's still with, we don't hang together. You know?"

I eyed Luscious.

"Uh-oh, there you go being judgmental again. I can see it all in your face, chick," she said with attitude. "You act like we were never friends. Best friends. Like sisters."

"You changed when we got to Rutgers," I told her truthfully. She wanted it, then there it was.

"So did you," she shot back.

"Yes, I did," I stressed. "But for the better."

Luscious looked down into her wine as she circled her wrist to twirl the liquid. "Here's the thing though. In the end we both wound up with an arrest record and a man in jail," she said, cutting her eyes to pierce me with them.

I smiled a little. "*Touché,* bitch," I said, taking a step forward to lightly touch my glass to hers.

Luscious looked off into the distance. "It's a damn shame it took the truth about what your father—"

"Victor," I corrected her.

Luscious nodded in acknowledgment. "Okay. The truth about what Victor did to make us talk," she said, her eyes filling with tears. "I been through some shit."

My heart tugged because the pain in her voice and her eyes was real as hell.

"I mean even more than what you know," she said, her tone soft and broken with emotion as a tear raced down her cheek to dangle on the edge of her face before it fell.

I felt awkward. I didn't know what to do.

"You remember how we would climb up on your father's car at night and tell each other everything?" she asked.

I smiled. "The first time we got up on the roof we were running from the Jefferson's dog," I reminded her.

Luscious smiled as she wiped away her tears. "Yes, I was so glad when his ass got run over. All he did was chase kids up and down the dang-on blocks."

"I think somebody hit him on purpose."

Luscious tilted her head. "I wouldn't doubt it."

We fell silent. It was like we were teenagers again in her mother's kitchen eating cookies and talking about nothing. I had been friends with this woman since kindergarten and all through the years until college. Over a decade.

Everything I been through in the last six months made me realize that we weren't all that different as I'd thought. And even now for her to be standing in my home and so open and friendly to me after I fought her . . . after what my father did. This was the Harriet I remembered and the Luscious I was getting to know.

"I miss my friend," I admitted.

"Why?" she asked, smiling as she opened her arms. "I'm right here."

I came around the island to hug her to my side. I needed a friend.

"So . . . you want your sister's number or not?" she asked, picking up her cell phone to scroll through her contacts.

I turned and got a pen and pad from one of the drawers. I pushed them toward her on the island.

Luscious wrote the number down. "Whenever you do decide to call and meet up with her, make you sure you swag the fuck out because *that* bitch stays on point."

I poured us some more wine and listened to her tell me all about my sister running a strip club out of her apartment in King Court of all places and her owning an apartment on New York's Upper East Side that she paid for with an ultra-exclusive prostitution ring catering to rich and famous clientele.

Long after Luscious left, with us making a promise to meet up for lunch real soon, I looked down at that paper. Everything Luscious told me about Goldie's life made me want to meet her. To see her with my own eyes.

On some real shit, the more Luscious talked, the harder it was not to see all the coincidences in our lives. It was like fate was trying to intervene but we kept missing each other. She lived in King Court but moved out before I became Johnica's mentor. We both shopped at On Your Back downtown—and how crazy was it that the man I saw getting yelled on by his wife that day used to be Goldie's lover . . . until that same crazy bitch he was still married to came and snatched his ass out of Goldie's apartment one day. Hunga (aka Coko) used to strip for Goldie and now she was the wifey of my man's best friend (who was now his enemy).

And then Luscious. My very best childhood friend was also my sister's friend at some point and none of us knew it.

This whole thing was a major mind fuck.

"Excuse me. Are you Sophie?"

I looked up from my seat in Tao restaurant on East Fifty-eighth Street in New York. "Yes," I said, standing up in my spiked heels to face her.

The woman standing there was just as fly and fabulous as Luscious said she would be. Honey complexion. Brownish-gold eyes. Shiny shoulder-length hair parted down the middle and highlighted with natural blonde streaks. Barely any makeup. Ivory lace dress with flowing skirt that came mid-thigh. Gold accessories. Sky-high white and gold sandals.

I was so happy for the effort I'd put in to wear a black sheer polka blouse with blouson sleeves and a pair of silk shorts that flowed together to appear like a short skirt.

But all of the fashion and flyness didn't matter.

I saw some of my father's features in her. A lot of the same ones I saw in me.

I reached in my bag and took out the envelope I discovered that day. I handed it to her.

"We look alike," she said as she reached out for the envelope with a diamond wedding ring set on her left hand that was flawless and flashy.

As Goldie looked down at the picture and nodded, I

couldn't believe just a few hours ago I pushed myself to call her and tell her that we shared the same father. That shit shocked her just like it shocked me.

She finally took the seat across from me. "I guess we have a lot to talk about," Goldie said.

I sat down too and crossed my legs at the ankle. *My sister.* "Yes we do," I agreed.

Goldie twisted her wedding band around her finger. She looked down at my hand and I realized I was doing the same thing. We both laughed a little and stopped. "I'll be honest, I have wanted to know who my father was for a long time," she said. "I'm grateful to you for reaching out to me, but there's a lot I want to say and ask about him. Who is he? What does he look like? How did he meet my mother? Did he know about me? Did he ever give a fuck about me?"

Bzzzzzzzzz . . . Bzzzzzzzzz . . . Bzzzzzzzzz . . .

I looked down at my phone. It was Detective Kotz. They were going to arrest my father—*our* father—today. I turned him in. It was right but it wasn't easy. Not easy at all.

She locked her gold eyes on me. "Everything okay?"

"I just need to take this call," I said, answering it before it could set off vibrating like a heavy-duty dildo again. "Hello."

I shifted my eyes away from Goldie's face to any random spot in the restaurant.

The detective's words were like background noise as I listened and answered him in monosyllables. Victor Alvarez had never been in the running for the greatest father but he was one helluva lot better man than the one he kept hidden from me in that trunk. That monster was not the father I knew.

I ended the call and clutched my phone so tightly I thought it might snap in my hand.

"Like I was saying, I hope you understand that I would like a paternity test just to be sure," Goldie was saying.

I locked my eyes back on her. She said she wanted to know who her father was and that had to mean the good with the bad. I had to come to grips with it and unfortunately so did she. "I'll be happy to do a sibling paternity test, but . . . but . . . but . . . our father is dead. He just passed away while in police custody," I admitted to her in a broken whisper, surprised at the sadness that overwhelmed me.

Goldie looked taken aback. "Police custody?" she asked.

I nodded.

"Tell me everything," she said.

And with one deep breath I did just that.

$\mathcal{S}$hit was completely out of control. No, no. Keno was out of control.

Yesterday, when I hadn't heard from Dane for two straight days, I hopped in my car and drove to Fairton. When I got there the security guard told me he was in an outside hospital recovering from getting jumped and then stabbed. Because I wasn't an immediate family member, they wouldn't give me permission to visit him and he wasn't allowed phone privileges in the hospital. They wouldn't even say what hospital he was in or when he was expected to be returned to the prison.

I tried everything to get info on him. I used the GPS to track the closest hospital to the prison and drove there. That got me nowhere. They weren't even allowed to confirm or deny he was there. And I fought the urge to run past hospital security and call out Dane's name as I hit every floor.

That was insanity . . . I seriously thought about doing that shit, but I finally gave up and carried my black ass home. That drive back to Newark had been hard as hell but I knew for sure it had something to do with Keno. And I had to do something about it.

In the days before Dane got "shanked" like a bad scene from *Penitentiary* or *American Me,* Dane got more info in jail than I got on the streets, and he told me the mob was indeed fed the fuck up with Keno's shit and had even reached out to him to remind him of the agreement. Keno sending back word for them to fuck off wasn't swallowed easily.

Just a few days before, someone drove by and shot up one of Keno's cars while it was parked outside a club. No one was hurt but the message was clear. The mob was not to be taken lightly—but anyone with good sense and a love of *The Sopranos* or *The Godfather* already knew that shit.

I couldn't help but think that Dane's stabbing was another message and the word was out on the street about my involvement.

Sliding my hands over my black leggings, I paced back and forth in Hunga's red living room as I waited for her to come downstairs. Ming had let me in and then disappeared. That had been damn near ten minutes ago. *What the fuck is she doing?*

I was tired of waiting on her and damned tired of pacing but I absolutely refused to sit my ass on that sofa after peeping in on their fuckfest. That couch would need a good bleach-down before I fucked with it.

It seemed like another ten minutes before Hunga finally came down the stairs in nothing but a wifebeater. Hair wild. Face puffy. Eyes crusty. And breath no doubt funky. It was damn near ten at night. *This bitch been sleeping all day?*

"What you want, Suga?" she asked, sleep still in her voice as she reached for a pack of Newports on the table to light one.

"Is Keno here? I need to talk to him."

Hunga eyed me through the cigarette smoke. "Okay, let's try this shit again, Suga," she said. "What you want?"

"To not get shot the fuck up would be nice," I snapped.

She laughed. "Trust me, Keno got total control of this shit. Ain't a motherfucker been born yet to stop him. Now . . . ain't shit happened to stop the cash flow—ours *or yours*—so roll with it and let him handle his business."

"Tell Keno to call me tomorrow." I turned and walked to the door as she sucked air between her teeth and turned on the flat-screen television on the wall.

When I reached the door I turned the knob but looked over my shoulder. Ming had already found her spot squatting between Hunga's legs and was slurping away. I ignored that psycho sex freak. "When Dane was in the game, I was so worried about him getting locked up and killed and shit was nowhere near where it is now. Don't you care that police already looking for him? This brings too much attention." I was enjoying that these motherfuckers still thought my ass was in the dark about their lies and manipulation.

Hunga exhaled a stream of smoke toward the ceiling as she twisted the fingers of her free hand in Ming's hair. "This month I paid all my mama's bills and mine. My son is good," she said, hissing a little bit as her hips arched forward on the chair. Ming must've hit a spot. "That's all I give a fuck about."

These bitches were really acting like I wasn't standing there . . . again.

"Yeah, but if he's dead or in jail that money will stop," I reminded her as she inched to the edge of the chair and raised her legs straight up to the sky.

Ming moaned and sucked away harder.

"Keno ain't Dane. He would leave shit in place for the business to continue on with him straight running shit from jail. Him getting locked up wouldn't change nothing," she said, letting her head drop back.

I eyed her. I sized her up. I detested her betrayal. I was sick of her. "You think you're smarter than me, don't you?" I asked her. "Huh?"

Hunga used her index fingers to push her hair back behind her ears. "No, you're the college girl with all the motherfucking sense in the world, right?" she asked, laughing a little.

The bitch was mocking me. In her head she thought they knew more than I did. That they were playing me. At one point they had but shit had changed . . . and they didn't know *that*.

I walked up and grabbed Ming's arms to pull her little ass up to her feet. "Could you do that later?" I snapped on her.

All around Ming's mouth was wet and her eyes glassy. "Dayum, bitch—"

I dismissed her skinny ass with my hand. "Do you eat anything *besides* pussy?" I asked her. "Ugh. Go eat a burger or something. Shit."

"Fuck you," she said, her voice slurred as she gave me the finger.

I had to do a double take at the tiny plastic penis with a pink tip glued to the end of her finger.

She licked the tip as she walked over to the sofa and slumped down on it.

Hunga just laughed as she finished smoking her cigarette. "You know, Hunga, don't be one of those chicks who makes the mistake of thinking everyone with 'book sense' can't top a motherfucker with 'street smarts,'" I told her, giving her a mocking smile. "See, the only people who believe that shit are insecure motherfuckers who feel less than because they ass didn't go to college."

"Bitch, you think you're better than me?" Hunga asked, coming to stand in front of me.

"No, I think *you* think I'm better than you," I shot back. "And to try and convince yourself that you're wrong, you make little smart-ass comments, always calling me bougie and boring and all kind of dumb shit. I mean, you think I give a fuck? Whatever helps you to feel better about yourself."

"Man, shut your lame ass up," Hunga said, eyeing me up and down.

"You know what else I think? I think I wouldn't fuck a nigga just so my bills get paid. I think I would raise my son regardless of *any* motherfucking thing," I said, stepping up to her.

See, on some real shit, I had had absolutely enough of Keno and Hunga's shit. For real. Keno betrayed Dane and she backed up the lies he told to cover it. And now his recklessness was putting us in danger. It was enough of his shit. *Their* shit.

"And I know I would never snitch," I added.

Her eyes shifted to the left for a hot second before she focused them back on me. "Bitch, fuck you," she said.

I gagged a little at the smell of her breath. "No, bitch, it's been fuck you before your Molly-loving ass even knew it. Believe that shit."

I left. Fuck them. I was going looking for Keno.

I climbed into my car and pulled off, heading toward the spot Keno used for the poker games. McCarter Highway.

Keno had to be at the warehouse. After that I didn't know where else to look for him.

I knew exactly where it was since I'd found it online and suggested using it to Keno. It seemed safer than another house or using a business as a front. Areas that housed warehouses usually had less traffic and barely caught anyone's attention. We rented out the entire first floor, using one unit for the gamblers to play and the other one for them to park in so the cars weren't on the street. To the unsuspecting eye the building was still empty and not in use.

Bzzzzzzzzz . . . Bzzzzzzzzz . . . Bzzzzzzzzz . . .

I turned the corner onto Grove Street to eventually hop on to I-280 East as I checked my phone. It was Luscious. *I'll call her back.*

I couldn't lose focus. This shit with Keno had to be handled tonight.

Dane was laid up in a hospital.

Shots were being fired around the city like confetti.

Who was the next target? Hunga? Ming? Me? *Hell to the no.*

I kept my eyes focused on the traffic as the red brake lights of cars ahead of me and the white headlights of the cars behind me stood out against the darkness of night, making it feel like a carnival or some shit. I was already anxious about confronting Keno because I had no idea just how crazy that son of a bitch was.

I pulled into the drive leading behind the two-story warehouse on the corner. There wasn't a game planned for the night and only Keno's new Range Rover was parked in the first unit. I pulled in and parked beside him, rolling my eyes at his vehicle tags: BOSS. *What the fuck ever.*

I glanced at the clock. *This has to work,* I thought, before I shut the car off and climbed out. My sneakered footsteps against the concrete were cushioned as I made my way out the first unit and over to the second to knock on the door.

After a few moments it opened and FuQuan, Keno's forty-year-old, Shaq-looking henchman, stood there looking down at me. I didn't know him. He hadn't been around when Dane was running the show and I had no clue where Keno dug his ass up. I did know that he didn't mind chopping off fingers or shooting out kneecaps.

I ignored him as I looked around.

The warehouse was large but only the half where Keno had the five poker tables and makeshift bar was lit by ceiling lights. The second half was so dark that a black cat would disappear in it. There was a row of windows around the entire warehouse but they were high above our heads and not letting anyone look in or out.

Keno was sitting alone at one of the poker tables using a counting machine. The shuffling sound of it working echoed inside the nearly empty building. He looked up as I came to stand beside the table. "Hunga called me and said you was on your way," he said, picking his lit blunt up from an ashtray to hit before he set it back down.

"That's her job to fill you the fuck in, right? So I'm not surprised," I said, pulling out one of the chairs to sit down across from him.

Keno was wrapping a rubber band around a stack of money and cut his eyes up to look at me. "You got something you need to get off your chest?" he asked, the overhead lights casting a spot of light on his bald dome. "She said you had a lot of shit to say to her."

"True, but that's between me and her," I said, rolling back to cross my legs in the black leggings I wore with a long-sleeved fitted black tee. "Now with me and you . . . I wanted to talk to you about shutting shit down until things cool off."

Keno made a face. "Nah," he said, taking the stack of money from the machine to wrap with a rubber band before he loaded it with another stack. "You can go 'head with that because it ain't gonna happen."

I twisted my engagement ring on my finger as I eyed him. "I let a lot of shit slide because I figured nobody really knew I was involved with this, but see, Dane got stabbed in prison and I think it had everything to do with whoever is trying to get at you," I said, licking my lips.

"Yo, no offense, but I handles mine out *here* and Dane got to learn to handle his while he in *there*," Keno said, standing up to pop open a duffel bag. "I can't watch my back out here and his in there. You feel me?"

Hatred for this motherfucker made my chest burn but I tried not to show it. "Did you have his back when he was out here?" I asked, my hands gripping the armrest of the chair, wishing it was his skinny tattoo-covered neck.

Keno set the bag on the table and eyed me before he leaned against the edge of the table. "You know so fucking much. You tell me, *smart ass*."

I arched a brow and leaned back from the hostility in his eyes and voice. "Why so angry?"

"I don't like you. Never did," Keno said. "I hate a bitch think she better than everybody. A bitch with her own head so far up her fucking ass that she can't tell nobody gives a fuck what she thinks. And that bitch is you."

FuQuan laughed.

Time to go. I rose to my feet. "Then you go your way and I'll go mine," I said, coming around the chair to walk toward the door.

A strong hand gripped my wrist and I turned around to eye Keno. He was standing behind me and holding a 9mm in his hand that he tapped against my temple.

My eyes shot in the corner of my sockets to eye it as my heart sounded off like a drum. "Don't do something you will regret, Keno," I said my voice slow and steady as I tried to step back from him and the look in his eyes.

Keno shook his head. "Shut up, bitch," he whispered to me, dragging the barrel of the gun down the side of my face to tap against my lips. "That's your problem. You yap your gums too fucking much and that's the last thing I need."

And I know I would never snitch.

I knew without a doubt that those words I said to Hunga put fear in this motherfucker and now I had plenty of fear in me. This wasn't how I imagined this shit going down. At all.

"Look, I'm out. It's not even this serious," I said, trying to free my wrist from his hand and shift my head back to break contact with the gun. I was nervous as hell.

"You ain't going no motherfucking where," Keno said, shoving me hard against my chest. "It's time to handle you just like my dude murked Dane's ass."

My eyes got big as shit and I reached out to slap the evil grin off his face. WHAP!

I hollered out at the feel of FuQuan's hands wrapping tight as hell around my upper arms. Panic set in as Keno just flexed his broad shoulders and laughed like I was a joke. *This motherfucker crazy!*

"Handle it, FuQuan," he ordered, turning back to sit his gun on the table and zip up the duffel before he crossed the warehouse to disappear into the darkness on the other side of the room. "I'll be right back."

I heard a door open and close as I tried to fight to free myself from FuQuan's strong hold. I tried to kick backward on his big ass. Major fail. "Let me fucking go," I screamed, raising my knee and bringing my foot down to stomp on his foot.

He hollered out and his grasp loosened enough for me to twist out of it and turn to try to run past him to the door.

I reached out for the knob and my fingers stroked it, just as he grabbed my ponytail and jerked me back so hard my feet came off the floor and I flew back and landed against his body.

One strong arm circled my neck and the other snaked around my waist, cutting off circulation and air around my rib cage and throat.

I brought my hands up to claw at his arm around my neck as I kicked my legs.

He laughed low in his throat. The smell of cigarettes, weed, and liquor surrounded me as I fought to breathe. He turned me around with rage on his face as he bit his lip and raised his arms to backhand me.

WHAP!

My face and jaw felt like they were on fire from his hit and my body dropped to the floor. I could taste blood in my mouth as I lay there on the dusty concrete floor breathing heavily and trying to get my mind right. *I gotta get out of here . . .*

One sneakered foot came down on my hand hard.

"Aaaaaaaaagh!" I hollered, tears filling my eyes as his foot ground my hand against the concrete.

"Maybe I should cut your tongue out your fucking mouth to keep you from screaming," FuQuan said, bending down to unlatch a switchblade.

I opened my eyes as blood and drool ran out my mouth and onto the floor. The light from the ceiling hit off the edge of the blade. It was sharp. Razor sharp.

Oh God. I'm going to die.

"Or maybe I should cut your fingers off and shove them down your fucking throat, bitch," FuQuan bit out through clenched teeth.

What the fuck was he so mad at me about?

He dragged his foot off my hand and then pressed the tip of the knife into the back of my hand.

I cried out.

It pierced my flesh and blood bubbled up from the break in the skin to run down the side of my hand as he drew a letter.

"Finish her, Fu, I ain't got all night," Keno said from somewhere behind his sadistic goon.

BOOM! BOOM! BOOM!

Gunshots suddenly filled the air and pierced the glass of the windows and door. *Oh shit . . .*

Still on the floor, I looked over my shoulder just as the warehouse door crashed open and four dudes with ski masks on stormed into the building. My heart stopped in the second before they all raised their guns.

Keno reached to grab his gun from the table.

FuQuan stood up, dropping his blade, to grab for a gun under his shirt.

One instantly put a bullet in FuQuan's heart and the force of it sent his big body a few feet away. I dived like I was headed into a pool and not across the floor into the darkness across the room.

Pow-pow-pow-pow-pow-pow-pow-pow.

The glass from the windows above shattered like tiny explosions. I felt shards of it hit, drop, and pierce any of my exposed skin and I squeezed my eyes shut but I kept moving, blind in the darkness, until I bumped into the rear wall. I lowered myself to the floor and prayed none of the bullets had my name on it.

And from my spot in the darkness I prayed I didn't get caught in the crossfire.

Pow-pow-pow-pow-pow-pow-pow-pow.

The gunmen all aimed for Keno, and the first bullet that entered his body detached his arm from his body. The pressure of the rest of the bullets into his body sent him back against the wall with jerking motions as if he was being electrocuted. Blood poured from the holes and the smell of it was thick in the air. The gun he uselessly held in his hand dropped to the floor just before he fell forward onto the poker table.

"Get any money you see!"

One of them carelessly picked up Keno's lifeless body. Sticky blood and plasma arced in the air as his body landed on the floor like a lifeless doll.

Damn.

"Shit, I'ma get all these diamonds too. Fuck that!" a tall thin one said as he squatted over Keno's bloodied body and began snatching off his diamond jewelry.

"Let's be out!"

Relief flooded me as I watched them head out the door. The side of my face and my mouth throbbed. My body ached from hitting the floor. My hand burned from where the knife sliced my skin. It felt like my heart couldn't slow down its fast pace.

But I was alive.

My eyes shifted from FuQuan's and Keno's dead bodies. More dead eyes.

I dropped my head to the tops of my knees where I sat and cried. From relief. From being overwhelmed by my feelings. From the death I saw.

"Thank you, Lord," I whispered into the hollow.

I sniffed the air. *Is something burning?*

I raised my head and I inhaled sharply at the sight of fire spreading across the warehouse. "They set the building on fire," I screeched, rising to my feet.

I turned and felt the wall until I found the door separating the two warehouse units. It was locked. "Shit, shit, shit!" I screamed, kicking the door before I turned and faced the fire. *I had to get the fuck out of there.*

I came across the room stepping out of the darkness and the fire warmed me from head to toe. The path to the front door was free and clear. I gave Keno's body one last look before I walked out.

The unjust never prosper.

I had to keep telling myself that.

Still aching from my wounds, I walked over to the next unit and pulled my keys from my pocket to unlock my car. My cell phone rang from where I'd left it on the passenger seat but I didn't bother to even pick it up as I drove out of the warehouse, flinching with the steady ache in my hand.

I can't believe my dumb ass got caught dead in the middle of a hit on the warehouse. Looks like the mob was absolutely not playing with Keno . . . and now Keno wouldn't be doing shit with no one else. I just wanted to get the fuck away from it all.

I was almost to the corner when I did a U-turn and headed back. The fire had spread in the second unit of the warehouse until you could see the smoke and flames engulf the entire unit. I rushed inside the first unit and covered my hands with the edge of my shirt to try and open the door to Keno's Range Rover. It was locked.

Humph, I gots the motherfucking key.

I grabbed the tire iron from my trunk and swung like I was going for a grand slam home run. The sound of the glass shattering echoed into the quiet. I unlocked and opened the door, snatching the duffel bag sitting on the passenger seat. *Fuck that.*

I hopped back into my car and sped off, digging my hand into the bag to pick up one of the rubber band–wrapped stacks of money. *Fuck it.*

Keno owed Dane and me way more than that.

KA-BOOM!

I hit my brakes and looked in the rearview mirrors just as all the windows of the warehouse exploded. I felt the explosion in the building rattle me and my car. The tips of the fire reached out the windows and the fire began to engulf the outside of the building as well.

I raced up the street, the light from the fire illuminating the inside of the car, but I didn't dare stop.

Epilogue

Eighteen months later

I glanced at the digital clock on the corner of my desk. It was a little after seven. I was beat. But it was completely worth it busting my ass to run my own business *and* finish up my first year pursuing my MBA in a few months. "So fuck you, Vickie," I said aloud, as I rolled backward in my leather executive chair and stood up to check my outfit in the full-length mirror in the corner of my office.

Life was good. Damn good. Finally.

I smoothed my hands over the dark metallic brocade pencil skirt I wore with a sheer tank and leather fitted jacket. With one last smoothing of my hair into its wide ponytail, I grabbed my favorite oversize leather clutch and the keys before shutting off the light and opening the connecting door leading into the hall and directly across to the other office.

I knocked once before entering. "Hey, I'm headed out," I said.

The office chair swiveled around and Dane held up one hand as he talked on his cordless office phone.

I looked around at his office with its black walls and leather furniture. It was a mini-replica of his man cave/basement at our house and I knew when I had it decorated three months ago that he would love it. It was the first place

I bought him after picking him up from the halfway house two months ago.

Because he was a first-time, nonviolent offender, Dane was accepted into an early release program under the state's Intensive Supervision Program. The guidelines for his release were stricter than ordinary probation or parole, but he was free. And home. And still catching up on fucking the hell out of me.

And our business was completely legit. We bought into a payday advance loan franchise that wasn't shit but legal loan-sharking on a smaller scale. We were still hiring staff and getting everything in place but the business was a go and I was happy that he was finally done playing around with the law.

Once Dane was released he surprised me with a mini-scavenger hunt over the city collecting five bundles of cash he hid years ago. Fuck a bank. Two hundred and fifty thousand dollars went home with us that night. We fucked on top of it. Straight hood shit.

But life was good.

And we were finally getting married in the summer.

He hung up the phone and I came around his desk to ease into his lap. I wrapped my arms around his neck and tasted his mouth. It didn't take long to feel his dick getting hard beneath my ass. I shook my head. "I have to go. I'm already running late," I moaned, shivering at the feel of his tongue circling my pulse.

"A'ight, but all this will be waiting on you when you get home," he said, raising his hips to double-pump my ass playfully.

I tasted his lips and hauled ass before he convinced

me to go home with him instead. The fall winds were cold as shit after the sun went down and I rushed into my car parked in the rear of the building we were leasing. The car was already warm and toasty. *Thank God for the self-start.*

It was two years since the day Dane and I were arrested. As I drove through the streets of Newark, I thought about everything that happened since then. Every day I said a prayer of thanks for being alive.

Keno and FuQuan were dead as dead could get . . . especially when the fire lit up the chemicals being stored on the second story of the warehouse and blew the building and them to bits and pieces. To this day no one knew that it was Dane and not the mob that sent goons to handle Keno's trifling snitching ass. I didn't even know about it until he was free. Let the streets think what they want. That just kept the heat off Dane. Fuck it. *It was him or us. Dane did what he had to do.*

I hadn't seen Hunga/Coko/Whomever or Ming since Keno's memorial service. I had no clue what those tricks were up to and could care the fuck less. I was just happy I didn't have to deal with their madness anymore. Goldie and I stayed sharing stories on just how dumb those hos act. *Fuck 'em.*

Lil Wil was our one and only employee so far. He stayed out of trouble after being shot in the neck and Dane promised to make sure his friend was straight. Dane said he didn't give a fuck if Wil just sat in the office all day every day doing nothing, he was on the payroll. I had no problem with that at all . . . especially since AaRon wasn't here for us to do anything for him. *RIP, AaRon.*

Johnica and her son, Kason, were doing real good at the

group home. She made sure to stay in touch with me and talking to her was totally different than before. Less drama and crazy-ass stories and more of her dreams and plans for her son and her. I promised her that once she graduated high school and moved into her own place, I would give her a part-time job. *I will not turn my back on her like her family*.

As I passed through downtown, my old work stomping grounds, I thought of crazy-ass Leo, my ex-coworker. Until I changed my number he was still sending me dick pics and begging to smell the seat of my panties. I could only send up a prayer to his wife. That *Negro is wild* . . .

I pulled into the parking lot of Fornos of Spain down in the neck on Ferry Street. I spotted Goldie's new silver Ferrari. It felt damn good having a sister. Although I was older than her by two months and had graduated college, I found myself turning to her for advice on things. Goldie had *lived* and she was smart. My sister didn't know that Luscious filled me in on her side hustle of selling sex to high-profile, wealthy clients who appreciated her discretion. *Make it do what it do, sis*.

I felt bad for her to finally find out who her father was and then not be able to be happy with the man that he was, but she was there with me when I released his ashes into the Hudson River—a small tribute to the man he was when he raised me alone and did my hair and made sure I graduated high school and college and sat with me that first night I got out of jail because he knew I didn't want to be alone. That's the memory of him that I mourned. Not the monster that he hid from me.

Shaking off any sadness, I walked into the restaurant and

was led to the small dining room. I stopped in surprise to see both Luscious and Goldie sitting at the table waiting for me. Together. Together? I asked Luscious to come but I didn't think she would show.

Wow.

It was awkward as hell knowing Goldie and Luscious's crazy-ass history and not being able to chill with both at the same time. They didn't hate each other anymore but neither one of them chicks were looking to be besties either and I could understand that from both viewpoints.

Luscious and I had slipped right back into our old friendship and it felt good having a friend again . . . especially since she was a hundred times funnier and wilder than when we were growing up. Her friends and business partners in their event-planning business, Michel and Eve, were just as crazy. Never in a million years would I have thought I would be chilling with a gorgeous transsexual like Michel or a hood chick like Eve. All the shit I'd been through knocked me off that pedestal I'd looked down on all of them from—including Luscious.

I took out my cell phone and snapped a few pictures of these bitches, because who knew when this shit would happen again. And they looked happy. Luscious all chocolatety and gorgeous and grinning. Goldie all golden brown and pretty with a relaxed expression.

Luscious was all giddy about Yummy Entertainment booking some huge gig or the fact that she was fresh off a trip to Fiji to celebrate her one-year wedding anniversary to Mr. Grown and Sexy, aka Jamal Jacobs.

Goldie was big and round with her first baby, so I knew that's what her glow was all about. She was already talking about naming my niece or nephew some variation of her husband's name, Has. Like Has Jr. or Haseema.

Judge not . . .

"What's up, bitches?" I said, setting my clutch along with their designer bags on the empty chair at the table before I sat down.

"Nothing much, just real bitches doing real things," Goldie said.

And she was right. Real bitches do real things. The three of us had been in long-term relationships with men but in the end something took them all away (be it a wife ending an adulterous relationship, a dude cheating, or another one getting locked up), and we all had to step up and get out there.

On the grind. Hustling hard. Getting money.

And that's the realest shit ever.

Acknowledgments

*G*od: Thank you for the gift of storytelling. It is so amazing to live out my childhood dreams every day. I know this is what You meant for me. I honor you.

My love, my heavenly angels, my family and my friends: Thank you for the constant support. I love you.

My assistant, Blair: Thank you for doing all the grunt work and giving me time to do absolutely nothing but create these stories. I acknowledge you.

Claudia Menza: Everyday we're hustling, hustling, hustling. LOL. Thank you for keeping me straight. I cherish you.

Allegra Ben-Amotz, Ashley Hewlett, and the entire Simon & Schuster/Touchstone team: Big thanks for laying eyes, hands, wisdom, and talents to this project. I appreciate you.

The readers, book clubs, reviewers, bookstores, and book bloggers: All authors should respect your support of the art of fiction. I thank you.

If I didn't name or remember someone please put it on my head and not my heart.

Forever grateful,

M. Mink

About the Author

*M*eesha Mink is the coauthor of the popular and bestselling Hoodwives series (*Desperate Hoodwives, Shameless Hoodwives,* and *The Hood Life*). *Real Wifeys: Hustle Hard* is the final book in her solo Real Wifeys trilogy preceded by *Real Wifeys: On the Grind* and *Real Wifeys: Get Money.* Mink also is the acclaimed and bestselling author of both romance fiction and commercial mainstream fiction as Niobia Bryant. The Newark, New Jersey, native writes full-time and currently lives in South Carolina, where she is busy on her next work of fiction.

CONNECT WITH MEESHA:

Websites:	www.meeshamink.com
	www.niobiabryant.com
E-mail:	meeshamink@yahoo.com,
	niobia_bryant@yahoo.com
Twitter:	InfiniteInk
Facebook Fan Page:	Niobia Bryant | Meesha Mink

And for more on the bestselling Hoodwives trilogy, please visit: www.HOODWIVES.com.

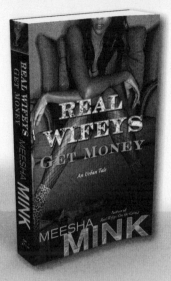
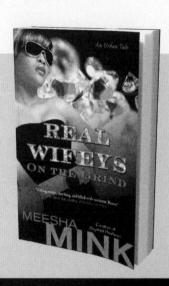

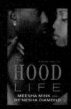